Fatal Embrace

Fatal Embrace

Aris Whittier

Five Star • Waterville, Maine

This novel is a work of fiction. Names, characters, places and incidents are either the product of the author's imagination, or, if real, used fictitiously.

First Edition
First Printing: December 2004

Published in 2004 in conjunction with Cambridge Literary Associates.

Set in 11 pt. Plantin by Liana M. Walker.

Printed in the United States on permanent paper.

Library of Congress Cataloging-in-Publication Data

Whittier, Aris.
    Fatal embrace / Aris Whittier.—1st ed.
      p. cm.
    ISBN 1-59414-178-9 (hc : alk. paper)
    1. Serial murders—Fiction. 2. Horse trainers—Fiction.
    3. Ranch life—Fiction. 4. Witnesses—Fiction. I. Title.
    PS3623.H58716P56 2004
    813'.6—dc22   2004043313

For my husband,
who always knew I had this book in me
and waited patiently while it came out.

Chapter One

Michael stumbled through the door and dropped his duffel bag to the floor; it was after four in the morning, and he had driven all night to get home. Running a hand through his hair, he hauled his stiff body up the stairs to his bedroom. The meeting with Windward Stables had taken a day longer than he had anticipated. However, he had won the contract and that was all that mattered. He would be the official trainer for the majority of their herd for the next five years. His entire body ached from the six-hour drive, but a little smile of satisfaction found its way to his lips.

In his room, he slumped to the cedar chest and began tugging off his boots, tossing them at the closet door. Then he peeled off his socks and left them in a heap by the chest. Standing, he slid out of the snug jeans and dropped the faded material on top of the socks. Finally he pulled the wrinkled T-shirt over his head and looked at the inviting bed before him.

But then a subliminal thought kicked in: he didn't have time to sleep. Only enough time to shower, change, and get some breakfast before his crew arrived. Wearily, he stepped out of his briefs and went into the bathroom. A cool shower would consume any and all thoughts of sleep.

Michael was sitting at the bar washing down his breakfast with a strong cup of coffee when his men walked into the kitchen. "Morning," he mumbled. He slid off the high stool and took his dishes to the sink. After rinsing them, he moved to the coffeepot, refilled his cup, and turned to the four men. "Where's Stanson? I thought he'd be with you."

"Sleeping, I think," Jake said as he adjusted the worn, green John Deere cap.

"What do you mean sleeping? Did you tell him that we need to ride the line and move the horses this morning?"

Jake shook his head and looked to Richard. "Did you tell Jess that we had to move the horses?"

"No." Richard rolled a toothpick to the other side of his mouth and then looked to John. "Did you?"

"Nope." John's green eyes fell on Tom who, at twenty-six, was the youngest of the group. When Tom shook his head, John looked back to his boss. "I didn't know that you wanted us to."

"Why the hell wouldn't I want you to tell him?" Through his weariness, Michael fought an impulse at irritation. The last thing he wanted to do was yell at his men. They were the best ranch hands around and one of the main reasons Pine Crest was so successful. He glanced at all four men and motioned toward the coffeepot. "Fill your thermoses and then get saddled up. I'll wake Stanson and meet you at the stables in twenty minutes." He paused. "I have to finish up early, I'm meeting with Dan this evening," he added, heading for the back door.

"Where are you going, boss?" Jake asked.

"To get Stanson." He was getting tired of this nonsense.

"Well, you're headed in the wrong direction." Jake pointed up.

Michael pushed past the group of smiling men. "Go saddle up."

No longer containing his irritation, he thundered up the winding stairs, ready to strike. What the hell was Stanson doing in the house? He had told Mrs. Mayfield to put the new foreman in the guesthouse on the other side of the property. Finding a good foreman who didn't demand all sorts of lavish comforts was hard, but Dan had assured him that this guy wasn't like that. Throwing every door open as he roared down the long hall, his fury doubled as each room came up empty. When he had come to the door across from his, he tossed it open and snapped, "It's time to wake up, Stanson."

Michael froze when his eyes caught sight of her full breasts heaving in alarm. The tall, slender woman who stood next to the rumpled bed froze.

His eyes burned a path from her big brown eyes wide with surprise to her unbelievably full lips, down to the hollow of her neck where they rested on the blue nightgown that didn't leave much to the imagination. The deep blue brought out the golden cream in her smooth skin. Her frame was delicate, well built, and very womanly.

Chestnut hair, which flowed freely around her shoulders, shone intensely. He swallowed hard as the heat traveled from his throat to his stomach and then lower. Who was she and what was she doing in his house?

He grabbed the rim of his black felt Stetson and tipped it. Nodding his head curtly, he said in a rugged voice, "Sorry ma'am." Why wasn't he reaching for the door and leaving? It was time to exit, he told himself. Reach for the doorknob, turn it, and get the hell out of the room. He didn't move. He couldn't.

"May I help you?" Her voice was soft and clear, with a slight touch of fascination.

Michael's eyes shot to hers when he realized he was staring at her body. "E-excuse me." He backed out of the room, closing the door behind him.

He descended the stairs, which were carved from logs, in a

daze. What had just happened? And where did that woman come from? If this was another one of his crew's sick jokes, he was going to fire them all. Movement out the window drew him out of his trance. He recognized Dan's car and went to the door to greet his long-time friend.

Dan was a lean, serious man. His long legs were clad in the customary, perfectly-pressed brown khaki pants. A dark brown, leather belt wrapped around his firm waist, holding in the white button-up shirt. When it was cold, he'd wear a tweed sports jacket. His dark hair that was receding just above the temples looked like the barber had just seen it. Dan looked as he always looked—neat and tidy.

"Mornin', Chief," Michael said as he opened the door and shook Dan's hand. "I thought we weren't going to go over things until this evening."

"We are. I stopped by to see how you like the new foreman I found you." Dan closed the door behind him and followed Michael into the spacious living room.

Michael opened a small cabinet and regarded the bottle of brandy that he feared wasn't near enough. It would have to do; it was all he had. He searched for a glass, knowing that he was lucky to have the meager amount left over from some barbeque his crew had hosted at the ranch. He looked to Dan. "Want one?"

"Maybe in nine more hours."

"Suit yourself." He filled the glass a quarter full because that was all there was.

"Is something the matter? Don't tell me the new guy isn't as good as they said." Dan's body language became very serious. "Mike, I know you're picky about who works for you, but I swear they said he was the best."

Michael shook his head and set the bottle down on the large coffee table, constructed out of the same timber as the staircase and the open, beamed ceilings. "No, it's not that. I haven't met him yet."

Relieved Dan asked, "Then what's up?"

Michael told Dan what had just happened upstairs. Dan slapped him on the back and laughed. "See something you haven't seen in awhile?"

"Go to hell."

Dan's sense of humor was quick to return. "I was merely stating a fact."

Michael glared at Dan as he sat on the sofa, which was facing a traditional-style open fireplace. "Well, you can take your fact and—"

"There's no need to get so defensive." Dan took a seat next to Michael. He only let a moment lapse before he decided it was safe to speak. "What was it like?"

Michael turned to him inquisitively. "What was what like?"

"Seeing her." Dan leaned, resting his elbows on his starched pants. "Just in case you don't know what it was that you saw, I'll explain it to you. It's called a woman."

"Are you finished?" Michael asked.

A wide smile pulled his lips back. "I've only begun."

"Hello."

Dan's head shot up, curious to see who was responsible for Michael's agitated mood. Michael didn't look at the young woman as she entered the living room. His eyes remained averted as he concentrated on his glass, swirling the golden liquid.

She crossed the room, stopping just a few feet away from Michael. "As a rule I like to knock before I enter a room; you never know what you'll be interrupting."

"I—I thought you were someone else," Michael said.

She smiled sweetly. "I gathered that."

Michael looked up slowly, working his way from the floor to her white, high-top shoes to her jeans. Her shirt displayed Hard Rock Café across her chest in bright red letters. When his gaze reached her face, her expression was not what he had anticipated. He thought she'd appear riddled with shock, or maybe anger. Perhaps embarrassment. Instead, she had a beautiful, wide smile that made her brown eyes crease at the corners. "I'm sorry," he said.

"Don't worry about it. I'm just relieved to know that barging in on sleeping women isn't a regular habit of yours."

Lifting the small glass to his lips for the second time, he drained it in one swallow, enjoying the liquid as it burned a trail down throat. He looked at the empty bottle. He was on his own now.

"Isn't it a little early for that?" she asked and glanced her watch.

"I thought you were a man."

The woman's brows shot up. "I hope you have changed your mind, considering what you—"

"Yes, I have changed my mind," he snapped as his cold stare bore into her.

"Good. Because if you need more proof, I would be more than happy—"

Michael swallowed hard. Her banter was fast. For someone who couldn't utter a word moments ago, she was doing a great job now. Could that smile of hers get any bigger? "No. I don't need any more proof." Proof was the last thing he needed. He hadn't forgotten what he had seen. He felt the hard stiffness return. He shifted his weight for comfort and glared at Dan, who laughed again, this time not hiding his amusement.

The woman looked from Dan and back to Michael, assumed a serious face, and said, "Look, it's no big deal. It was an honest mistake. I was only kidding." She shrugged. "It's kind of an awkward situation, and I thought we could laugh it off. My mistake."

Michael just stared at her.

Not knowing what to do next, she extended her hand. "I'm Jessica Stanson."

"You're who?" Both men shot up out of their seats. The smile that had been painted on Dan's face from the moment Michael had told him what had happened was replaced with a twisted frown.

After discarding the possibility that she was a result of his men's sick sense of humor, Michael had assumed the woman standing before him was a guest of Mrs. Mayfield's. His housekeeper occasionally had a relative stay at his house when hers became overcrowded.

"Jessica Stanson, the horse trainer." Her words were slow as she spoke her name for a second time.

Michael didn't take his eyes off her. He couldn't.

"You did need a horse trainer, d-didn't you?" She looked from one man to the other, pleading for an answer. "I was hired by Dan Walker."

Suddenly able to break his gaze, Michael turned to Dan. "What the hell is going on?"

Dan raised a calming hand. "Mike, I'll straighten this out."

"I sure in the hell hope so."

Dan looked at Jessica. "I'm Dan Walker. I was the one that hired you for Mike. I remember speaking to a Mr. Ronald Stanson. He said that his kid Jess was the best."

Jessica nodded. "That's my dad."

Dan blinked, trying to comprehend the turn of events. "I don't recall him mentioning that you were a woman."

Jessica thought for a moment. "Are you sure?"

"I think I would remember it if he did."

Michael was pacing in front of Jessica, trying to organize his thoughts and make sense of everything. His shoulders were straight, his hands planted on his hips, and his eyes drilling into the floor. How could he have let Dan find his replacement? If he'd done it himself, none of this would have happened. He cursed himself for making such a foolish mistake.

"This isn't going to work," he said.

"What?" Jessica turned her attention from Dan to the man pacing in front of her. A few wisps of blond hair escaped from under his hat, situated carelessly across his forehead. Piercing blue eyes focused intently on the hardwood floor. His body was strong and tight, and she got to view a small portion of it through his shirt that was open just below his tanned throat. If it weren't for his angry disposition, he'd be very handsome.

"I'm sorry, but there is a mistake." Michael didn't look at her; he didn't want to see the disappointment that filled her eyes. Besides, he couldn't erase the big brown pools from his memory.

"What do you mean a mistake?" She held her hand against her chest. "I'm Jessica Stanson. That's who you hired, isn't it?"

"I hired a Jess Stanson," Dan said.

Jessica patted her chest again. "That's me."

"I thought you were a man," Michael said flatly.

She moved her hands to her hips as she looked at the harsh man who would be her boss for the next few months. "I thought we already established that."

"You're a woman." Too many things were happening at once. Michael was thinking about the meeting later that evening, riding the line, Jess—Jessica, whatever her name was.

He couldn't focus. Damn he was tired.

"That's the way it usually works. If you're not one, you're the other." She rolled her eyes. "Mr. Carven, you catch on quick."

"I think it will be best if you return home. I'll pay you for your time. I'm sorry for the inconvenience." His cynical gaze touched her as he stalked past. "Now, if you'll excuse me, I have work to do."

Dan stepped in his path and spoke under his breath, "What are you doing? You can't send her away."

"Watch me," he said, his eyes gleaming with fury. There was no way that he was living with a woman. Especially *that* woman. It wouldn't work. He had only known her for a few minutes, but he knew that it would never work.

"You're being unreasonable. Where are you going to find someone else?"

"I don't give a damn where I find a new replacement. I don't even care who the replacement is, just as long as it's not her." He lifted his hat and raked his hair with his fingers before slamming it back on again. "I don't know what in the hell you were thinking."

Dan raised his shoulders as he stuffed his hands in his pockets. "I didn't know she was a woman."

"Well, she is and I'm not living with her." He stared out the window, finding it hard to look at Dan. "I'll find someone this time."

"We were lucky to get her on such short notice and you know that." Dan looked over Michael's shoulder and glanced at Jessica. "I hate to remind you, but we have other things that need to be done."

Michael knew that Dan was talking about the investigation. Riverside, the small town they lived in, was paralyzed with fear. The media had played up the recent serial killings to the hilt. They spoon-fed Riverside's fifteen thousand people, along with several other nearby towns, with as much of the gory details that were allowed on television. It rested on Dan's shoulders to end the nightmare and return the town to its original Norman Rockwell–like charm.

"Look, she has excellent references, if that's what you're worried about," Dan persisted.

"That's not what I'm worried about."

Dan lowered his voice. "Mike, you'll never see her. You'll be too busy. She'll be too busy."

Jessica marched over to the two men. Her eyes settled on Michael's. "I'm not going anywhere until you give me a good reason why I should. And don't give me any crap about me being a woman. I'm a good trainer, and for you to judge me without seeing me work is outrageous and very shallow."

Michael held his hand up. "Like I said, Ms. Stanson, I'm sorry to inconvenience you, but I don't have the time or the patience to discuss this." He turned to leave again.

Jessica clenched her fist and bit her bottom lip. "I think that you just better find the time, Mr. Carven, because you're going to discuss this whether you like it or not. And as for patience, I seriously doubt that you have any." She threw her hands up. "Or manners for that matter. I don't know who you think you are, but your behavior is appalling."

Dan slipped out of the room, not wanting to get caught in the crossfire.

Chapter Two

Michael turned until his face was only inches from hers. "What did you just say?"

His eyes were like small volts of electricity as they burned through her. Somehow she held her ground. "You heard me. I think you owe me an explanation for your decision."

"You are a woman, for God's sake." He never blinked. "I don't think it would be proper for you to stay here."

"Proper?" she bit out in a curt tone. "What century do you think we're living in?"

"Yes, proper."

Jessica stuck her chin out. "I hate to be the one to break this to you, Mr. Carven, but Mrs. Mayfield is a woman too, if you hadn't noticed, and she works here."

"That's different." He couldn't believe that she was comparing herself to his housekeeper. She was thirty years older and thirty pounds heavier. The only thing they had in common was their temper. From the looks of it, all three of them had that same trait in common.

"Different?"

"Yes, different," he drawled nastily. "Jesus Christ, don't you get it?"

"No, I don't get it," she yelled. "Just what the hell are you trying to say? Please don't hold anything back because I'm a woman. Whatever is on your mind, come out and say it."

Michael tossed his hat on the sofa. He had gotten himself

into this, now how in the hell was he going to get out of it? Was she really unaware of what he was talking about?

Jessica took a little step closer, placing herself inches from him. "You get this, Mr. Carven. I'm not in the habit of accepting a job, driving hundreds of miles to get there, and being fired upon arrival for no apparent reason."

"I've already told you. I will pay you for your time."

The idea that he thought she could be paid off made Jessica even madder. "I don't want to be paid for my time. I want the job."

"I'm sorry, that isn't possible," he said sternly.

"Is the position already filled?"

"No."

"Then it *is* possible," she said.

He had the urge to take her by the shoulders and shake her. "I don't think you are listening to what I'm saying."

"I'm listening to what you're saying. I just can't believe you're saying it."

Michael ignored her comment and continued with what he was saying. "The discussion is closed."

"What discussion? We haven't discussed anything." Jessica licked her lips slowly, trying to control her anger. "I've been here for two days. During those two days I've met and worked with the crew. They have already shown me around and informed me how you like things done. They didn't seem to have a problem with me. Why do you?"

How had things gotten so out of hand? He had left town for two days to take care of some business before he went to work with Dan on the case. Somehow, in those two days, his calm, quiet life he had worked so hard for turned completely upside down. The high-spirited beauty standing before him was the cause of the majority of it.

"Boss?" Jake said entering the room.

18

Michael turned. "What?"

Jake stopped at the demand. "Everything's ready. We better get going if you want to finish early."

Jessica turned. "I'll meet you boys outside."

"You're not going," Michael said. His fingers dug into her biceps when he grabbed her as she walked past. "I obviously didn't make myself clear."

The tight grip knocked Jessica off balance, and as she whipped around, anger flashed in her eyes. "Mr. Carven, you hired me to do a job. I don't think you should fire me before you have had the chance to see me do that job."

Michael slowly released his grip as she spoke through clenched teeth. The look in her eyes told him she wasn't going to back down. He would give her a chance, he decided, and when she proved she couldn't handle the job, he would ask her to leave. That was the only way he was going to get her to go away. "Get saddled up."

Michael met the crew by the stables. As he walked to his horse that was tethered, he spoke. "I want Stanson to come with me. We'll ride the south and west lines. Jake and Richard, you ride the north and east lines. John and Tom, I want you to check the upper pasture." He swung himself onto the saddle. His horse danced in the gravel as he worked the reins. "Make sure you have all your supplies." Kicking his horse, he rode away.

Twenty minutes into the ride, Michael rode up beside Jessica. He watched her with a skillful eye. She looked at home in the saddle, like she was born in it. He spoke to pass the time. "I know you've met the staff, but I want to give you a quick rundown of everyone's positions, so you know what to expect of them. Richard is the stud groom. He takes care of all the breeding records and stallions. Jake is in charge of all the broodmares and foaling. Tom and John are responsible for all colts, gentling and green-breaking, feeding, and selling." He stopped. Dismounting, he tightened the top wire in a section of the fence. Mounting, he continued, "I'll make all the policy and budget decisions." He glanced at her. "Your job description isn't going to be as generalized, due to taking my position. You're to be responsible for all training. That means preparation of all horses for the track or their designated field. You'll be buying feed and any other supplies that are needed. You'll also supervise the rest of the staff. And two days a week I offer riding lessons; I would like you to handle that too." He stopped his horse. "Your pay will be adjusted according to the added responsibilities."

"Thank you, Mr. Carven."

"And you can cut the 'Mr. Carven' crap." He kicked his horse into a trot.

"Excuse me for being polite," she said.

Michael halted his horse and waited for her to catch up. "Is that what you call it?"

"Yes."

He gave her a sharp glance. "I don't need 'polite.' I need a horse trainer."

"Well, lucky you. You've got the best one around."

"We'll see about that."

Jessica sighed. "Listen, why don't we split up? It would cut our time in half." She pointed to the fence line they were riding. "I could ride the west line and you could ride the south."

"We're going to ride the line together."

Jessica didn't argue. Besides, what was the use if she did? They were going to be stuck with each other for the better part of the day, so she might as well make the best of it. She kicked her horse and followed Michael and the line.

When Michael left Jessica, she was talking soothingly to a stubborn stallion as she stroked his neck. Her soft words echoed off the massive building's walls and followed him out of the stables. He rounded the corner and headed towards the house. He had a few minutes before he was to meet with Dan.

"Hey, boss. Over here." Jake waved Michael over.

Michael looked to his left and saw his men sitting at a picnic table.

"How did everything look?" Michael asked.

Each man gave a report on how the fence lines were and the health of the herd.

"You got us," Jake said, slapping Michael on the back.

Michael looked confused. "What are you talking about?"

"Jess. It was a good joke. She was a good joke."

Richard spoke up. "Look, we've already figured it out. So, you can tell her to leave now."

"You figured what out?"

John tapped the side of the can of chew that he'd pulled from his back pocket. "You're getting us back for what we did to you at the bar a week ago." He tucked the pinch of snuff into his lip. "She's not blond, but she's a hell of a lot prettier. Damn, boss, I'm not sure how you got a looker like that to go along with this, but she's been nice to have around."

"It's been nice looking at her, but it's time she leaves," Richard said.

Michael realized what they were talking about. It was one of the few times he had agreed to go out with them. His crew had deviously fed a voluptuous blond cocktails throughout the night, asking the bartender to tell her they were from him. He had found out later they had even passed her a few one-word innuendoes scribbled on a napkin to keep her interest.

21

When he had gotten ready to leave, she had assumed she was leaving with him. "This isn't revenge."

The four men looked confused.

"I'm sorry, this isn't a joke. She isn't a joke." Michael shrugged his shoulders. "What's the big deal? You've gotten along with her for the last two days."

"The big deal?" Tom said kicking the dirt with a well-worn boot. "We thought it was all some big prank. We didn't want you to think you got the best of us, so we went along with it all."

Michael wanted to laugh but thought better of it. "That's why you didn't say anything this morning."

Jake nodded. "We thought you were just acting."

"Sorry, that was no act." Michael turned and headed toward the house. How he wished it were all an act. He let out a long breath as he followed the rock-edged gravel path that twisted and turned its way from the stables to the house.

"Boss."

Michael stopped as Richard came up behind him.

"You didn't need to hire someone else. We could have held down the fort until you were finished."

Michael not only sensed the irritation in Richard's voice but saw it riddled in his expression. Dark eyes that matched his tanned skin held the bulk of the displeasure. They narrowed and creased at the edges with discontent. "I have no doubt that you could have," Michael said simply as he watched Richard run a hand through his dark, wavy hair that had been ruffled from the long ride. Michael could tell that he was uncomfortable with the confrontation.

"I've been here the longest and I think I should have been next in line for the position." Richard lifted his shoulders. "I don't understand why you need to hire the position out."

Michael knew that none of his men wanted to play second-fiddle to a woman, especially Richard. "I didn't want to take you or any of the others from your present positions. You all are too good at what you do to be pulled from one area and put in another. Besides, then I'd just have to find someone to fill that position and I'd never find anyone as good. It's easier this way."

"She's a chick. Why'd you have to pick a chick?"

"It's just the way it worked out." Michael glanced at the house. "I need to be going." As he made his way to the house, he couldn't help but think of how Jessica would have reacted to being called a chick.

Chapter Three

Michael sat at the big oak desk in his study and watched Dan open his briefcase and pull out several thick files. He spread the cream-colored folders across the desktop and waved a hand over them. "It's all there. Everything I've got."

Michael's hands skimmed over the top of one of the folders before he flipped it open. He sorted through the file until he came across what he was looking for—the crime scene reports. "Give me a quick rundown on the victims."

"All three of them are young women between the ages of twenty and twenty-five. They are raped and strangled. The bodies are found in semi-remote areas. They are fully clothed, except for their underwear. Apparently he keeps them for himself." Dan gestured to the files. "As you'll soon find out, he doesn't leave much to work with. He's good. Leaves no prints of any kind."

Michael slipped on the light-framed glasses and listened carefully to Dan. His knowledge about the case was limited to what he saw on the news and read in the paper. He made a point not to watch or read either that often. Dan spoke about the case occasionally whenever he stopped by, but like the television and newspaper, he never paid much attention. His attentions had been focused on Pine Crest; he let very little of the outside in.

He jotted words in his notebook as Dan continued to fill him in. He hated starting a case in the middle of the investigation. It was like coming into a movie after it had already begun. You could be told every detail, but it was never the same as seeing it yourself.

Michael glanced up at Dan. "No witnesses?"

"Not a single one."

"Who were the last to see them?"

Dan rearranged the folders in chronological order. He placed his hand on the first folder. "Victim number one was last seen by her three girlfriends as she left a night club around eleven-thirty p.m." He moved down to the next folder. "Victim number two was last seen by her boyfriend around ten p.m. when he dropped her off at her house. And number three was last seen by a cashier at a gas station around ten p.m."

"He likes to work at night." Michael dropped his pen and asked, "Who do you think he is?"

Dan sat on the edge of the desk. "To tell you the truth, I don't know. He has to be friendly or else he wouldn't be able to get these women to go with him." He thought for a moment. "Level-headed, because most killers will drop something or forget something out of sheer excitement of committing the crime. He hasn't done that. Calm; you can't be nervous and do what he does. He builds trust somehow."

Michael cut in. "If we could decipher how he does this, it would narrow the margin of suspects."

"I agree."

"Do we have any suspects?"

"No. We've ruled out the possibility that the killer is a personal friend of any of the families or victims. These women didn't even know each other. The possibility that they know the same people is highly unlikely. All the family members check out fine."

"Tell me what you think a typical night for this guy is like."

Dan shook his head. "I've gone over this in my head at least a hundred times. I don't know. That's why I came to you. You could always get into their head and think like them." He paused and shrugged his shoulders. "I think he goes to a public place. A bar, a store, or a park, and pretends to accidentally bump into a woman. He could also use some slick pick-up line to strike up a conversation with her. And from there he gains her trust. Maybe he talks her into having a drink, dinner, or even just going for a walk with him. I think he chooses these girls at random. If he's lucky enough to get one to go with him, that's when he strikes. If not, no big deal; he moves to another."

Michael nodded in agreement. "Sounds reasonable. But he doesn't just pick any woman. She has to be between twenty and twenty-five and white."

"Yes, that seems to be what he likes."

"Is there anything that stands out about him?"

"Yeah a lot of things. The underwear for starters. But the mere fact that he can dump a body in the middle of nowhere and leave no evidence that he was even there is astounding. It's like the body appears out of thin air. I'm not shitting you. The crime scenes are spotless."

"Trained maybe?" Michael added.

"He could be. He might just be really efficient. I don't know." Dan gathered up his briefcase. "After you read everything I'll be curious to hear what you have to say about him." He looked at his watch. "It's getting late. I need to get home to the wife." He smiled. "I don't like the thought of sleeping on the sofa. By the way, she says hi and welcome back."

"Tell her I said hi, but I'm not back."

"She seems to think you are."

He ignored the comment. "I'm going to leave first thing in the morning and re-question the families."

"Let me know if you need anything." Dan stopped. "Thanks for doing this for me, Mike."

"No problem." He raised his hand. "But remember. I'm giving it two months. If I can't find him in two months, you're on your own."

"You'll find him. You always did." Dan laughed and shook his head. "You're the only detective I know that would go to crime scenes and the station on your own time, chase down every lead, and follow up every tip. Nothing laid dormant while you were on it. You were dedicated." Dan blew out a long breath and raised a finger. "I wish I still had one of you around."

"I'm not making any promises."

Dan moved to the door. "You don't have to." He stood quietly. "That's the thing about you. You never had to." He raised his briefcase. "What are you going to do about her?"

"I'm assuming you're referring to Jess."

"Yeah." Dan looked at the papers on Michael's desk. "As you can tell, I need you. I assure you I'll keep you so busy, you won't even know she's around."

"I'll know."

"Yeah, but you won't care. Let her stay. It's not her fault that she got mixed up in this. If there's any fault, it's mine. You've had a long day, Mike. Get a full night's rest before you decide to send her packing."

Michael lifted some photos and fanned them out like a deck of cards. "I don't think I'm going to get much sleep tonight either."

"Is she going to stay?" Dan asked as he opened the door.

"Maybe. Now, let me get to work." Already lost in his thoughts, Michael didn't even hear Dan leave. He went to a cabinet across the room and sifted through several maps before finding the one he wanted. After clearing off the desk, he spread the map out, then placed a red dot where the bodies were found and measured the distance from the first victim to the two others. They were all located in a fifty-mile radius. That led him to believe that the killer was local or knew the area well. He used a blue marker to locate the victims' residences. He put a green dot where the victims were last seen. Satisfied with differentiating each victim's information, he tacked the map to the wall behind his desk where he could refer to it throughout the investigation.

Three hours later, he had gone through only a fraction of the local police reports and hadn't even touched the pathologist's and coroner's reports. He took off his glasses and rubbed the bridge of his nose. He hadn't slept in twenty-four hours and he was beat. Time to call it a night.

He turned off the lights, shut the door behind him, and moved to his recliner in the living room. Closing his eyes, he stretched out, in the prone position, and allowed his body to relax for the first time in two days.

Several minutes later he heard someone walk in the room. He opened his eyes to see Jessica standing a few feet away in front of the sofa. He watched as she balled each hand up into a tiny fist and rubbed her eyes vigorously. She then unclipped her hair, ran her fingers through the soft tresses, separating the strands, let out a faint sigh, and flopped onto the sofa.

"Please, make yourself at home," Michael said, and he brought his arms up and folded them behind his head, using them as a makeshift pillow.

"Thank you, I will," she said as she yawned.

With her face slightly tilted, she reminded him of something a fine artist would produce. Her skin was flawless, her

28

hair was full and shimmered in the soft overhead light. Relaxed, she looked as harmless as a spring butterfly, but her true colors had been exposed this morning. She was full of spunk, wild as a mustang.

She had impressed him riding the fence line. He didn't have to explain or repeat himself once. She had completed every task he had given her. In fact, she'd been so efficient they had finished two hours before the rest of the men. She knew her way around a ranch—that was obvious. He had watched her closely all day, trying to find fault. He had looked for a reason to let her go, but he had found nothing. To send her away would be plain stupid, because he'd never be able to find a better replacement.

Dan needed his help; there was no doubt about it. Even though Michael had looked over only a fraction of the reports, it was enough to know that this case wasn't going to be easy to solve. Dan had said that he wanted him—it could be no one else—to look at the case from a fresh, new angle. Michael would do it, even if it meant living with a woman.

He looked at Jessica sprawled out on his sofa, an odd feeling grew in the pit of his stomach. He shifted uncomfortably as he recognized the slight pain as loneliness. Why? Anyone would feel lonely when looking at Jessica Stanson. The woman was so full of life. He had noticed that from the first time he'd seen her.

The odd feeling grew into a terrible ache. God forbid, but he knew no matter what he did or how he handled her, she was bound to create quite a stir in his house. The crew was either going to fight over her, worship her, or be at complete odds with her. He cringed at the thought of any of that happening. Then there was Mrs. Mayfield. She would protect Jessica like a mother hen from all of them, if need be.

He moved to a sitting position, resting his hands on his

knees. "Please, don't think I'm sexist. Even though I came off that way this morning."

Jessica opened her eyes. "Does that mean I'm staying? Or is this just an apology?"

"It's both. I'm sorry for this morning." And this afternoon, he thought. "I've had a lot of things on my mind." He sat forward. "I didn't mean to doubt your capabilities or offend you."

She rolled to her side. "Apology accepted. And I'm sorry for losing my temper." She smiled. "How about we start over?"

"That'd be nice." He drummed his fingers. "I didn't get a chance to show you around today. You know where all the tack and feed is, right?"

"Yes."

"Good. There's an office in the stables. I'll give you a key. In there I keep a list of all breeding records. I have individual records of mares that have bred two consecutive times and mares that have not conceived. I also keep a record of mares due to foal in thirty days. That helps keep an accurate cumulative inventory of the herd. Do you understand everything?"

She nodded. "How often do you update the records?"

"Once a month."

"Do you chart every session?"

"Yes. Only to show the owner what is being done and the progress that the horse is making." He clasped his hands together. "That's about it. The crew will handle the rest."

Jessica nodded.

"Mrs. Mayfield takes care of everything that has to do with the house. So, if you need or want anything, go to her." He paused a moment. "Why don't you tell me a little bit about yourself? Where you're from and how you got into horses."

Jessica sat up before she spoke. "I grew up in Richville.

30

That's about three hundred miles south."

"I know where it is."

"My dad has a small ranch. Locals board and come out when they have free time. A few small shows on the weekends, you know the kind. My mom died when I was six, so it was just me, my dad, and my three older brothers."

"When did you start training?"

"When I was eighteen. I went and worked for a rancher in Wyoming as a favor for my dad. It snowballed from there."

"Do you like traveling around?"

"Not really. But I love what I do, so it makes it easier. I hope to own my own ranch some day. That's the only reason I work for other people."

"People like me?"

"Yes. It pays well, and I'll do whatever it takes. I was excited about this job because this is the closest I've been to home in awhile." She paused. "You have a beautiful home."

"Thank you. I designed it myself."

"Really?"

"Yes, I have a friend, Nathaniel Marshall, who happens to be an architect. He gave me some pointers."

"When I arrived it was dark. It was amazing as I pulled into the driveway; the house was litup like a gigantic jack-o-lantern. The huge window seemed to glow in the dark." She looked at the floor-to-ceiling sheet of glass. "It seems to reach the stars."

"Then my efforts weren't wasted." It didn't surprise him that she felt the same about the house as he did. The house was exceptional—there was no denying that, but what did surprise him was how much it pleased him to know she liked it.

"It's like the house is cut in half. Don't you worry about privacy?"

"No, not out here. That's why I chose to build here; it's secluded."

Jessica looked around the room. "I love the fact you left the wood natural instead of painting it. And the stone fireplace is magnificent."

"I hand-picked the rocks from the river."

She looked up. "I like sitting in the loft. I feel like I'm sitting in the tree tops when I look out the window."

Michael smiled and said, "I'm glad you enjoy it."

"I must admit this is by far the nicest place I have ever worked. And I have never stayed in the main house before." She shook her head as she looked around the beautiful room. "And to think I almost didn't take this job."

Curiosity that was so much a part of him surfaced instantly. "Why wouldn't you take the job?"

"My dad didn't want me to."

"Why is that?"

"Because there is some maniac on the loose out here." She crossed her arms over her chest and rubbed her shoulders.

"Serial killer is the proper term."

"I know. I just hate the way that sounds." She inched forward and gave him a strong stare. "Have you been following the case, Detective Carven?"

"Yes, I'm actually working on it." He raised a questioning brow. "How did you know I was a detective?"

"I don't take just any job. I check the employer out first."

"That's smart."

"Thank you. You can never be too careful, in my book."

He was curious to know how much digging she had done. "What else do you know about me?"

Jessica shrugged. "Not much. Your grandparents raised you a few miles from here. You were a football hero in high school, and in college you graduated at the top of your class. As a detective you were—how did they put it?—brilliant and intuitive."

Michael laughed. "Brilliant?"

"That's what they said. I can't take credit for that information. You owe that to your local fan club. I had to stop in town and ask for directions. When they found out I was going to be working for you, they were more than happy to tell me about my new boss."

"I never knew anyone was keeping track. Please continue."

"You're now thirty-six. You went into the horse business three years ago. You have not only built a successful business, but a beautiful ranch."

"Thank you."

Jessica smiled because he sounded so pleased with what she said. Their newfound alliance must have agreed with him because his handsome features held none of the anger she'd seen this morning. He actually looked like he was enjoying the conversation with her.

"Go on."

"You have no family, at least none I could find." She raised a brow. "And you're a little superstitious."

"How so?"

"You never buy a horse with white hooves." She lifted her hands. "That's all I managed to find out."

Michael was impressed. She had been right about everything. "I think you should be the detective."

"There's only one thing."

"Which is?"

"I thought you were retired," she said.

"I am. I'm doing this as a favor for a good friend."

"Dan?"

33

"Yes. We were partners in the old days. I owe him a few favors."

"So, you hired me to take your place while you work on the investigation."

Michael nodded.

"I hope you don't mind if I ask, but what made you quit in the first place? You seem a little young to retire."

Michael got up and moved to the huge rock hearth. He lifted one leg and rested his foot on it. "My fiancée was murdered three years ago. Her killer was never found."

Her breath caught in her throat. The ghastly statement left her head reeling. In all her digging, she hadn't discovered he had been engaged. "I'm sorry." She met his gaze. "If her killer was never found, then why did you quit?"

How could he explain that? He was the best in his line of work, yet he couldn't find the one person who had torn his life apart. Sure, thousands of cases went unsolved, but not when it's the chief's fiancée. He had gone crazy. The investigation had become his obsession to the point of near-destruction. His only salvation had been his ranch, Pine Crest. He had stepped down from his job and Dan had been next in line to take his position. It was nice knowing that someone as competent as Dan was filling his shoes. It made it that much easier for him to leave.

He looked at her and spoke with impatience. "Do you have any more questions, Stanson?"

Jessica knew from his reaction that she'd overstepped her bounds. She hadn't meant to dredge up painful memories. "Yes," she said as she stood up slowly. She eyed him carefully as she waited for him to look at her. When he did, she said, "Are you always so charming in the morning?"

"I beg your pardon."

Her smile grew as she watched Michael's lips twitch. "I'm

asking purely to prepare myself for what might be in store for me tomorrow morning. I'm afraid that my attire was not appropriate for the unique wake-up call."

"There won't be any more wake-up calls."

"Why?"

"We're not roommates, we're employer and employee."

"We're living under the same roof, so technically that makes us roommates."

Michael stuffed his hands in his back pockets and tapped the point of his boot on the hearth. "Questions about the ranch, Stanson."

She nodded. "Oooh, those kinds of questions."

"Next time I'll specify." He lowered his glare. "I forgot I was speaking to a woman—or is it a comedian?"

She would let that one slide for the time being. She had gotten him over the hump of pain that she had so blindly led him to. "No, I think that's it. The guys explained everything to me." She winked. "And then some."

"I'll bet they did," he said.

"Excuse me?"

He shook his head. "Nothing. Let me give you a little warning about the men. They're a little rough around the edges."

Jessica shrugged. "They seemed to be fine."

"They're just being polite because you're new. When it wears off, watch out."

"Don't worry about it. I think they've met their match." She had grown up with three older brothers who had tormented and tantalized her nonstop. She knew exactly what to expect. A little teasing from the men that she worked with was nothing new to her. She'd always managed to get along with them.

"Don't get me wrong, they're good men, but they get a

little competitive and like to try and outdo each other. Occasionally they take it a little far." Michael paused, remembering some of the shenanigans they had pulled on him. "However, there's never really any harm done."

"No harm. That's good to hear." She made a smacking sound with her lips. "Are you as misbehaved as your hired help?"

A rough wrinkle shot across Michael's forehead. "Since you have no other questions concerning the ranch, I will excuse myself. I have work to do."

Jessica held up a finger and said, "There is one other thing."

He blew out a long breath. "Dare I ask?"

"Jess or Jessica is fine."

"Good night, Stanson." He walked to the study without looking back.

Chapter Four

Michael flung his hand across the bed at the ringing phone, fumbling with it before he managed to get the receiver to his mouth. "What?"

"Mike, another body has been found," Dan's voice was strained as he spoke the words.

Michael swung his legs around and sat on the edge of the bed. It was still dark out. He glanced at the clock: seven minutes past four. "Another body? Where?"

"In a field in Cutler Creek. The girl is in her early twenties."

Cutler Creek was fifteen miles south from the main part of town. "Is she from around here?"

"I don't know. They haven't identified her yet. I pray she's not."

"Have they moved the body?"

"No."

"Tell the M.E. not to move her. I want the best crime scene team you've got. I don't want a bunch a pansy-ass idiots wandering around messing shit up."

"It's done."

"Where are you?"

"At home. I just got the call. I thought it would be best if I called you first to see if you wanted to tag along," Dan said.

"Of course I want to go. I'll pick you up in a half hour." Michael hung up the phone and didn't move. He stared into the darkness. Did he really want to do this? When he had given up being a detective, he had also given up a part of himself that he wasn't sure he wanted back.

God, how he loved being a detective. It was all he ever wanted to be. All he dreamed about being. But the dream turned into a nightmare one terrifying night. It still amazed him how one day his life had been wonderfully fulfilling, and he had everything he could possibly want. Then a mere twenty-four hours later, it was a struggle just to go on.

Pine Crest had been his savior. He had bought the run-down ranch right out of college. It was where he went during summer vacations and weekends. Over time he'd managed to fix the place up, built a house with his own hands, and eventually state-of-the-art stables. Over the years, he'd also managed to acquire the surrounding land.

When shit had hit the fan, he had fled to the haven located in the backwoods, as everyone would call it, to begin a new life. It was the perfect place to escape the media. The story of his fiancée's murder smothered the front of every paper in the state, the gruesome details printed for everyone to read. He had quit his job and moved to the ranch when it became too much. Now, three years later, he was going back. Not forever, he told himself, only for this one case. He had no choice; he had to do it for Dan.

Dan had stood by his side through it all. He had put up with more shit than any good friend should. More than once, Dan had found him locked up in his apartment, shades pulled, drunker than a skunk. His normally spotless living room was littered with papers, files, and folders. An array of empty beer cans filled the gaps that the papers, files, and folders missed. Unlike the dirty dishes piled in the sink and on the counters, the refrigerator was empty. Dan would never say anything. He would come in with a bag of food and clean the place up.

A little unnerved, Michael turned his light on and pulled on a pair of jeans. "Here we go."

Michael and Dan drove up on a swarm of patrol cars. The Photo Unit and Medical Examiner teams were hovering everywhere. Cops were prowling the bushes, writing reports, and cordoning off the area with yellow ribbon.

Beyond the yellow ribbon was a group of media vans. The press shouted out questions to anyone who would answer. The normal number of civilians was low due to the remoteness, but there were still at least a dozen or so people scrambling around. Flash bulbs and spotlights were everywhere, competing for the best photo. The story was top news and everyone wanted a piece of it.

"Looks like a God damn zoo," Dan said.

"It always does." Michael motioned to the crime scene. "This place needs to be restricted. No wonder there is never any evidence found. I only want detectives and the M.E. in this area. Send everyone else in the field to look for evidence."

The deputy inspector walked up to Dan. "Good morning, Chief."

"Good morning," Dan said to the deputy, who was compactly built with a military buzz cut.

The deputy turned to Michael. "Well, I'll be damned. Michael Carven. It's nice to see you again, sir."

"Morning," Michael said.

"I thought you got tired of the business and built yourself a nice ranch up in the hills."

"I did."

"Got bored and came back?"

Michael looked around and laughed. "Miss all this? Nope.

I'm just here to help out the chief."

"Fill us in on the details," Dan said.

"We have a twenty-three-year-old white female. We identified her about twenty minutes ago. Her name is Nichole Blake."

"Where is she from?" Michael asked.

"Riverside, sir."

"Shit. Who found her?" Dan asked.

"That man over there." He pointed to a man in a long brown duster leaning against a squad car. "He was moving his cattle early this morning when he came across her."

"Who took his statement?" Dan asked.

"Freeman."

"Tell him I want to speak with him. And get this God damn place cleaned up or you're going to find a pink slip with your name all over it. This isn't a fucking circus."

"Yes, sir." Before the deputy inspector left, he looked at Michael. "It's nice to have you back. We've missed you."

"I'm not back," Michael snapped.

"Whatever you say, sir."

Michael moved to the bright yellow blanket that covered Nichole Blake. He lifted the cloth and stared at the woman. People thought he was cold-hearted because he could look at a corpse and feel none of the normal emotions. He was there to solve the murder, not feel sorry for the woman. He supposed that was what made him so good. He never got involved with the victim emotionally. Once it became personal, that was when you started making mistakes.

The dark blue jeans and light sweater that she wore were smeared with damp mud. He moved to the end of the body and looked at her shoes. The tops were soiled; however, the soles were relatively clean. "She didn't walk here." He mumbled the words to himself as he moved to the upper part of the body.

Debris from the ground stuck to her lifeless face and clung to her hair. He did a visual search over her body. Her clothes weren't ripped or torn. There didn't appear to be any marks on her body, at least the parts he could see. He looked on the ground next to her for any evidence. There was nothing. Just like Dan had said, everything was perfectly in place. Everything from her clothing to the ground cover was in order. There was no evidence that anyone had been there.

The M.E. walked up to Michael and said, "It's a shame."

Michael looked at the lean, bald man. "How long has she been dead?"

"Can't say. Not until I do an examination."

"I want that A.S.A.P."

"I'll do my best."

Michael's eyes remained fixed on the body. "What do you think the cause of death was?"

The man crouched next to the body. He pulled down the collar of her sweater and pointed to a black ring around the small neck. "Looks like she was strangled."

"Can I have a pair of gloves?"

The man reached in his coat pocket. "Here."

Michael put the gloves on and reached for the woman's pants. He struggled as he unbuttoned and unzipped the damp jeans. A patch of pale white skin appeared as he pulled back the material. He continued on tugging the denim until he saw a patch of dark pubic hair. She wasn't wearing any underwear. Michael knew for sure that he was looking at victim number four.

"You can take her now." He looked over his shoulder toward Dan. "It's him."

"Shit."

"It was only a matter of time before he hit again," Michael said.

"Yeah, but I was hoping we would get him before then."
Dan looked over his shoulder at the bright lights. "How about talking to the press for me?"

Michael laughed. "You've got to be kidding."

"Do I look like I'm kidding? I'm too old for this. Besides, it's too God damn early."

"It's not going to happen, old man."

"Come on, do this one favor for me."

Michael glossed over his attempted guilt trip. "I'm already doing a favor for you, and talking to the press isn't part of it."

"Thanks," Dan grumbled as he walked away.

Michael walked up to an officer from the local police who was searching the field. "Find anything?"

"Yes, sir. We found some footprints over there." The officer pointed about twenty yards from the body.

"Get a mold made immediately." The light sprinkle they had last night was possibly the best thing that could happen. "And don't let the press know about it."

"Yes, sir."

"And drop the 'sir.' "

"Yes, sir."

Michael looked at the man seriously. "Do I call you 'sir'?"

"No."

"Then don't call me 'sir.' "

"Yes, sorry."

Michael wandered back to his truck. He watched the dozen or so police scout the field for a few minutes and then he looked down to write in his black note pad. He glanced back up when Dan approached the truck.

"I'm all finished here. You ready to go?" Dan said.

"Yeah."

Dan climbed in the truck. "Are the prints all they found?"

Michael took a sip from the lid of his thermos and watched

the crime scene disappear in his rear view mirror. "Yes, so far."

"Well, at least we can finally get an estimated height and weight," Dan said.

"Has the girl's family already been notified?"

"Yes, they sent someone out when they identified the body."

"Okay, I want to start questioning her friends, co-workers, and family. I want to know everything about her. What she did last night, who she was with, if she has a boyfriend, where she works, where she hangs out."

"Got it."

"And make sure no one talks to the press."

Jessica watched Mrs. Mayfield as she worked efficiently in the spacious kitchen. Using two bowls and a wooden spoon, she was scrupulously preparing something at the island. A soft, yellow, embroidered apron hung around her large waist. Her graying hair was pulled tightly back in a bun at the base of her neck. Come to think of it, Jessica hadn't seen her wear her hair any other way. It suited her though, and in its own way it matched the high-collared shirts she always wore.

The older woman finished with her task and bounced around, cleaning and organizing the mess she'd made. Jessica moved to the breakfast bar. "Good morning."

Mrs. Mayfield looked up. "Good morning, dear."

"What is this?" She pointed to the table loaded with food. Platters filled with steaming potatoes and pancakes were surrounded by tableware, fresh orange juice, and milk.

"Once a month I fix a breakfast for the guys and Michael. I guess you can call it a meeting. They talk about how things are going, and if there are any problems they discuss them."

"Great idea. Can I help with anything?"

43

She handed her a bowl of scrambled eggs. "Put those on the table and I'll get the salt and pepper, and the pot of coffee."

While Jessica was rearranging the table of food to accommodate another dish, Jake and Richard came in.

"Morning Jess," Jake said.

Richard just mumbled as he found his seat.

"Good morning," Jessica said.

Within a few minutes Tom and John came in. Jessica glanced at the empty chair at the head of the table. Where was Michael? He didn't expect her to head the meeting, did he? He hadn't informed her that there was going to be a meeting. She looked at the guys. They were so busy shoveling food onto their plates they hadn't even noticed his absence.

"Can you pass the eggs, Jess?"

Jessica looked to Tom. "Sure." If they weren't going to worry about it, neither was she.

"Mornin'," Michael said, walking into the room.

Jessica stuffed a fork full of pancakes in her mouth. "Good morning."

Michael poured himself a cup of coffee and looked down the table. It was strange seeing Jessica there. It had always been just him and his men. There had never been a woman at the table. He waited until everyone had served themselves before asking, "Anyone have anything they would like to discuss?"

Jake said, "I think Sassy is going to deliver in a week or two."

Michael nodded. "Leave her in the pasture for a few more days and then put her in the foal stall."

Jake took a bite of his biscuit. "Okay. Can I have the day off tomorrow like we discussed?"

"Yes. Make sure that you make arrangements with

Stanson. You want to pass me one of those?" Michael motioned to the basket full of biscuits.

Richard was the next to speak. "Cash is losing weight."

"Is he breeding?" Michael said.

"No."

Michael thought for a minute. "Does he have any symptoms of being sick?"

Richard shook his head. "I even checked for a fever."

"I'd check the feed. It might be damaged," Jessica said.

Michael looked at Jessica. "I agree. It might have been a bad batch. Keep him on the same feeding program, just try some new feed. If that doesn't work, let me know. Is there anything else?"

Jessica watched Michael as he poured an ungodly amount of gravy over his biscuit. She waited until he was finished before she spoke. "I think we should have a radio installed in the barn. Nothing elaborate, of course. Just a few speakers at each end."

"Your job is to work, not sing, Stanson," Michael said.

"Thanks for reminding me." She puckered her lips and she took a drink of orange juice as she watched Richard stifle a laugh. "But it's not for me; it's for the horses."

"Horses?"

"Yes."

"And what type of music do horses listen to, Stanson?" Michael asked.

"I don't think it really matters, just as long as there is sound."

"Why?"

"Because they get lonely just like the rest of us," she said.

Michael lifted a chunk of gravy-soaked biscuit to his mouth. "Are you lonely, Stanson?"

Jessica ignored the snickers from the guys. "I read an article on it. Would you care to hear about it?"

"Of course. Please enlighten us on the harmonious sounds that horses prefer."

Jessica wiped her mouth and tossed her napkin on her plate. She glared at Michael. Words were not needed to get her message across. It was clearly written on her face that she didn't need his shit.

"Several doctors studied hundreds of horses and found the ones exposed to a radio twenty-four hours a day were less restless." Since reading the article, she had put a small portable in her father's barn.

Jake said, "I read something like that, too. It said that most horses suffer, at least slightly, from boredom and a lack of mental attention. They're used to being in a herd where there are other horses to interact with. In the stalls, there's nothing for them to do. The radio is supposed to fill that emptiness."

Jessica nodded. "I also read that goats, cows, dogs, and cats often serve as companions. The company makes their day a little more interesting."

Jessica and Jake compared the articles they had each read. Both pieces had said just about the same thing.

"It sounds like a good idea to me," John said.

"I'll look into it." Michael glanced at his crew.

Jessica offered to Michael, "If you like, I could give you the article. I still have it."

Michael swung his eyes back to Jessica and glared at her. "I said I would look into it. Is there anything else?" Everyone muttered no and kept eating.

"There they are. Hand-delivered." Dan tossed the lab results on Michael's desk.

"That was quick."

46

"Yeah, when I told them who wanted them, they suddenly appeared on my desk the next day." Dan sat down. "The killer is approximately six foot, a hundred and eighty pounds, and his shoe size is eleven and a half."

Michael didn't look at the results; he would go over them later. "His shoe preference?"

"Nike."

"What type?"

"A cross-trainer," Dan said.

"Check it out. I want to know where they are sold."

"I already did. It's the most popular type. It can be bought anywhere."

"That figures." He shoved the results aside. "What did you find out about the girl?"

Dan pulled up a chair. "She was a loner. No boyfriend and not many friends. She worked at Winters' Market downtown. She clocked out Wednesday at four p.m. That was the last time anyone saw her. She wasn't supposed to be back to work until Saturday at eight a.m."

"Where did she live?"

"She lived alone in an apartment complex three blocks away. She walked to and from work every day."

"Has it been searched?"

"Yes. Nothing was found."

"Did any of her neighbors see her come home Wednesday night?" Michael chewed on the end of his pen.

"See her, no, but we have a little old man who saw her lights on around five."

"Five? Well, it shouldn't take her but a few minutes to walk home. She must have stopped somewhere along the way. I want every business between the market and her apartment questioned. Ask them if they know any of her habits. She might stop off every day after work and get a cup of coffee or dinner." As he spoke, he took notes. "See if anyone was passing through the area at the time she got off work. Check out if there were any service people who were en route. There has to be someone who saw her."

Michael walked Dan to the door. "Call me if anything comes up. If someone did see her, I don't want him or her questioned. I want to do that myself."

"Sure thing."

Michael went back to the study. He jotted down a list of things that he wanted to check out in the morning. If Nichole Blake was home Wednesday, that would mean she was murdered between Thursday and late Friday because she was found early Saturday. He would have to call the M.E. and push for a report. Her time of death would help tremendously.

He put his pen down and tried to envision what the killer would look like. Of course he wanted to picture a man who looked like a monster, but he knew that couldn't be possible. His appearance was average. How he conned the young women to go with him was also puzzling. What kind of promises did he make to insure their cooperation and instill their trust?

He glanced at the clock: one-thirty a.m. He was exhausted. He had better get to bed before it was time to get up. Putting a few papers in a folder, he turned his desk lamp off and shut the study door.

Walking slowly to the kitchen to get a drink, he stopped in his tracks when he saw Jessica's elegant figure outlined by the refrigerator light. The sheer cotton nightgown cast a glowing aura around the same delicate body that he had seen a few mornings ago, only this time the dark, round curves and supple skin were more pronounced. The silhouette looked to be cut from fine black satin. She resembled a glowing an-gel—all she needed was a halo and a set of wings.

"Midnight snack?" His voice shattered the quiet of the night.

She jumped and turned around. The small saucer of food dropped to the floor. "You scared me half to death." She fell back against the refrigerator. Both of her hands were pressed against her chest.

He took her by the shoulders to steady her. "I'm sorry. I didn't mean to—"

She shoved his hands away. "What do you think you're doing, scaring me like that? You could have given me a heart attack." She felt as if her cheeks were on fire. She was glad it was dark and he couldn't see her.

He snorted as he took a step back. "I seriously doubt that."

"You were probably hoping for just that."

Michael regarded her impassively. "Is that what you think?"

"You make it no secret that you don't like me," she tossed back at him. "Don't pretend otherwise."

He stared at her through squinted eyes. His hands rested on his hips, one leg shoved forward in a relaxed stance. It was becoming more apparent just how much he had startled her. No one had ever been afraid of him, at least no one on the right side of the law, and he didn't like it. "Come here." His voice was warm with regret. Regret for scaring her and regret for the way he had been treating her. He honestly hadn't intended to do either.

"Come here," he said again.

She took a few steps, then stopped as if she were contemplating going any farther. Michael made up her mind for her. In one fluid motion, he went to her and closed his arms tightly around her small frame.

He held her body close to him as he rubbed her back. His hand glided over the satiny material in long slow strokes. The words he whispered were said without thought. "Shh, it's okay. I didn't mean to scare you." It upset him, seeing her frightened. When she wrapped her arms around him, he realized that it had been a long time since he had held someone. The press of another body against his felt good. He moved his hands up her back until he found her hair and weaved his fingers through it momentarily before uttering under his breath, "I don't hate you. Don't ever think I hate you."

"Well, you don't like me," she said against his chest.

"Why do you say that?"

"Because you don't want me here. You're stuck with me. That's the only reason—"

"I didn't get stuck with you. And if you'll recall, I asked you to stay. I want you here." He felt her give in to his embrace after a few seconds. Her breathing slowly returned to normal as she nuzzled her head into the crook of his arm.

She pulled away and looked at the food on the floor. "I'm sorry." She went to the sink to get a washcloth, knocking over a glass as she did. It shattered as it hit the floor. Jessica's hand flew to her mouth. "Michael—"

"Don't move or you'll get glass in your feet."

Jessica froze when Michael snuggled his arm around her waist.

"You're going to be fine." He stepped over the glass and carried her to the foot of the stairs. "You go back to sleep. I'll clean up." His voice was now hard and sharp.

Jessica didn't move. Her eyes locked with his. "I don't know what has gotten into me. I'm not usually this clumsy."

"Go," Michael said. He didn't know how much longer he

could stand those big brown eyes looking at him with such innocence.

"I'm sorry, Michael," she said again.

"Please go." He watched as she turned and climbed the stairs. He was going to have to be careful around her.

Chapter Five

Michael leaned back in his chair as he stared at the case file for Nichole Blake. All he needed to do was answer: who, where, when, why, and how. If he could answer those questions, he could find her killer and close the case.

Easier said than done, he told himself as he took a piece of paper and wrote *HOW* in large letters at the top. He knew how she had died: by asphyxiation. When had she died? He was sure between Thursday and Friday, but he would have to wait for the M.E.'s report for that. Where? Judging by the neatness of the ground, she wasn't killed where she was found. Now came the hard part. Who had killed Nichole Blake and why?

He had mulled that over and over and had come up with nothing. The simple fact was that he didn't have anything to go on. Just like the three other murders, the evidence was next to nothing. He was going to have to wait until something or someone turned up. This was the hardest part, the waiting. He shoved himself away from his desk; the wheels of his chair squeaked loudly in protest as it slid across the room. He stood, and in one swift movement he sent the chair reeling back toward the desk. Helplessness consumed him. "I should be doing more." The words were slightly more than an audible whisper as he moved to the other side of the room.

He examined the map on the wall he had marked earlier.

Maybe there was a pattern to which towns the killer chose. He ran his finger over the map as he studied the locations. After rechecking the towns, the distance between them, and the location of the bodies, there still didn't seem to be a pattern.

The killer preferred larger towns, but not cities. He steered away from them. It was just an hour drive to Coburn, with a population over a hundred thousand. He had spoken to the chief of police there, and he said that they hadn't come across anything, but they were keeping their eyes open.

He concluded there was no pattern and if the killer, heaven forbid, killed again, it would more than likely be in one of the smaller towns that surrounded Riverside. He looked at the clock. Past midnight. He left the paper spread across the desk. He would pick up where he left off in the morning.

Michael gripped the rail as he climbed the stairs. He was tired. As he passed Jessica's room he noticed that the door was open and there was no one in the room. "Stanson?" He flicked on the light. The bed was still made and she wasn't in the bathroom. He went downstairs and checked the kitchen. Finding it empty, he looked out the window and saw there was a light on in the barn. He took his coat off the peg by the back door and shrugged it on as he stepped out in the cold night air.

When he opened the door to the stables, he was greeted with a face full of warm air from the glowing heat lamps and fans circulating the air. When he had constructed the stables, he had the horses' comfort in mind. The skylights and a few panels on the side of the arenas were removable to allow the summer breeze to blow through when it warmed up. He walked to the foaling stalls on the other side of the building, where he spotted Jessica leaning over the stall. In a loud whisper he said, "How is she doing?"

Jessica looked down the wide hall. She didn't speak. She pointed and waved him down.

Michael saw the light reflect off her tears and knew Sassy had lost the colt. But how? The vet had said she was doing great. He lengthened his strides to reach Jessica. "What happened?"

Jessica wiped the tears from her cheeks.

Then he saw the long-legged colt burrowed in the soft hay next to his mother. He looked back to Jessica, his brows pursed. "What's wrong with you?"

Her hands came to her mouth as she smiled. "Isn't it exciting? We're the first to see him."

"And this triggered you to cry by—"

"It's a miracle. And I got to see him being born. Oh, Michael, it was beautiful."

Michael nodded his head like that explained it all. "Do you cry every time?"

She sniffled and nodded. "If you would have come out just a few minutes earlier, you could have seen the birth."

"You should have come and gotten me."

"I didn't want to disturb you while you were working," she said. "It was magnificent. Sassy did a great job."

"I thought she wouldn't deliver for a few more days."

"Me too. But when I checked on her at the end of the day, I noticed that she was having strong contractions."

They both turned their attention back to the bonding that was taking place in the stall. Jessica looked to Michael and started laughing because a fresh stream of tears was spilling down her cheeks. "I'm sorry. I can't help it."

Michael laughed when he looked at her. Her cheeks were streaked with tears, yet she had a smile on her face. He fished in his pocket, produced a handkerchief, and handed it to her. "Here."

She took the white cloth and wiped her eyes. She glanced back into the stall. "Isn't he just beautiful?"

Michael stared at the bloody, slimy colt. "I guess."

"What do you mean, you guess? He's perfect."

"Maybe when he dries he'll be cuter."

Jessica leaned her head over the stall. "You don't listen to him, little fellow, he doesn't know what he's talking about. You're adorable and don't let anyone tell you different." She smacked Michael in the chest with the handkerchief as she gave it back. "We have to celebrate."

"Celebrate what?"

She looked at the colt. "This new life."

Back in the kitchen Jessica searched the cabinets for wine or champagne. "You don't even have any beer," she said as she looked in the refrigerator.

"Sorry."

"What kind of ranch is this?"

Michael didn't keep beer in the house; he didn't want history to repeat itself. He sat at the breakfast bar and watched her rummage through his kitchen. Her eyes were puffy from crying and the tip of her nose was red from sniffling. The few hairs that had escaped from her ponytail lay softly against her cheek and neck.

"You can't tell me this huge house doesn't have a wine cellar."

"Afraid not."

Jessica ran out of the pantry. "Look what I found. We have a choice, red or white." She tossed an evil grin his way. "Or both."

Michael took the bottles from her. "Cooking wine?"

"Why not?" She was now searching the cupboards. "Where are your wine glasses?"

"I'm not drinking this."

"Why?"

"Have you ever tasted this stuff?"

She shook her head. "Wine is wine."

"You don't drink much, do you?"

"No. Look, I found them." She had to stretch to reach the glasses stored over the refrigerator. She washed the dusty glasses and then filled them. Raising her glass, she said, "Come on, Michael."

He reluctantly picked up his glass.

Jessica tapped it with hers. "To Criss Cross."

"Who?"

"That's what I named him. His legs were all tangles when I first saw him." She smiled meekly. "I know you'll give him a name, but that was the first thing I thought of when I saw him."

He raised his glass and took a big swig, then made a sour-looking face. "This is disgusting." He set the glass down. "I'm not drinking this."

She took another sip while willing her bitter expression back. "You must not be a real cowboy."

"Excuse me?"

"Real cowboys don't care what they drink." She shrugged and took another sip. "It's a well-known fact."

Michael drained his glass in one swallow. "How's that for a real cowboy?"

She giggled as she refilled his glass.

A half hour later Michael picked up the empty bottles of cooking wine. "We don't have to celebrate every birth, do we?"

"Yep."

He swirled the last swallow of wine in his glass. "Do you realize how many births we have?"

Jessica hiccupped. "Nope."

"Well, I can tell you I'm not drinking this stuff for every one of them."

She looked at him like he was being ridiculous. "It's not that bad."

"Famous last words. You remember that tomorrow morning."

She put her glass in the sink, and when she turned she stumbled into him. For some reason she didn't step back. She didn't want to. "Developed" and "firm" was the only way to describe his chest. Well, she could toss "broad" in there too. His scent was a drive-you-crazy combination of fresh, woodsy, and rich spices. Stifling a groan, she resisted the urge to bury her face in his shirt. Instead she sucked in a deep breath.

Michael looked down at the innocent, brown-eyed beauty staring so hopelessly at him. Warm pink swept across her cheeks, lighting her face into a healthy glow. He wasn't sure if the flush was a result of the wine or the close proximity. Her lips captured his gaze and held it. Their shape was sensual because of their natural pout. And their fullness only enhanced the incredible appearance. Would they taste as good as they looked? He had half a mind to find out.

On their own accord, his eyes found their way to her hair. It looked heavy and soft. It was a mass of thick tresses that a man could get lost in and he wanted nothing more right now than to touch it—

God, what was he doing? There wasn't enough alcohol in that wine to make him lose all his senses. "I'm gonna check on Sassy."

Jessica nodded in stunned silence as he walked out the door.

The next morning, Jessica came in the back door.

Michael was sitting at the kitchen table. "You're up. I thought you were still sleeping."

Jessica slid into a chair and buried her face in her hands. "I've been up for two hours and the dull pain in my head hasn't eased any. Don't you have some ancient remedy to cure this?"

"Afraid not."

"I thought cowboys had remedies for everything."

"Not for hangovers caused from cooking wine." He looked at her when she removed her hands. "You want to know why? Because any cowboy with a lick of sense wouldn't touch the stuff."

Jessica covered her ears. "Point made. You don't have to yell." She went to the coffeepot and poured herself a cup. She decided against cream—the blacker the better.

"It's not going to work," Michael said. "I'm on my third cup."

"I have to try something." She lifted the cup to her mouth. "How about aspirin? Coffee and aspirin, that sounds like it would work."

"Tried it."

"Coffee, aspirin, and Pepto Bismol."

"Are you trying to make it worse?"

Jessica sat back down at the table. "No, I'm desperate. Just the thought of galloping a horse around an arena makes me want to throw up."

"It's not that bad." Michael mimicked her words from last night as he took a sip of his coffee.

Jessica shot him a dirty look.

"Good morning, you two." Mrs. Mayfield came in with a basket of laundry. She set it on the table and began folding. "What sounds good for breakfast?"

"Oh God, I couldn't eat if I wanted to," Jessica said in a low moan.

"I'll pass too," Michael said. "The thought of food makes me sick."

"You two aren't feeling well?"

"That's an understatement," Jessica said.

"What's the matter? Catch a bug? You know that twenty-four-hour flu is going around."

"Let's just say that we had a long night and leave it at that," Michael said.

Mrs. Mayfield looked at each of them out of the corner of her eye. "I'll fix a big pot of homemade soup for lunch then. That'll fix you right up." She put the neat, categorized piles of clothes back in the basket and left to put them away.

Jessica pressed her fingers into her temples. "It's going to hurt, but we have to talk."

"About what?"

"Wes."

"What about him?"

"He's not dependable," Jessica said. "He was supposed to be here an hour ago. He did this to me last week also."

Michael knew the topic of the dependability of his shoe farrier was going to come up sooner or later. "But he does good work."

"I agree, but you have to wait a day or two for him to show up and do the work."

"A day or two—hell, he's getting better. Before you started working, we used to wait weeks for him. You're giving him a reason to get out here sooner. You should be happy."

"Happy? I never know when my horses are going to be

shod. Which makes it hard when you work by a schedule and the horse you want to work with you can't because it threw a shoe that was supposed to be fixed two days ago."

Michael didn't care what she said; he wasn't going to let Wesley go. Wesley had shoed his Grandpa's horses when he was little. He could still remember how Wesley used to let him be his helper. If he did a good job, Wesley would walk back to his truck and take a candy bar from his lunch and give it to him. He would praise his good work and declare that he couldn't have done it without his little helper. Just as he had when he was younger, Michael still looked forward to his visits. Even more so now because they reminded him of when he was younger and living with his grandparents.

"Do you know he comes to work drunk? Do you want a drunk man shoeing your horses?" It seemed ironic she should be saying this. The pressure at her temples didn't seem to be doing any good, so she pushed her thumb between her eyes.

"I have never seen Wesley drunk a day in my life. And I don't care if he was drunk, sober, or asleep. He is the best around."

"You own one of the most elite ranches in the state of Montana, you hire only the best to work for you, but you'll settle for a drunk to shoe your horses," she said.

Michael glared at Jessica over the rim of his cup. "Stanson."

"If I'm to do my job to the best of my ability, I need cooperation from him."

"Fine, I'll talk to him."

"I don't think talking is going to work."

"Then what do you want me to do?"

"Get someone dependable. I'm simply asking for someone I have a little confidence in."

"I have confidence in him and that's all that matters."

"But—"

"You're not going to win this one, Stanson."

"Fine. You're the boss, do what you want," she said as she got up and left, slamming the door behind her.

Michael watched Dan as he considered his words. He wasn't sure if his friend was going to go along with his idea. "So, what do you think?"

"I don't know."

"I'm open for suggestions if you have any other ideas." Michael shifted his weight as he sat on the edge of his desk.

"I'm all out of ideas; that's why I came to you," Dan said as he stood and moved to the other side of the room.

"Well, then in my opinion, I think the sooner we release the portrait of Nichole Blake the better. If I was still in charge, it's what I would do."

"I think it's a good idea."

"But?" Michael said, sensing his hesitation.

"But, I don't know how the people are going to react when they realize that we are turning to them for help."

"They're going to think we're doing everything in our power to catch this guy. Besides, we *are* turning to them."

"They're going to think we have no control over this case; that's what they're going to think. They're afraid as it is, Mike; this could cause major hysteria. Do you know what I read in the God damn paper this morning? It said something to the effect that the officials need to start doing their jobs instead of acting like they are doing them. Who in their right mind would print that? As far as the public is concerned, they don't think we're doing a damn thing right now."

"I understand what you're saying, but do you think we really have a choice?"

Dan exhaled an exhausted sigh. "No."

"I could see if we had a few leads that we wanted to pursue on the low, but that's not the case. We have nothing." He moved around his desk. "Everyone is hysterical as it is. It's not going to cause more hysteria. I think it's worth a shot. It's our only shot." Michael held his hands up. "No one saw Nichole since she left work Wednesday. We have a man who saw her lights on in her apartment later that evening, but he didn't see her. What we need is to find someone who actually saw her during her last few hours or days of her life. There could be someone out there who might have seen her and not even know it."

Dan stared into space, contemplating. "How do you want to do this? It's your call."

"I think we should release it to all the local newspapers and the television stations. The more they broadcast it, the better."

Dan shrugged in agreement. "On my way back to the station, I'll stop by and speak to her parents and get that out of the way. Then I'll call all the newspapers and the television stations. I'm sure we can get this out by tomorrow night." Dan stood up and put his coat on. "They're going to have a fucking field day with this."

"Don't they always?"

"Yeah, but it's not usually in my jurisdiction." He rubbed his stomach. "I think I'm getting an ulcer."

"What's the matter, Chief, can't you take a little heat?"

"I'm not like you." Dan laughed. "I remember you used to eat this shit up. Nothing bothered you. Interrogation, checking statements, searching records, all the hours spent in court, and even dealing with the press never produced a single complaint. Man, I loved working with you." He shook his head. "I wish all my men were like you."

"You don't want your men to be like me."

"Why is that?"

"Because when it boiled right down to it, I couldn't handle it. I couldn't take the heat."

"That's not fair to say."

"It's the truth."

"I was there Mike; the circumstances were completely different. Don't be that hard on yourself."

"Let's hope someone recognizes Nichole and can give us some information that will help us get this guy."

Dan reached for the door. "I'll be in touch."

Chapter Six

Jessica turned around as she rinsed the last of her dinner dishes and was surprised to see Michael. She had seen his headlights when he had pulled in, but he usually went straight to his study after spending the day with Dan. "Hi, you want some dinner?"

"I'll fix it." Michael went directly for the refrigerator. He peered at its contents.

"Sit down. I can fix it," she said as she pointed to a chair at the bar.

"You are my trainer, not my cook." There was an edge to his voice.

"I know what my job is." She picked up the casserole Mrs. Mayfield had made earlier. Michael looked exhausted. "Mrs. Mayfield has already fixed everything. All I need to do is heat it up. It's no trouble, really," she said.

Michael closed the door and jerked the dish from her hand. His face was like stone. "I can heat it myself." He turned his back to her and thrust the dish into the microwave.

Jessica didn't push the subject any further. As Michael prepared his meal, she dried and put the dishes away. She took a wet sponge and wiped down all the counters. Once she was finished tidying up, she slid into the stool beside him. She used the palm of her hand to prop her head up and sat for a moment. "How was your day?"

"Fine."

She waited for a few seconds to see if he was finished speaking. When he took another bite of his dinner, she realized that he was. Apparently he didn't feel any elaboration was needed. She tried once again. "Tom and I worked with the new quarter today."

Nothing.

"She is a great horse. Nice disposition. I think she'll go far."

Nothing.

She drummed her fingers. "Yep, everything went smoothly."

Nothing.

"Yes, other than Richard breaking his leg falling off a horse this morning and Mrs. Mayfield cutting her finger off this afternoon making that very casserole, I think it's safe to say everything went smoothly today. However, the night is still young; you never can tell what might happen next."

If he noticed her attempts at conversation, he gave no indication of it. He ate his food without taking his eyes off his plate.

Jessica gestured to his plate. "Good isn't it? Who would of ever thought that lima beans could be good in anything? I've got to hand it to Mrs. Mayfield; she's amazing in the kitchen."

As the fork dropped, it clattered loudly against the ceramic plate. He stared straight ahead as he spoke. "What are you doing?"

"What do you mean?" Her face went blank.

He shook his head and lifted his hands indicating the space between them. "This."

Jessica's brow furrowed. "It's called conversation."

He looked at her with wild eyes. "I know what it's called.

The question is, why are you making it?"

"Because that's what most people do when they sit down for a meal. They talk about the events of the day."

"I'm not like most people." He picked up his fork and continued to eat.

Jessica rearranged the placemat until it was perfectly straight. She then inspected a small spot of dried food on the tile. Using her thumbnail to scratch it off, she then wiped it clean, folded her arms, and leaned back in her chair.

"What are you doing now?" he asked.

"I don't understand."

"Why are you sitting there?" His face remained impassive while his eyes made contact with hers.

"I thought you'd like some company while you eat. Most people don't like to eat alone. I know I don't."

"I'm not—"

She scooted the tall stool back and stood up in frustration. "Like most people. All I was trying to do was be friendly. I should have known it would be a waste of time." She stared down at him. "I don't know why I even bother."

"I didn't mean—"

"Forget it." She walked out of the kitchen.

Michael shoved his plate aside. "Shit."

Michael found Jessica sitting on the swing at the far end of the porch. She was bathed in almost complete darkness, and the porch light strained to light her. He could make out Quest's head resting in her lap. The dog's tail thumped rhythmically as she stroked the soft area between his ears.

"Quest, you have the strangest owner. I can't believe he likes to be alone. He eats alone, works alone, sleeps alone; he does just about everything alone. And he doesn't like to talk.

66

Who doesn't like to talk? Imagine never talking. I sure can't. It gives me the goose bumps just thinking about it." She gave the large black lab a sturdy pat on his shoulder before she continued, "How do you live with him, year after year? I've only been here a little while and I feel like grabbing him and shaking some sense into him."

"Do you always talk to animals?" Michael askcd.

Jessica looked up in surprise. She had pictured him in the kitchen eating alone, staring blankly at his plate, enjoying his isolation, and thinking about whatever it was he thought about.

"When there isn't anyone else to talk to."

He held the door open. "Come inside. It looks like it might rain again and it's starting to cool." He didn't want to be the one to kill her liveliness; it wouldn't be fair.

Jessica didn't move. She pushed the deck with her tiptoe, setting the swing in motion. Why should she do as he asked? Or even answer him, for that matter? Hadn't he just made it perfectly clear he didn't want her talking to him or sitting with him? She scanned the sky for the moon. She wished it wasn't so cloudy.

Michael watched her for a moment before closing the door and walking to the swing. He stopped the swing and sat beside her. "I'm sorry, I wasn't trying to be rude. I have a lot on my mind."

"The case?"

"Yes." He watched her for a moment. "But that's not all. I'm not like you."

"In what way?"

He thought for a moment. "I don't allow myself the pleasure to indulge in leisurely chit-chat or the wonders of spontaneity." He took a deep breath. The life had been sucked out of him, but he wasn't going to let that happen to her. "What

I'm trying to say is I'm not used to having someone around. I'm not used to eating a meal or watching TV with someone. It's been a long time since I've lived with anyone." He paused. "I'm used to spending my time alone."

Jessica didn't understand. "You don't have to spend your time alone anymore. You have Mrs. Mayfield and me." She looked at the black dog and smiled. "And Quest to keep you company."

"Look at me," Michael said.

Jessica turned to him.

"I like to spend my time alone, Stanson. I don't know how to make it any clearer than that."

His disclosure shocked her. She got the feeling that he had to force the words from his lips. She studied his face for a time before she said, "So, you're a hermit?"

"No."

"Loner?"

"No."

"Monk?"

"Stanson." His voice was a growl.

Amusement danced in Jessica's eyes as she watched him. He was very cool and very detached. Maybe that's why he didn't find humor in anything. "I'm just joking. Do you know what that is, Michael? Joking? You should try it sometime."

Michael walked back to the front door. She would never understand. How could he explain and put into words the loneliness he faced every day, which he created himself? That, unlike her, he didn't welcome the crazy commotions of life. The surprises, joys, friendships, anticipations of life were not wanted. He didn't have the time or the gumption for such things.

He stared at the moths circling the porch light. Yes, letting her in would be the worst thing he could do to her. It would mean dragging her into his isolated world of regret and pain. She would never survive. At times it was hard for him to survive. The only things that kept him afloat were his ranch and his horses.

Jessica patted the dog on the head before she stood up. She walked to Michael and grinned. "I think Quest wants to come in too."

"I don't think he does," he said.

"Sure he does." She looked up at him with big eyes that were impossible to resist. "He's cold."

"He isn't cold."

"Yes, he is."

"No, he isn't," Michael said.

She gave him a sideways glance. "How do you know?"

"Do you see that black stuff that covers his body? That's called fur. The fur keeps him warm. And I know that we've had a bout of storms lately, but it's not like it's winter yet."

She rolled her eyes at him then squatted down to the dog. "I still think he should come in with us. Quest, do you want to come in where it's warm?" The dog barked. "See?"

"He's not coming in."

"Please, Michael. I promise I won't talk to you anymore tonight."

"Peace and quiet?" He doubted that was possible.

"Guaranteed."

Michael stepped aside as Jessica and the dog strolled past him. He watched her take the dog into the den and prop herself up on a pillow she had taken from the sofa. Resting the dog's head in her lap, she flicked the television on and scanned through a few channels before she stopped.

"There are still no leads on the mysterious, phantom-like killer whose horrible crimes have frightened—" The newscaster's voice rang through the room.

Jessica looked over her shoulder to see Michael standing behind her. "It's him, isn't it? She's talking about the guy you're trying to catch."

Without thinking, Michael sat in the recliner. He thought the story wasn't going to be aired until tomorrow. Dan must have decided the sooner the better.

Jessica's eyes remained on the television as she spoke, "They found another woman murdered, didn't they?"

"Yes."

"I can't watch this. This is why I don't watch the news."

Michael raised his hand. "No, leave it there."

The newscaster's face was grim, as if the top story was too much to deliver. "Police departments from three different counties are working together to try and find the killer. They have asked us to show a picture of Nichole Blake, the fourth victim, in hopes someone could shed light on the last few hours of her life."

"I'm not watching this. It's too depressing." Jessica stood up and started to walk away.

Nichole Blake's face flashed on the screen. Her smile was big and bright. She wasn't beautiful, but she was attractive in a simple way. Michael didn't know how the woman on the screen could be the same one he had first seen lying under a bright yellow blanket in the middle of a field. He closed his eyes. Please let someone recognize her.

"You can change it now," Michael said. When the station didn't change, he looked at Jessica. Her gaze was fixed on the screen. He could clearly see the alarm in her eyes. "Stanson?"

"Oh, my God," Jessica whispered as she stood in the

70

middle of the room, her hand over her mouth.

"What? What is it?"

"Oh, my God."

"Talk to me, Stanson."

She turned to Michael as she raised her hand and pointed to the television. "I've seen her. I've seen her before."

Michael was immediately on the edge of the recliner. "You've seen Nichole Blake?"

Jessica looked and him and then back to the television. "Yes, I'm positive."

Michael went to Jessica and led her to the sofa. He wanted her to sit down. Her face faded from deep golden-brown to a pasty white. She was going to faint any minute. "Are you okay?"

"I think so."

"Let's take this nice and slow."

She just nodded her head.

"When did you see her?"

"Tuesday." She shook her head. "No, it was Wednesday. Yes, Wednesday." Her eyes darted back to the television. "It's her. I know it's her."

"Stanson, look at me."

Jessica had to fight to tear her gaze from the face on the television. She looked over to Michael, her eyes big and bewildered.

"Where did you see her?" Michael could see the shock she was experiencing. The emotion was erupting from deep within and rapidly consuming her.

"I was at Green's getting feed. I remember going outside to wait for the boy to load it. I've only been in town one other time and didn't get to see much. So, I took the time to look around at the different stores. I looked across the street and saw an antique store. That's where she was standing."

"Was she alone?"

Jessica's eyes darted to the television. Nichole's picture had been replaced with a phone number and an address. She was dead. The woman she saw a few days ago was dead.

"Stanson," Michael repeated for the second time.

"No, she wasn't alone. There was a man with her. They were talking."

"Did you get a good look at him?"

"Yes. There was a beautiful roll-top desk being displayed in the window of the antique shop, and they were standing right in front of it. I had to wait for them to move before I could see it."

"Can you give me a description of what he looked like?"

"There was nothing that stood out about him. He's white. He looked like he was average height and build. He had brown hair. Oh, and he had facial hair." She thought for a moment. "A mustache. He was wearing a jogging suit, I think."

"What were they doing?"

"Talking."

"Just talking. They weren't fighting?"

"No, they appeared to be having a nice conversation."

Michael noticed the lightning-fast change in Jessica. She was now trembling and her shock turned into unadulterated fear. "What?" He took a seat next to her and then reached for her. "What? What are you remembering?"

"He looked at me."

"What do you mean?" He ran his hands up and down her arms, stopping at her shoulders to give them a gentle squeeze.

"I didn't think anything of it at the time, but he looked at me. Before they started to walk away, he looked at me." Jessica tried to swallow but her mouth was too dry. "I need a drink of water."

Michael led her into the kitchen, where he got her a glass of ice water and pulled a chair out at the bar for her. "You said they walked away."

"Yes."

Michael stood on the other side of the counter and watched her closely. "Did they walk away together or separately?"

"I'm not sure. I was too busy looking at the desk. They might have been together. I don't know."

"That's okay." He waited for her to take a few drinks before he asked the next question. "What time was it when you saw her?"

"A little after four-thirty, maybe even five."

He could get the exact time from the feed store. He always had them bill his account when anyone bought anything for the ranch. They would have the time the purchase was made. "If I have a police artist come out tomorrow, do you think you could work with him?"

"I could try."

"I'll also have him bring a book of mug shots. You might recognize one of them." Michael watched Jessica. She looked like she was dizzy. Her head was supported by her right hand propped under her chin. Her left hand gripped the counter as if she needed it for support. "You better get some sleep. Tomorrow is going to be a long day."

Jessica nodded in agreement. She finished her water and put her glass in the sink. "Good night."

"Good night."

As Jessica left, she stopped abruptly and turned to Michael. "This could be it. I could be the one to identify this guy."

Michael nodded.

She turned to leave but stopped again. "Michael?"

"Yeah." She didn't have to speak; he knew what she was thinking. "Stanson, I won't let anything happen to you. That's a promise." He took a step toward her and touched her hair. "Trust me."

"I barely even know you," she said.

"Then I'll tell you a little something about me. I've kept every promise I've ever made."

Chapter Seven

Michael was still leaning against the counter staring at the spot where Jessica had stood moments ago, looking at him with such uncertainty. Physically she had appeared strong, with her head held high and her shoulders straight and tall. But he had seen the confusion and worry in her eyes when she had looked at him.

The ringing of the phone snapped him out of his thoughts. He crossed the room in three strides. "Hello."

"Hey, Mike. Airing that picture was a good idea. I just got word that someone saw her walking past the deli around four-thirty."

"I can beat that. I have a witness that saw her a little before that with a man."

"No shit. Who?"

"Stanson."

"You're kidding me?" Dan said.

"I wish I were." Michael filled him in on all the details.

"Did she get a good look at the guy?"

"She was on the other side of the street, but I think we can get a description. I'm going to have someone come over first thing in the morning and see what we come up with. I didn't want to push her."

"How is she doing?"

"She's a little shook up." He picked up his pen and began doodling. "I think it's him, Dan. I questioned all her male friends personally. Not one of them had seen her in days."

"We'll just have to wait and see."

"If we have a witness who saw her alone just minutes after Stanson saw her with a man, where did the man go in that short of time?"

"Your guess is as good as mine. Do you think Nichole made it home that night?"

"She must have; we have a neighbor who saw her lights on at five."

Dan cut in. "That still leaves about fifteen minutes unaccounted for, even if she did stop and talk to someone."

"I'm going to walk her route tomorrow and see approximately how long it takes."

"Do you want me to send someone out to question the new witness, or do you want to do it?"

"I'll do it," Michael said.

"I'll stop by in the morning."

"See you then." Michael turned off the lights and went to his room. He flicked the bathroom light on and started the shower, then stepped in and adjusted the water. The burning water pounded on his back, softening his tight muscles. He tilted his neck so the water could work on the sensitive area. Every muscle in his body seemed to contract the instant Stanson had told him that she recognized Nichole Blake. He looked up and let the water pelt his face. "Why Stanson? Why couldn't it have been someone else? Anyone but her." He disclosed the words into the hot spray as if waiting for someone to answer.

He stood under the water, thinking. How was he going to deal with Jessica being his number one witness? Would he be able to handle it if something happened to her? Just the mere thought of injury to Jessica caused his fists to ball and a surge of infuriated energy to shoot through him. No harm would come to her. He had promised her and that was one promise he wasn't going to break.

He remained under the water until his skin was bright red and his emotions were under control. He dried off. Not bothering to put anything on, he slipped into bed.

"How did you sleep?" Michael asked as he moved from the cabinet under the stovetop to the refrigerator, gathering contents to prepare breakfast.

"I didn't. I can tell you exactly how many knots are in the knotty pine on my ceiling in my room."

"I know this isn't easy." He gave her a soft smile. "It will get easier in a few days. The shock will wear off."

"I hope so. I dozed on and off, but I keep having nightmares." Jessica dropped her head in her hands. "Why can't this just be a bad dream?"

"I wish it were too."

"Can I do anything to help?" she asked as she looked up.

"I've got it under control." Michael handed her a cup of coffee. "You have a headache?"

"Is it that obvious?

"Worse than the hangover?"

She forced a lopsided grin. "I don't think anything could be that bad."

"No, I don't think I have experienced anything quite like it myself."

She looked up to see him smiling at her. "I didn't force you to drink it."

Michael put two pieces of toast in the toaster. "I didn't say you did."

Jessica sat through a period of silence. "I can't believe this is happening to me."

"That's the reaction of most witnesses."

Jessica shook her head. "But I'm not most witnesses. I'm a horse trainer who works up in the mountains. I rarely see anyone unless it's a customer." She exhaled noisily. "It figures, one of the few times I go to town I see a killer. I guess that's what I get."

"Get for what?"

"Not listening to my dad. He told me that he didn't want me to come out here."

Michael laughed. "Since when do children ever listen to their parents?"

Jessica sipped her coffee. "I'm starting. I guess I'm going to have to call him. He is going to flip. I haven't even told him that you were working on the case."

"Why?"

"He would freak. He's a little protective." She shifted in her seat. "I should go out and tell the guys I'm going to be late."

"I already did. The police artist will be here any minute." He looked up to see Dan at the back door. He motioned for him to come in.

"Good morning." Dan wiped his feet before he took his coat off and draped it over a chair.

Jessica looked over her shoulder and gave him a soft smile.

"Coffee?" Michael asked.

"Sure."

"How many eggs?" Michael said.

"Three." Dan came up behind Jessica and took a seat next to her. "How are you holding up, Jessica?"

"Fine, I guess. How am I supposed to be?"

"Nervous, shocked."

"I am. How can you guys be so relaxed about this?"

Dan looked to Michael before he spoke, "We've done this hundreds of times."

"I feel like there is a swarm of butterflies in my stomach." She folded her arms across her midriff and looked at the slice of dry toast Michael had set in front of her. "I don't think I can eat."

Michael moved to her side. "That's normal. But I want you to try." The doorbell rang and Jessica looked to him. "That's him." He squeezed her shoulder. "You ready?"

"I guess."

Before he left he gave her another gentle squeeze. "Piece of cake."

She looked at Dan as Michael walked away. "Yeah, piece of cake."

Michael reappeared with a young man. "Stanson, this is Officer Parker."

Jessica smiled slightly and extended her hand. "Nice to meet you."

"Likewise. Mike, here are the mug shots you wanted." He handed Michael a thick black book. He looked to Dan. "Morning, Chief."

Dan nodded.

The officer motioned to the kitchen table. "This looks like a good working space."

Jessica sat to the side of Officer Parker. Michael stood behind both of them. "Okay, Ms. Stanson, I want you to close your eyes and picture the man that you saw with Nichole Blake."

"I don't know if I can do this. I've never tried to describe someone's face before."

"I'll walk you through it." He picked up a pencil and positioned the pad of paper in front of him. "Go ahead and close your eyes. You'll be surprised with what we come up with."

Jessica looked to Michael before she closed her eyes.

79

"You ready?" the officer said.

Jessica nodded.

"Let's start with the shape of his face."

"It's long. Thin, but not too thin." Jessica opened her eyes. "I'm sorry. That didn't make much sense, did it?"

The officer smiled. "Sure it did. His face was long and narrow, but it wasn't because he was thin physically."

"Exactly."

"Just trust me. You're doing fine." The officer asked Jessica another question. And within a few seconds he was sketching again. Michael stood over his shoulder and watched as he worked. With each description Jessica gave him, a face began to appear. Within minutes, the features started to come to life, actually becoming a person.

The officer filled in a few details before letting Jessica look at the composite. "Does this look like the man you saw?"

Jessica stared at the picture. "Yes. But his nose wasn't that pointed."

The officer made the correction. "Does that look more like it?"

Jessica stood up and took a few steps back. She studied the picture. "It looks like him to me."

"I think that about does it." The officer began to collect his supplies.

"Thanks for coming out." Michael looked to Jessica. "Stanson, you feel up to working? It might take your mind off things."

"I thought you wanted me to look at some photos."

"We can do that later."

When Jessica had left, the officer spoke to Michael and Dan. "I know it's sketchy, but it's the best I could do. Since she was so far away, she couldn't see a lot of detail."

"I know. At least it's something." Michael walked the officer to the door. When he came back, he picked up the composite. His eyes crinkled at the corners as he studied it. He looked at Dan and spoke. "So, the suspect we're after has a medium complexion, short brown hair, a mustache, and sideburns. His build and face are average. So basically he's no different from the typical man."

"Well, you know how it is. Most composites have a kind of generic quality to them. We're not going to identify the killer with it, but it will help us rule out suspects. I say let's go ahead and distribute the composite to all the police stations, newspapers, and the television stations."

Michael ran his hand through his hair and started collecting the breakfast dishes and stacking them by the sink.

"What's the matter, Mike? You don't think that's a good idea?" Dan said.

"No, it is a good idea."

"Then what is it? Is it because of Jessica?"

The welfare of Jessica or any of his witnesses was a great concern to Michael. It was a slim chance, but if he released the composite the killer might know it was Jessica who identified him. If that happened, it would be a situation he didn't have control of, and he liked to be in control at all times. He gathered up the composite and handed it to Dan. "Get copies of these out as soon as you can. I'm going to the auction tomorrow."

"I thought you were sending Jessica and the men."

"I was, but I decided to go with them."

"What's up, Mike?" Dan asked.

"I just get the feeling the killer is the kind of guy that wouldn't hesitate to take out the person responsible for identifying him. Stanson is just his type, all the more appealing."

"Just because he saw her doesn't mean he could identify her."

"I'm just being careful."

81

"Then why have her go?"

"She'll want an explanation if I tell her she can't go. And I don't want to worry her over nothing. It's just a precaution, nothing more."

"You've read all the files. Who do you think this guy is? What is he like?"

Michael turned to Dan. He had thought about that non-stop. "He's clean-cut. Intelligent. I think he went to college. He probably has a steady job that requires thought and skill. I agree with what you said about him being calm and level-headed. That's the only reason we haven't caught him. I don't think he is just some nut doing this just because."

"What makes him different?"

"I'm not saying he's completely different. I'm sure he has some of the textbook traits of a serial rapist and killer. He was probably sexually abused as a child; he obviously has a deep anger against women."

"But?"

"But, I think it's much more than that. I think that ninety-nine percent of it is a game to him. A game of control, a game that he likes to play."

"What do you mean by a game?"

"Do you know why he keeps the underwear?"

Dan thought about it before he spoke. "He wants to remember each girl."

"No, he doesn't give a shit about the women."

Dan shrugged his shoulders. "Behavioral science was never my strongest area."

"He keeps them so at any minute he can relive the killing. He has a taste for it. It goes much deeper than wanting to be in control; he likes to kill. It excites him. So, now we're dealing with control, obsession, and ego."

"Ego?"

"He is cunning, and he knows it. That's where the game comes in. He is so perfect at his obsession and so in control of it that it is almost a game to see if he'll get caught doing it. He's walking a fine line and he knows it. Killing involves careful planning and thought. That's why he does it. Each murder is an attempt to fine-tune his skill."

"So, we're dealing with someone who is on the borderline of being in complete control and almost out of control?"

"You got it."

Dan shook his head. "How the hell did you come up with this? I look at the files and I see a whacko who gets off on killing young women."

"That's basically what he is. He's just a whacko who's in control."

"That's a scary thought. What about the shoe prints?"

"That's part of his game. Did the shoe print help us? No, not really. He'll never get that lazy."

"We're dealing with a real pro."

Michael slid on his glasses and held the composite before him. "This guy isn't going to stop. At least not until we stop him. And that is going to take a big mistake on his part for that to happen." He looked at Dan over the top of the drawing. "I think Lady Luck is going to have to step in for us to get him."

"Then we'll just wait for her."

Chapter Eight

Jessica sat in the truck with her hands in her lap and her legs pressed tightly together. Her bottom was slowly growing numb, her neck was stiff, and the rest of her body was in pain. Every muscle hurt from trying not to touch either man on each side of her.

Why did Michael have to come along? Yesterday morning at the stables he had informed her that she had to go to the auction with the rest of the hands because he wasn't going to be able to make it. He had given her the money and instructions about what kind of horses he was interested in, but this morning he had changed his mind, insisting that he go with them. She wrinkled her nose with vexation at the thought that he probably didn't trust her judgment.

Her shoulder brushed Michael's as she leaned away from Jake when they rounded a corner. The sensation brought her attention to his arms as they expertly steered the truck. When she grabbed the dash for assistance, her eyes moved to his chest and then to his lap where they rested on the fly of his tight jeans. She continued her travel down to his thick thighs that flexed each time he manipulated the gearshift. Her eyes followed the length of the faded blue denims that extended and disappeared under the steering column. She closed her eyes; she couldn't look at him anymore. "This cab is shrinking." It had slipped out before she knew it. She prayed that no one heard over the twang of the radio.

Michael had heard her remark loud and clear. He had to force back the laugh that threatened to surface. She had been twisting and turning since they had gotten in the truck. This was a side of her he hadn't seen before, except for the night in the kitchen. She was usually relaxed and in control. He fully enjoyed watching her squirm for the rest of the trip. He took the corner into the auction parking lot a little too fast, sending Jessica scrambling to keep from touching him. He looked forward to the ride home.

Climbing out of the truck, he waited for Richard, John, and Tom to park the truck and trailer in the overcrowded parking lot. When they walked up he said, "Go ahead and go in." He grabbed Jessica's arm. "We'll be a minute."

They nodded and went into the big blue building that had "Auction" printed in large red letters across the top of the roof.

"I want you to stay by me." His tone was flat.

"Why?"

His stance was firm as his eyes pierced hers in all seriousness. "Don't argue. Just do it."

Jessica nodded, not really understanding his demanding request. She would agree to anything as long as it meant avoiding a quarrel. Besides, she could care less what he requested right now. She was happy to be free of the confines of the undersized cab she had spent the last two excruciatingly long hours in.

The huge building was packed. The seating had overflowed, leaving men standing shoulder to shoulder around a big arena. Seeing was next to impossible unless you were at least six feet tall. Between the auctioneer and all the shouting, you couldn't hear yourself think.

Jessica stood close to Michael as he looked around, not because he had just told her to, but because she was afraid if she didn't she would lose him in the mass of people. When they paused to look for the crew, three men stepped between them, then four more, and then two and three breaking a path for a walkway. Michael proceeded to walk. He hadn't noticed they had been separated. Jessica tried to forcibly push through the stream of people, but her efforts were wasted.

Michael must have finally sensed she wasn't behind him because after a moment or so, he abruptly stopped and whisked around. He shoved through the crowd of people and found her searching for a different route. Grabbing her hand, he stressed his words as he spoke them. "I told you to stay by me."

"I tried."

Michael dragged her unkindly behind him as he found their seats. The dirty look she gave the back of his head compensated a little for his behavior. It made her feel a little better too.

They hadn't been seated longer than a few minutes before several horses came into the arena.

"You remember the only rule," Michael said.

"You never buy horses with white hooves."

Michael smiled. "That's it." He leaned back and pulled his hat over his eyes. "Have fun. Wake me when you're finished." He looked over toward Jake, Richard, Tom, and John. "Don't let them get too crazy. Last year they bought two horses too many and we had to hire someone to bring them home." He leaned over so his men could hear him. "Remember, we only have room for eight. Not ten."

Each man winced and diverted his attention to something else.

"That's it? You're not going to have any say in what I buy? I can buy any horse I want just as long as it doesn't have white hooves?"

"Yep." He motioned toward the arena that had several horses trotting around restlessly. "Time's a wasting. Things move fast around here."

As the auctioneer's voice bounced off the massive walls, Jessica began to study each horse, assessing his or her health and potential. Eager to become a part of the bidding, she moved to the edge of her seat.

After hours of bidding, Jessica felt satisfied with the choices she had made. She was confident that Michael would approve once he saw how well the horses would be when they got them home and they actually worked with them.

Jessica jabbed an elbow softly at Michael's ribs. "It's over."

Michael sat up, rubbed his eyes, and looked at his men. "Let's load 'em."

"I'm going to the restroom while you load the horses." She stood up and looked down at Michael.

"Can you wait?"

"No I can't wait. I've been waiting all morning." She turned and headed toward the sign hanging from the ceiling with "Restroom" printed on it.

When she finished in the restroom, Jessica stepped back into the crowd of people; she looked for Michael but couldn't see over everyone. Glancing up at the seats where they had been sitting and finding them empty, she searched the crowd. There was a man wearing a blue denim long-sleeved shirt and black hat with his back to her. She was sure it was Michael waiting for her.

Jessica touched the man lightly on the back. "Mich—" She jerked her hand away. "Excuse me, I thought you were someone else."

The man smiled as he looked Jessica up then down, while

giving a twisted grin of approval. "Why, ain't you a sweet thang? There ain't nothing to be sorry for, darlin'."

"Have a nice day," she said in disgust. She turned to go, but was caught by her wrist.

"Now where do you think you're going?"

"Let go of me now." She yanked her arm out of the man's harsh grip.

He clutched it again. "I like feisty women."

"If you know what is good for you, you'll let go of me now." Jessica's back was straight and her chin tilted.

"Is that right?"

She kicked him in the knee as hard as she could with her pointed boot. As he doubled over and grabbed it, she smiled at him. "That's right." Her brothers had always taught her if you can't get him in the balls, the knees were the next best thing.

She found out all too soon he was quick to recover when he grabbed her by the wrist once again. This time his grip and expression weren't as gentle. The pain she had caused was evident and he wasn't pleased.

"Let go of her."

Jessica's head shot up in surprise. Michael was standing beside her. But when she looked into his eyes, she didn't recognize him. Anger had turned them a coal gray. Hate twisted his features into a grueling scowl. She didn't know if she should feel relief or fear. She had never seen such revulsion in a person's face as she was witnessing now.

"And who the hell is goin' to make me?" the man asked.

"Michael, don't. Let's just leave," she pleaded in an awkward voice.

Michael didn't acknowledge she was speaking to him.

She tried to shove past the large man who had tossed her aside, but someone caught her by the arm. This time when she turned around it was Jake's face she was peering into.

"Let's go. Now."

"But, what about Michael? He might need help."

Jake towed her through the mass of people that had formed around Michael and the stranger. "He can take care of himself."

"And so can I." She tried to stop but was only pulled harder.

"This is not the time to argue, Jess."

"Why does everyone keep saying that? I don't argue. Now, let me go."

Jake didn't release her arm, he only moved faster in the direction of the door, which he opened and guided her through in one swift movement. Once they were outside he loosened his grip, but it wasn't until he had deposited her safely in the seat of the truck that he released her arm completely.

Michael looked at the stranger before him. The crowd had squeezed them together so tight he could smell the alcohol on the man's breath and see every tiny vessel in his bloodshot eyes. Michael cursed under his breath; there was no chance of him getting out of this one without a fight.

He balled his fist and watched as the stranger's head bobbed around. He figured the other man was so drunk it wouldn't take much to knock him out. One good hit and he would be done.

When the stranger's hands dropped slightly, Michael saw his chance. His fist connected with the hard angle of the stranger's jaw and he watched as the man fell to the ground, grabbing his face in pain. Satisfied that was all it took, Michael turned to leave.

The crowd started to yell and Michael didn't look at any of them. Instead he put his head down and pushed his way through. Before he'd gotten far, someone grabbed the back of his shirt. He spun around, ready to knock out the next punk who wanted to fight, but surprisingly he was looking into the same bloodshot eyes. Before he could respond, his head flung back as pain shot through the right side of his face and the crowd turned into a slow moving blur. His whole world began to spin.

His hand went to his face. "Son of a bitch." Squinting his eyes and gritting his teeth against the pain, he forced himself to gain control. He tasted blood from where the inside of his cheek ground against his teeth. Cocking his fist back, he threw his entire body weight into the hit. His fist smashed into the man's jaw. The stranger stumbled back but didn't fall. He came back charging into Michael's stomach with both fists. A gush of air flew from Michael's mouth. He gasped for air, fighting the nausea that rapidly engulfed him. His anger built and spread through him like a wildfire. He took a deep breath and pounced, hitting the stranger with a right hook and an upper cut. The man fell to the ground.

"You ever treat a woman like that again—" Michael let his foot finish the sentence as he kicked him in the ribs for good measure. He then placed his boot in the middle of the man's back and gave a shove. The stranger sprawled on the concrete, motionless.

Michael picked up his hat, dusted it off, and adjusted it on his head. He straightened his shirt and moved to the door. The crowd gathered around the groaning man on the ground.

Michael squinted at the sunlight when he stepped into the parking lot. Both trucks were idling and loaded. Jessica sat in one while John, Tom, and Richard sat in the other. Jake was leaning against the hood of the truck.

He started walking toward Michael. "You okay?"

Michael walked past him. "Ride in the other truck."

Before Jessica knew it, Michael was sitting in the driver's seat. She watched him fasten his seat belt before he put the truck in gear and spun out of the parking lot. She threw her seat belt on, but didn't dare look his way.

They drove in awkward silence for several miles. Jessica couldn't look at Michael because the guilt that filled her was too overwhelming. How could she have been so stupid? She should have stayed by Michael like he had suggested earlier.

"Michael." She turned to look at him. "I'm sorry," she whispered.

"Why didn't you listen to me?" Michael's voice was sharp with anger. "Damn it, I told you to stay by me."

"I tapped the man on the shoulder, thinking he was you. How was I to know he would go crazy?"

Michael took a deep breath. "Let's just forget about it."

"I don't want to forget about it. Why are you so angry with me?"

He looked out his window, hoping to ignore her. Unfortunately, they were driving down a deserted highway, in a truck that was no larger than a coffin. He should tell her. He should let her know the danger she put herself in. He didn't want to scare her, but maybe that was what she needed. It might be the only way he could make her listen to him. "What if that man back there was the killer?" The statement was cruel but effective.

Jessica moistened her lips and then swallowed the lump that formed instantly in her throat. "Do you think that could have been the killer?"

"No. I think he was just a drunk, horny bastard." He looked at her. "But it could have been. We don't know who

91

he is, what he looks like, or where he'll show up. No one can be trusted."

Jessica had never even considered that the stranger at the auction could have been the killer. Panic washed over her in an overwhelming intensity. "Does he know who I am?"

Michael shook his head. Sensing her fear, he almost regretted mentioning the possibility at all. But he had to. What other options was she giving him? She needed to know the danger that was out there.

"Then why do you think that might have been the killer?" She took a deep breath and said, "Don't lie to me, Michael."

"I'm not lying to you, Stanson. I just want you to be careful. I can't stress that enough." He eased into a restaurant parking lot, glancing in the rear view mirror to make sure the crew followed him. "I think we could use some dinner."

Michael removed the keys from the ignition and opened his door. When he noticed no movement coming from the other side of the truck, he looked toward Jessica. "What?"

"Thank you for what you did back at the auction house." She turned to him. "Thank you for caring too. I promise I won't be so careless next time."

"I didn't want to scare you, Stanson, but I think you should know what we are dealing with."

"Now I do."

A heavy-set blond, who looked like she applied her make-up with a roller, took their orders. After she left, Jessica excused herself. "I'm going to wash my hands."

Michael winced at the pain as he rubbed his hand lightly across his jaw. He had taken a few good hits.

Jake removed his tattered green hat, placed it on his knee, and then fiddled with the Tabasco sauce. "Where did he hit you?"

"Square in the jaw." He lightly touched the soft spot again in disbelief. He hadn't been in a fight in years.

Jake tried to hold back his laugh but couldn't resist. He smacked his hand on the table. "I would have given anything to see that fight." He started humming the theme song to *Rocky*. Soon the rest of the guys joined in.

Michael had to smile. "That was one tough bastard. I couldn't get him to go down."

Plucking the toothpick from his mouth, Richard said, "From all the yelling going on, it sounded like one hell of a fight. I heard it all the way outside."

Michael looked up and saw Jessica standing at the edge of the table. He could feel her distress as she approached. She looked faint as her eyes darted to his. "Are you all right?" He stood up. "Stanson?"

She tried to put on her best "I'm okay" smile for everyone. She had them all fooled but Michael. Willing her hands not to tremble, she spoke. "I'm fine. Michael, I need to talk to you."

Michael forgot all about the men. Reaching for her hand, he ushered her across the room to the counter, out of hearing distance. "What's the matter?"

Jessica looked around the room for the stranger with lost hope. He was just there. Her eyes darted around the room. Where was he?

"Stanson, answer me." Michael's wide eyes revealed the tension he felt throughout. "Stanson?"

"A man was following me."

He looked over his shoulder and didn't see anyone. They were the only people in the small diner. "Who was following you?"

"I don't see him," she said. "He's gone."

"Tell me what happened." He put an arm around her shoulders and pulled her close.

"I was walking to the bathroom when I noticed that someone was watching me." She shook as she got the goose bumps. "Everything about him made my flesh creep. He just kept staring." She pointed to the booth by the door. "He was sitting there. I could feel him watching me, but I didn't want to look at him. When I finally forced myself to, he gave me a weird smile and got up and came across the room toward me."

"Did he talk to you?"

"I didn't give him a chance to. He seemed kind of odd so I turned around and came back to the table."

"Did he look like the man you saw with Nichole Blake?"

"No."

"What about the guy at the auction?"

"No. This guy was much taller and heavier. He was wearing a navy blue shirt and a black ball cap."

Michael pulled her closer. It tore him up to see her frightened. "It's okay, honey." He pulled away. "Come on, I'll walk with you."

Jessica nodded. "I think I've been watching one too many horror movies."

After Jessica disappeared through the restroom door, Michael went back into the dining area to take another look. Except for his men, there were no other patrons in the dining area. He walked outside and looked around. Two men were getting into a tow truck.

"Excuse me, gentlemen."

The men turned around. The one at the driver's side spoke. "What can we do for you?"

Michael looked them over. Neither one was wearing what Jessica had described. "Have you seen a man in a blue shirt and a black cap?" Each man looked nervously at the other.

"No, we haven't seen anyone."

"I'm Detective Carven, can I see some identification?"

The men dug into their back pockets and produced two driver's licenses. "Are you sure you haven't seen anyone fitting that description?"

"No, sir. We just came to pick up some supper." The man reached into the truck and pulled out a brown paper bag of food.

Michael looked over the identification cards. The addresses were local; he doubted if either one was his man. He handed the cards back. "Thanks for your time. Have a nice evening." He watched the men climb into the truck and drive away.

As he opened the heavy glass door, he heard the crunching of gravel coming from the other side of the diner. He walked around the building. A car shot out of the darkness onto the highway; it didn't turn its lights on until it was a half a mile down the road. There was his man.

Michael went back into the diner and asked the waitress if she had seen the man before.

"Yes, he comes in occasionally."

"Do you know his name?"

"No. Is there a problem?"

Michael shook his head. "No, no problem." He waited for Jessica. She came out of bathroom looking better. "Are you all right?"

"Yes. I think I'm just a little jumpy because of what happened at the auction."

"Let's get some dinner, then get home. It's been a long day."

Chapter Nine

By phone, Michael gave Dan a blow-by-blow description of his trip to the auction. He didn't leave anything out, not even the fight or the incident at the diner.

"It sounds like you had a fun-filled day," Dan said with a hearty laugh.

"Fun's not the word. It was the trip from hell." Michael pressed the ice pack to his jaw. "That's the last time I go anywhere with that woman. She's nothing but trouble."

"You weren't too hard on her, were you?"

"Whose side are you on?" Michael knew it wasn't her fault, but it was easy to blame her.

"I know you. You're short-tempered, you blow up at anything."

"I am not."

"Just go easy on her, Mike, she doesn't know what's going on. She's probably a little scared and confused."

Dan changed the subject. "Do you think either might be our guy?"

"I don't think so. Stanson didn't recognize them. I'm going to check them out anyway. Has anyone called about seeing Nichole?"

"No, but my men are pounding the pavement."

"I showed the composite to Nichole's friends this morning, and none of them had ever seen the guy before. Her parents didn't recognize him either."

"Were they close?"

"Yeah, from what everyone says. Since her parents didn't recognize him, I really don't think he's someone she knew. If he was a friend, I think they would have known."

"Did you get the chance to speak to the witness that works at the deli?"

"Yes. She said there was nothing out of the ordinary that day. Apparently Nichole walks past the store every day on her way home from work around the same time. She didn't see anything that looked suspicious."

"How about the guy?"

"She didn't see him," Michael said. "But there were three other people in the store around that time. She gave me their names. I'm going to talk to each of them as soon as possible."

"I had someone distribute the copies of the composite to the local police stations. I haven't got any calls on it yet, but when I do you'll be the first to know."

"Okay. I'll call if I come across anything."

Michael hung up the phone and followed the savory aromas, which had been seeping under his door for the last hour, to the kitchen. Jessica and Mrs. Mayfield huddled around the huge island busily preparing a meal. "What's for supper?"

"Lasagna. Ten minutes," Mrs. Mayfield said.

He rubbed his hands together, anticipating the meal. "In that case, I'd better get washed up."

As he turned, Jessica looked up and caught a glimpse of the dark purple bruise on his cheek and jaw. The injury looked painful. She hoped that the slight swelling and dark coloring were only cosmetic, making it look much worse than it really was.

Jessica caught up with him in the hall. "Michael."

He stopped. Turning halfway around, to hide the bruise, he answered, "Yes?"

"Is there something I need to know?"

"No." He turned, still concealing the right side of his face.

"Well," Jessica twisted his head until his jaw was in perfect view. Her fingers traced the tender spot. "Then what is this?"

"It's called a bruise."

"Michael, I'm serious. Are you okay?"

"Nothing an ice pack won't heal." His hands went to his hips as his gaze fell to the floor.

"Did this happen yesterday?" She remembered when she had come back to the table hearing Richard saying something to Michael about how he would have a nice bruise to show off.

"It doesn't matter when it happened." He didn't want to remember the terror in her eyes when she was grabbed and tossed aside like a rag doll.

"Of course it does," she said.

Michael's features softened. "It's okay. It looks much worse than it is."

"Did you put ice on it?" She had an urge to kiss him. To take him in her arms and protect him from everything that could hurt him, both physically and emotionally. She also had the urge to beat the crap out of the guy who had done this.

Michael nodded.

"Why didn't you tell me?" she asked.

"I didn't see any reason to."

"Is that so? You get hurt defending my honor and you don't see any reason to tell me?"

When he saw the doubt in her eyes, he covered his hand over hers and said reassuringly, "I'm fine. Really."

His hand felt heavy and hot over hers. Her knees weakened, threatening to buckle under her. She couldn't take her hand away nor stop staring at his rugged face. Again, she couldn't bury the overpowering urge to kiss him. She wanted him to know she cared and she was sorry for what had happened. She stood on her tiptoes and gently kissed the bruise.

Michael froze, enjoying her tender lips on his skin. He couldn't have moved if he wanted to. Her touch and affection immobilized him. The burning bond the kiss had created between them consumed all his senses. The beating of her heart echoed in his ear, her breath bounced softly off his cheek, the fiery warmth where their skin touched was magnificent. There wasn't a sane thought in his head when he felt her lips move down the length of his jaw. The trail of kisses ended at the corner of his mouth.

Jessica felt him pull away as her lips brushed his. His movement was inconspicuous, but she noticed it nonetheless. She took the gesture as her cue to stop, and she stepped back. "You better get washed up."

Michael returned to the kitchen five minutes later. They both ate in silence and seemed anxious to finish the meal. Jessica wished that Mrs. Mayfield hadn't left. She would have enjoyed not only her conversation but also her presence. Michael looked as if he were miles away. At least he hadn't taken his dinner and fled to his study like he had done before.

When the meal was finished, they stood side by side at the sink and did the dishes. The process was done without thought. When the dishes were finished, Jessica grabbed a towel and started drying. "There's a good horror movie on in about five minutes. Are you up to it?" She bumped him as she bent down and put the pan under the stove.

He turned his head and coughed uncomfortably.

When she rose, she watched the change in his face. "Are you getting sick?"

"No, to both of your questions; I have work to do," he said as he closed the cupboard door and walked out of the room.

Jessica went into the living room and flopped on the sofa. Why did she even bother asking him? She decided against the movie. Her imagination was getting out of hand, and she wasn't in the mood anymore.

Grabbing a magazine off the coffee table, she flipped through the pages and stopped to read a poorly written article on how to lose ten pounds in five days. Disgusted, she tossed the magazine on the table. She was bored. Looking around the room, she noticed the stereo. Country music roared out of the speakers when she turned it on. She loved music.

She danced around the room, singing at the top of her lungs. She was having so much fun that she didn't see Michael come in. When the song ended, she heard clapping coming from the corner of the room. She turned around; her face was flushed when she saw Michael smiling. "Enjoy the show?"

"Yes."

"When did you come in?"

"Just a minute ago."

His stance and the boyish look on his face made her smile. "The music too loud?"

Michael walked over to her and held out his hand, offering a dance. "No, it's not too loud."

"You dance?" She started laughing.

"What's so funny?" Michael asked.

He took her in his arms and began moving to the soft beat. Their bodies melted into one when they touched. The barrier that kept Jessica at bay dissolved and vanished into the words and melody of the love song.

He held her with care as she followed his lead, twisting and turning as they glided through the room. His body moved smoothly and gracefully, keeping with the beat. Missing the lamp and end table by inches, Michael pressed Jessica's body snugly against his.

When they had made their way back to the center of the room, Michael put his hand in the middle of her back. He pushed her slightly, sending her spinning away from him.

Jessica was about to curtsy but Michael pulled her back again. She landed against his chest with a thump. She laughed as he tossed her out again. This time she was prepared and when he pulled her back, she snuggled against his chest. When the song ended, he dipped her long and slow.

"You were great," she said, slightly out of breath.

"So were you."

"Where did you learn to dance like that?"

"My mother taught me." Reluctantly he released her hand.

"She did a wonderful job. What was her name?"

"Anneliese. I was young when she died. I don't have a lot of memories of her, but I do remember there was always a lot of singing and dancing. She loved to sing me to sleep."

"If you don't mind me asking, how did she die?" she said.

"My father and she were killed in a car accident."

Jessica sensed him draw back from her. He had lost everyone he loved: his parents, his grandparents, and his fiancée. She ached for him. Pain and sadness had essentially followed him throughout his life, never giving him time to heal. She couldn't imagine having loss upon loss like that. "I was six when my mom died. She was killed in a car accident too."

The shared experience seemed to reduce the tension. "Were you close?"

"Very."

Michael's eyes fell to the floor. "How did you manage?"

"The pain was unbearable at first, but it eased over time."

Michael knew the kind of pain she was speaking of; he lived with it every day. A month after Cathy's death, he asked Dan: When would it stop hurting? How long until the pain went away? When would he stop expecting her to greet him at the front door? When would he forget her magical smile or the feel of her lips against his? He knew it would take longer than three years. The dim ache in his soul refused to fade. He would never really forget. The guilt and pain were branded in his memory.

Jessica allowed him a moment of silence. She knew he needed it. "It was my dad who got us through it. He had four children and he knew he had to be strong for us."

Michael nodded. "I don't know what I would have done if I didn't have my grandparents. I had no other family. If it wasn't for them, I would have gone to a foster home."

She smiled. "You loved them a lot, didn't you?"

"Yes, they were all I had. My grandpa died when I was sixteen and my grandma died four years later."

"What did you do?"

"I sold everything we had and used the money for college."

"And became the brilliant detective."

"I don't feel brilliant right now."

"Have you ever dated since Cathy?" How the words rolled off her tongue she'd never know. She hadn't meant to ask such a personal question.

"Don't pry, Stanson."

Chills of regret moved up her spine, resting in her throat. What did she say? What could she say? "You're right. I had no right asking that."

"No, you didn't."

"I said I'm sorry. What more do you want?"

"I want you to stay out of my private life. I hired you to do a job, and inquiring about my personal life is not in the job description." Michael left the room.

She wanted to yell back at him: "But dancing is in the job description." Would she ever understand his quick anger and unexpected gentleness or his well-hidden vulnerability? One minute they were sharing a dance and laughing, and the next they were fighting like cats and dogs.

Moving to the sofa she yawned, tucked her feet under her, and rested her head on the arm. She grabbed the remote and flicked the TV on, turning it up several notches more than necessary. She didn't care if he was working.

"We found another witness," Dan told Michael over the phone.

"Who?" Michael put a finger from his free hand in his ear. The reverberation the horror movie Jessica was watching made it hard for him to hear Dan. It must be at a climatic part, he decided.

"Jean Camp. She lives in the same complex as Nichole Blake. She is positive Nichole didn't come home Thursday night."

Michael swore under his breath. He hated when there was more than one witness and both had different stories. "Well, that is just the opposite of what the first witness told us."

"I know. She works nights, so you could go question her now."

"What's her number?"

Michael hung up the phone and gathered a few papers. When he opened the study door, he was greeted with a snappy jingle from a commercial. He walked into the den looking around for either Jessica or the remote. When his eyes had adjusted to the darkness, he could see her curled up in a ball on the sofa sleeping soundly, the remote nestled beside her. Aiming it toward the television, he turned it off.

He pulled a blanket off the back of the sofa and covered her. He sank down on his knees and studied her young face. He felt both passion and serenity when he looked at her. Her full lips that loved to smile looked as soft as satin. Her long eyelashes fanned out over her round cheeks like rays of sunlight.

As he brushed the stray hair from her forehead, she stirred. Jessica represented everything that had been taken away from him. Peace, love, and most of all, life. The freedom to laugh and be carefree no longer existed. He felt trapped after Cathy died. Trapped between the loneliness of losing someone he loved dearly and the self-hatred he felt for never finding her killer.

He had thought he was happy living on the ranch. He had convinced himself keeping busy twenty-four hours a day would cure his pain; but now that Jessica was here, he realized it hadn't.

He didn't know how long he sat there and watched her sleep, but it wasn't until the clock chimed on the hour that he reluctantly forced himself to leave her.

Michael gave the door one loud tap and then took a step back. A woman opened the door several inches and peeked through the crack to get a glimpse of him. One hand was on the knob while the other remained on the gold chain that prevented the door from opening any farther. "Ms. Camp?"

"Who are you?"

Michael could tell the woman was nervous. "I'm Detective Carven." He looked at the number on the door. "Are you Ms. Camp?"

The woman nodded.

"I called a little while ago. I'm here to ask you a few questions about Nichole Blake."

"Yes, just a minute." The woman closed the door and then reopened it. "Please come in. I'm sorry, I didn't mean to be rude. I'm just a little nervous. I live alone." The words came out in rapid succession. She waved a hand in the air. "The whole complex is shaken up. You don't know who you can trust and who you can't."

Michael stepped into the small combination living room and dining room. The apartment might be little, but it was spotless. The light scent of Pine Sol and potpourri permeated the air. Assortments of houseplants were efficiently placed in areas where the sunlight was likely to reach them. The coffee table in front of the sofa was littered with home and garden magazines. "I understand. No need to explain."

Ms. Camp closed the door and fastened every lock. "Would you care for some coffee?"

"Sure." Michael sat at the small dining table and evaluated the room. From the front window you could see into the courtyard and the other apartments below. However, the parking lot and the entrance and exit to the building were on the back side, but he was sure one could view them from a bedroom or bathroom window.

He watched Mrs. Camp in the kitchen, which was as tidy as the rest of the house. She looked to be in her mid-fifties. Her slightly graying hair was twisted into a loose bun. What make-up he had noticed was applied with as much meticulousness as she put into her home. As far as witnesses go, she was ideal.

He waited until the woman came back with the coffee and sat across from him before he spoke. "Did you know Nichole Blake?"

"We spoke casually whenever we saw each other, that was all. She was quiet. She kept to herself."

"When was the last time you saw her?" Michael watched the woman as she thought.

She gave a quick look over her shoulder at the calendar that was tacked to the wall. "Wednesday morning. She was leaving for work just as I was coming home. She walked to work." She shook her head. "I don't think she owned a car."

"Did you see her come home?" Michael asked.

"No."

"What leads you to believe she didn't come home Wednesday night?" He sipped the perfectly brewed coffee as he wrote on a small, black note pad.

"I went to do my laundry around seven. Her apartment is right above the laundry room." Her hands moved erratically in front of her as she spoke with them. She explained where the laundry room was in relation to Nichole's apartment. "There weren't any lights on at that time." She shook her head again. "I'm sure of it."

Michael made certain that his expression implied that he wasn't the one doubting her. "We have a man in sixteen-A who saw her lights on around six-thirty or seven."

"Mr. Daniels." The woman laughed. "He doesn't even know what year it is. He couldn't see his hand in front of his face. I know for sure that there were no lights on at seven. I don't care what that old coot thinks he saw."

Michael finished his coffee. "Thank you for your time. Here is my number." He handed her a piece of paper he'd just written on and then ticked the note pad into his pocket. "Call if you remember anything else."

Chapter Ten

The loud rap on the door made Michael look up. "Yes."

Jessica opened the door and smiled. "I thought you would like some dinner."

"Is it that time already?"

"It's way past that time. You've been in here all day." She set the tray of food on his desk in front of him. "Chili and corn bread, made by yours truly."

"How did you convince Mrs. Mayfield to let you cook?"

"After begging didn't work, I told her that my only joy in life other than horses was cooking. She didn't want to give in at first, but I managed to talk her into it."

"Did she give you the line of bull about how after a long day's work the last thing you want to do is cook?"

"Yeah, she tried that. But I told her cooking is how I unwind. Surprisingly, she went for it." Jessica laughed a little. "Or maybe it was my pathetic excuse that changed her mind." She set a mug of hot black coffee beside his chili. "This is to help you stay awake until dawn."

The meal was a peace offering. It was the only way she knew of saying she was sorry for prying into his personal life without bringing the topic up again. She hadn't intended to overstep her bounds. She had only wanted to get to know him a little better. Opening up wasn't something that he set out to do. She had hoped that a little encouragement would be all that was necessary to close the distance between them.

"Thank you. It looks good." There was sincerity in his voice as he pulled the tray of food toward him. "And it smells wonderful."

Worn out was the only way to describe him. His shoulders stooped. His hair was ruffled because he most likely had spent the day running his hands through it in frustration. The grimace that had been fixed on his face since she had come in caused deep lines around his eyes and mouth.

Jessica moved to the front of the big oak desk and looked around. The tall bookshelves that lined the walls were filled to capacity. A mess of papers covered every square inch of his desk. "How is the case going?"

"It's not." His hand immediately threaded through his hair.

She gestured to the papers spread across his desk. "You haven't learned anything more?"

"Not much."

Jessica sat in a soft leather chair. "Didn't you say something about a new witness?"

Michael nodded as he took a bite of the chili. "I went and saw her today. She saw Nichole in front of the deli minutes after you saw her."

"Did she see the man?" She folded her arms closely against her.

"No."

"That means they must have gone separate ways after I saw them."

"True. But the question is what happened after that?" He shook his head. "I can't piece it together."

Jessica thought for a moment. "Do you think he followed her home?"

"I doubt it. Someone would have seen him if he did. Besides, I don't think he would go to that length. This guy wants to find a quick target; he's not going to hunt someone down. It would be much easier to move on to someone else." He broke apart a square of corn bread and dipped it into his chili.

Jessica considered what he said. "It might have been easy. She might have made it easy for him."

He finished swallowing before he spoke. "How so?"

She slid to the edge of her seat. "Did she make it home?"

He rolled his eyes in irritation. "We have two conflicting stories. A man who lives right across the hall from her says that he saw her lights on."

"And the other witness?"

Michael told her what he had learned when he questioned Jean Camp.

"Did you ever think that both of them could be right?" she said bluntly.

"What do you mean?" He pushed aside the empty bowl.

"When I saw them, they were having what appeared to be a nice conversation."

"Agreed."

Jessica thought a moment, envisioning what might have happened. "I think he might have stopped her and asked for the time or perhaps directions. We agree that the conversation I saw them having was a friendly one, so they might have hit it off. He could have complimented her or thanked her for her help and then asked her out or something."

"Even if he did, she didn't leave with him."

"Maybe not right then. Being a woman, I would want to go home and change, freshen up a little before I went out on a date. Nichole had just gotten off work. Even if they were just meeting for coffee, I'm sure she would have at least wanted to change her clothes."

"Are you saying the first witness saw her lights on because she was home and the second witness didn't see any lights because she had already left to go meet this guy?"

"It makes sense to me. What do you think?"

"It's possible." Michael started piecing everything together. He could have picked her up at the apartment complex. He scratched that idea instantly. The killer wouldn't have been foolish enough to go to Nichole's home. He wouldn't risk someone seeing him. Nichole could have met him back at the antique store. That would make more sense. All the stores would have been closed, so no one would have seen them. He calculated how many hours they would have spent together. They had around six hours together. They had to have gone somewhere and done something in that amount of time.

Jessica chewed on the possibility herself. It did sound like it could have happened that way. Thousands of people met their mates by a happenstance on the street. "Do you think he'll kill someone else before you find him?"

His face filled with complete earnestness. "I hope not."

"Has the composite helped any?" Jessica asked.

"Not yet. But we have to give it time." He said nothing for a moment. He was mentally taking in the new details. He pushed the thoughts aside and looked at her. "How are things going with work?"

She relaxed a little at the change of subject. "Good."

"And the radio?"

Jessica smiled. "Great. I think it has made a difference. You'll see. When you start working again, you'll notice the changes. I think it's good for us, too. I can't count how many times I've come out of the office hearing one of the guys belting out a song."

Michael smiled for the first time that evening. "Singing. I can't picture that."

"It's funny. You should come out and visit us sometime."

"I'll have to do that," he said.

"I better let you get back to work." Jessica stood up and moved to the door.

"We're going to have to go over the mug shots sometime."

"Okay. Just tell me when." She leaned against the door, not really wanting to leave. She wanted to stay and talk about the ranch. In the last ten minutes his disposition had changed from completely serious to a little more relaxed. She didn't want him diving right back into work. He needed a break. But she would never be able to convince him of that.

"Thanks for the dinner, Stanson."

"You're welcome."

Michael reached for the coffee when she shut the door. Mentally he had been ready to submerge himself deep into work, but when he heard the television come on, the case slowly drifted away. Cradling the cup, he took a long sip. Knowing Jessica was only a few rooms away from him gave him great comfort. The huge house had transformed into a home since she had arrived. It was the little things he liked most. Seeing her sneakers on the back porch or her jacket hanging in the closet next to his. The clatter of noise throughout the house was no longer annoying. The soft voices from the television as she watched her nightly programs, the way her feet pounded on the floor, and the slamming of the cabinet as she got a snack was just as much anticipated as the opening and closing of the front door as she let Quest in and out.

The ringing of the phone brought him out of his thoughts.

"Mike, you better get down here now," Dan said.

"What's up?"

"Just get down here."

Michael took his coat from the closet and tossed it on. He grabbed his keys off the table and shouted, "Stanson."

111

Jessica appeared at the railing in the loft.

"I'm going to the station."

She moved toward the stairs. "Is everything all right?"

"I don't know."

When Michael entered the squad room, it was unusually crowded for the time of night. Officers lined the walls and gathered on cluttered desks. The atmosphere was prickly as people spoke in low voices. All eyes followed him as he walked through the room. He recognized several men standing around, and there were some faces he had never seen before. He shook his head as he walked past a desk where four men picked apart a pizza. This wasn't some damn slumber party. He fought his irritation.

As he moved toward the back of the room near Dan's office, he spotted a group of detectives from three different counties, along with some of Dan's best. He nodded as he walked past them into Dan's office.

Dan looked up with a smile. "Look what the cat drug in." He gestured toward his face. "Nice bruises."

"What's got you in such a good mood?"

Dan's smile grew bigger. "You aren't going to believe this."

"Are you going to just sit there and smile or tell me what's going on?"

Dan got up and went to the door. He called two men in and made quick introductions. "Carven, Sawyer, McBee."

Michael nodded.

"These two guys, they're from Norman County, picked up a man for shoplifting today."

Michael looked at the two men standing to the side of him. "What the hell does that have to do with me?"

Dan raised his hand. "Hold on, let them explain."

The officer named McBee stepped forward and spoke. "During the suspect's questioning, he openly confessed to the killings. He said he was actually at the store looking for women."

Michael looked to Dan, and without much thought he said, "It's not him."

"He knew a lot," McBee said.

Michael didn't look at the young officer. His glare remained on Dan. "He wouldn't confess. He has no reason to."

Obviously getting irritated for being ignored, McBee cleared his throat. "Maybe his conscience got to him."

Michael swung around and looked at the officer, who was several inches shorter than he. "I don't think that's possible."

"And why not?" McBee challenged.

"Because he doesn't have a fucking conscience."

"We found him in the lingerie department," the officer countered.

Michael could clearly see where he was going with this. "I don't care where you found him." His brows arched in aversion. "I don't care if his damn pockets were stuffed full of underwear."

The officer stumbled back as Michael turned to Dan. "I'm telling you it's not him."

Dan stood up and spoke. "That's why I want you to interrogate him." The flare-up of Michael's anger hadn't put a damper on his mood. He slapped him on the back. "If it's not him, you'll know."

Michael moved in the direction of the door. "Let's get this over with."

As the group of men filed out of the office and into the squad room, all talking ceased. Michael felt his irritation grow as the room of officers collectively watched them like they were observing a parade. He could hear conversation picking up once again as they left and entered the interrogation room.

The young officer who had been sitting with the suspect left the room. Sawyer and McBee stood in the corner while Dan pulled out a chair and offered it to Michael. "He's all yours."

Michael looked at the man sitting across the table from him. His eyes remained averted. His disposition was that of nervousness. He didn't look like he could have killed and raped four women. Something about this guy didn't sit well with him. He fit Jessica's description, but so did a lot of men. This wouldn't take too long. "What's your name?"

The young man looked up slowly. Studying Michael's attire. He probably thought his old jeans, sweatshirt, and worn leather jacket looked out of place against the other men's slacks and ties. "Jeff Webb."

"Jeff, my name is Michael Carven. These two men claim you confessed to killing and raping four women?" Michael threw his thumb over his shoulder, indicating McBee and Sawyer.

"I did. I killed them."

Michael eyed him. "How do I know you killed them?"

"You don't."

"You're right, I don't." Michael leaned back in his chair. "You know Jeff, there are a lot of insane people out there who get off on confessing to crimes they didn't commit."

"Are you saying I'm lying?"

Michael watched as Jeff started to get agitated. "Maybe."

"I'm not. I killed 'em. All of 'em."

Michael played with the pen in his hand. "Do you know you could be sentenced to death for killing those women?"

Jeff just shrugged his shoulders.

"You don't care?" Michael asked.

"Nope."

Michael stood up and began pacing in front of Jeff and the table. "Why did you rape and kill them?"

"Because."

"Because why?"

"I don't know."

Michael spun around. "You don't know?" His voice bounced off the walls, sending loud echoes in every direction. "You don't kill four women and rape them and not know why you did it. You know why." He watched him intently. "Now tell me, Jeff, why did you kill and rape them?"

Jeff looked startled.

Michael slammed his hand on the table. His eyes leveled with Jeff's. "Give me a goddamn answer. If you want me to believe you, convince me."

"I just wanted to."

Michael ran his hand across his face. This wasn't him. Where was his control? He was too nervous. "Tell me about the women you killed."

For an hour Michael questioned Jeff about the women he claimed he killed. His answers came easily, well formulated. It was as if he had planned and rehearsed the conversation. He was prepared for every question tossed at him. His knowledge and descriptions were believable. But there was one thing he hadn't said anything about: the underwear.

"What did you kill them with?"

"A cord."

Michael took a sip of bitter coffee in a white foam cup before he spoke. "What kind?"

"I don't know. Just a piece of cord I found around the house."

"How did you get the women to go with you?"

"I just started talking to them and they came. They wanted to come."

"Do you keep anything from the victims?"

"I keep lots of stuff. But I'm not telling you."

Michael wanted to smack the sickening smirk of his face. Instead, he stuffed his hands deep into his coat pockets and moved to Dan. He leaned into his ear. "It's not him."

"What do you want to do? It's your call," Dan whispered.

Michael moved away from Dan and looked at a uniformed officer. "Have someone get me a copy of the composite." Michael turned back to Jeff abruptly. "You want to know what I think? I think you're a goddamn liar."

Jeff only flinched slightly at the accusation. "I don't give a fuck what you think. I killed 'em."

Michael looked at Jeff's hands in his lap. The tops of his knuckles were white as he squeezed them together. "Then I'm sure you wouldn't mind if we have a witness come in and identify you."

The statement got Jeff's attention and his eyes grew big. "A witness?"

"Yes, a witness."

Jeff started laughing. "I know what you're doing. There isn't no witness. No one saw me commit those murders."

Michael looked over his shoulder to Dan. "Have someone get the witness."

Jeff watched as Dan spoke to a man standing by the door. "The witness is here?" he asked.

Just as Michael was about to speak, a man walked in with a copy of the composite. Michael ripped the paper out of the officer's hand and shoved it in Jeff's face. "Tell me who the fuck this is."

Jeff studied the picture frantically for a minute before shouting, "Me. It's me. I killed them."

Michael was inches from his face. "Bullshit. You didn't kill them, did you Jeff? And don't lie to me. I got a witness who is going to be here in thirty seconds to say you didn't."

"I did," Jeff shouted.

"No, you didn't. You don't have the balls to kill someone," Michael shouted back. "Isn't that true?"

"No."

"You're such a pansy ass that you had to lie about—"

Jeff stood up so fast that his chair fell. His face was red with rage. "Okay, okay, I didn't. But I wanted to. I wanted to kill them. All of them."

Michael threw the paper at him. "Get him out of here."

Chapter Eleven

Jessica sat in the living room with only a lamp on. The book she had attempted to read was flipped over on her lap. She had spent the last two hours arranging and then rearranging the sofa cushions and magazines. If it wasn't bolted down, she fiddled with it. If Mrs. Mayfield weren't so efficient, she would have scrubbed every square inch of the house to try and contain her edginess.

She was staring out the sheet of glass into the darkness ready to find something to do in the stables when she saw headlights stream through the trees. She raced to the door and flung it open.

"You're still up?" Michael asked as he got out of the truck.

"I couldn't sleep." She closed the door behind them and handed Michael a hanger when he took his coat off. "What happened? Please tell me someone else hasn't been killed."

He kicked off his shoes and set his keys on the table. "No, no one else has been murdered."

Jessica expelled the breath she felt like she'd been holding since Michael had left. She placed her hands against her chest as it collapsed. "Thank God."

Michael found his way to the fire. Positioning his backside toward the flame, he began to warm himself. "We just had a guy confess to the murders."

"It's over? You have him?" Jessica's excitement almost

bubbled out of her. She had the urge to rush to him and throw her arms around him.

A strange giggle seethed from Michael's lips. "No, we don't have him. It wasn't him."

"What? Why?" Had she just misunderstood everything he had just said? Someone had confessed to the murders. What more did he need? "I don't understand." She gawked at him.

"This guy isn't who we're after."

Without thinking, Jessica moved to the sofa and sat. She was utterly taken aback by what Michael was telling her. "Then why would he confess?"

"For attention, because he's crazy, I don't know." He placed his hands behind him to deflect some of the heat that was beginning to burn him.

"How did you know he was lying?"

"He didn't know about you." He looked at her. "He didn't know there was a witness. When I threatened I was going to bring the witness in, he started to break down."

"I can't believe this. Does this happen all the time?"

Michael rolled his head, stretching his neck. "More than you would think."

Jessica moved next to him. She wanted to ease the tension he was obviously experiencing. "Would you like some coffee?"

The words came out in a sigh. "Real coffee, I would love some. The stuff at the station should be called motor oil, not coffee."

"That bad?"

He moved to his recliner. "Worse."

"I'll be right back."

When Jessica came back with a tray of coffee, she fixed Michael's first, then her own. They talked about the case for a little while. Michael tilted his head and closed his eyes. He was tired.

She pushed the coffee table aside with her foot. "Come here."

Michael lifted his head and opened his eyes.

Jessica pointed toward the floor in front of her. "Come here and sit."

He sunk down to all fours and moved to her. When she opened her legs, he slid between them, pressing the middle of his back against the sofa. He extended his longs legs and crossed them at the ankles.

"Close your eyes and relax," Jessica said near his ear.

Michael did as she suggested and when he felt Jessica's hands come to his shoulders, he thought he would melt. He could feel each individual finger working out the tension in his neck. He sank down even farther.

While manipulating the area around his neck, Jessica allowed her knees to rest against his shoulders. Using her thumbs, she prodded the tender area at his hairline. After several minutes she felt the tension ease so she moved down to the base of his neck and allowed each hand to spread out to his shoulders. They were so broad she could barely span her fingers across them. She decided to use both hands on one shoulder.

"You're good at this." Michael's words came out in a soft moan.

"Thank you. I've had many years of practice. My brothers used to make me give them rubdowns after they came in from working." She worked a knot for a second. "I hated it."

He didn't know if he should groan in pleasure or pain. "Why?"

"Because I would have rather been outside playing or riding my horse."

"What was it like growing up with three brothers?"

She stopped momentarily and then started again. "I got teased a lot, beat up on an occasion or two, but I was never lonely and they always looked out for me."

His shoulders shook as he laughed. "Sounds like fun."

She gave him a final knead. "Better?"

"Much." He turned and looked at her. His face was only inches from hers. Her expression was serene and kind. "Thanks."

Moments passed before she spoke. "Do you have a deck of cards?"

"Yes."

"How about a game of poker?" she asked.

He didn't conceal his surprise. "Poker? You know how to play poker?"

"My brothers taught me."

While Michael went and got the cards, Jessica made more coffee and got a bag of pretzels. She set the tray on the floor in the middle of the brightly-colored area rug.

"What do you want to play for?" Michael asked as he handed her the cards to shuffle while he sorted the poker chips.

"Not for money. I'm trying to save all mine up." She thought for a moment. "I know. Massage minutes."

Michael stopped sorting and looked up. "What?"

"The white chips are worth one minute of massage, the blue are worth five minutes and the red are worth ten minutes. And whoever gets the most minutes wins and the other has to give the massage."

He continued to sort the rest of the chips. "Sounds good to me."

An hour into the game, Jessica was twenty minutes ahead of Michael. "I have a full house," she said. "I win again." She reached out and scraped all the chips towards her pile.

"You do that well."

Jessica was counting up her minutes and tallying them on a piece of paper. She fanned it in front of him. "Look at that." She pointed to the number under her name. "Aren't your fingers just cramping looking at it?"

"You're a graceful winner."

"You're a horrible loser," she countered.

"Did you say your brothers taught you how to play?"

"Yes."

"Remind me to never play with them." He pushed his cards toward her in defeat. "I give up."

Jessica laughed. "This was a lot of fun, thanks." She picked up the tray of coffee and the bag of pretzels and carried them into the kitchen. "I'll let you know when I'm going to cash in."

Michael gave her a weary smile. "I'm sure you will."

Michael stood in one of the tack rooms and listened to the music while he watched Jessica lead a sorrel mare into the washing unit. She placed the horse in cross ties before turning the water on and then held her hand under the water, waiting for it to get warm. Moving to the horse's head, she lifted the hose. "Here it comes." As she spoke to the horse, she ran the hose over her head. The horse opened her mouth to get a taste. "You like that?"

Michael stepped out. "Need some help?"

"Sure." She tossed him a bottle of conditioner. "Put that in her mane and tail." She lifted the hose to the horse and soaked its body. She dipped the brush in the bucket of soapy water and began to scrub. "What are you doing out here?"

"I needed to stretch my legs."

"You should stretch your legs more often."

He looked up at the small black speaker nestled in the corner. "I like the radio."

Jessica moved the brush to the horse's neck and worked the lather. "So do the horses." After she finished speaking, they heard the soft echo of whistling bounce down the hall. They looked at each other and started laughing. "Can you hand me the hose?"

As Michael lifted the hose over the horse, he doused Jessica's face. "Sorry—"

"Oh, I can't believe you did that," Jessica sputtered as she wiped her face off. The water was warm but it was still a shock.

The look on her face was amusing. Michael could not help but laugh. "I didn't mean to."

Jessica picked up the bucket of soapy water and tossed it on him. Half of its contents landed on his stomach and ran down his legs. "Oops, sorry. I didn't mean to."

Michael stuck his thumb in the end of the hose and aimed the spray at Jessica. She crouched behind the horse as the spray shot over her head. She had no other weapon but a wet sponge by her feet. She grabbed it, popped up, and tossed it at him. It landed in the middle of his chest with a loud thump. Surprised, he dropped the hose and gaped at his chest in disbelief.

Jessica gained control of the hose, and before she knew what was happening, Michael dove around the horse and caught her by the waist. Holding her from behind, he pinned her arms at her side and lifted her feet off the ground. "Truce?"

"You started it." She kicked her legs, trying to break his hold.

"It was an accident." He was laughing in her ear as she tried to get away. She still had the hose in her hand but couldn't do anything with it.

"I don't believe you."

"Drop the hose."

Jessica stopped struggling. "Let me go first."

"No way. You drop the hose and then I'll let you go."

"You don't trust me?" She tried to turn and look at him.

"Not on your life."

Grudgingly, Jessica dropped the hose and Michael released her. He reached out and gently tucked the wet hair that was plastered to her face behind her ear. He ran his thumb over her lips. "Your lips are trembling." He lazily stroked her bottom lip and watched it shudder under his fingers. Could his touch cause her to respond like that? As he caressed her plump bottom lips, desire shot through him.

"Why do you look at me like that?"

"Like what?"

"Like you're trying to figure me out." Her fingers were nimble as they glided over his brow, his temple, and his cheek. "I'll tell you whatever you want to know."

He took her hand and held it. He knew she would. But he wouldn't be able to handle hearing what she had to say. "Let's rinse the horse and sit under the heat lamps with her."

Together they rinsed the horse thoroughly. Michael used a sweat scraper to get the excess water off, while Jessica brushed the tangles out of her tail and mane.

They took the horse to a large stall and turned on the heat lamps. They piled straw in the corner and sat down.

"This feels good," Jessica said as she looked up at the bright lights that carried warm waves of heat to them.

"Come here." Michael fiddled with a piece of hay in her hair. When he untangled it, he put it in his mouth and chewed on it. "Smell that? I love that smell."

"Are you referring to me or the horses?" A giggle threatened to escape from her throat, but instead it danced in her eyes.

He shot her a look.

"I love it too. The sweet scent of oaks and grain, the musty smell of horse, and the bitter fragrance of hay are wonderful. I could never get tired of it."

The horse snorted, swishing her tail from side to side as it dried. "I think she agrees too."

Chapter Twelve

"What happened?" Michael looked at Jessica's foot that was propped up on two thick white pillows. Another one supported her back, as she lay lengthwise on the sofa.

"Mugger stepped on me. It was my fault. I wasn't watching what I was doing." She set the book down she was reading.

Michael lifted the ice pack. Her foot was red and slightly swollen. There didn't appear to be any bruising or lesions. "Is it okay?"

She couldn't resist. "Nothing an ice pack won't heal," she said with a wink.

The look he sent her was void of any type of amusement. "Stanson."

"Yes, it's okay. It doesn't even hurt. The ice pack wasn't my idea. Mrs. Mayfield insisted." She lifted the ice pack and set it on the coffee table to prove her point.

"Do you need to see a doctor?"

Jessica's voice crackled in annoyance. "This isn't the first time I've been stepped on. I don't need to see a doctor. I'm fine."

Michael raised his hands. "Okay."

"There's dinner in there if you want something." She hiked a thumb over her shoulder. "Mrs. Mayfield left twenty minutes ago with strict instructions that you eat."

"I grabbed a bite with Dan in town." He raised the black

book. "I thought we could go through this if you feel up to it."

She twisted until she was sitting and both feet were on the floor. "Sure."

"We should do it at the kitchen table; there's better light in there." He offered her his arm when she stood. "Do you need help walking?"

"You're insulting me," she said in a biting tone.

In the kitchen, Michael chose a chair beside her and sat down. "Take your time and look at every one of them."

"I will."

For an hour she turned page after page, looking closely at each individual black-and-white photograph. She didn't recognize any of them until she skimmed over a face in the lower right corner. His features caught her eye. He looked familiar.

After a stretch of time Michael noticed that Jessica hadn't turned the page. "What? Do you recognize someone?"

Jessica tapped her finger on a picture. "He looks familiar."

"Is it him?"

She shook her head. "He looks like my cousin."

Michael fell against his chair. "Damn it, Stanson."

She examined the headshot even closer. "I swear he looks exactly like my cousin Phil."

"Just look at the book."

Two hours later Jessica could barely hold her head up. "Can we stop and look at the rest some other time?" She cupped her hand over her mouth as she yawned. "I'm dead tired."

"We haven't even gone through half the book yet. Are you sure you haven't recognized any of them?"

"I'm sure." She pushed her hair to the side and yawned for a second time. "Let's call it quits for the night."

He reached for the book and angled it in front of her. "Just a few more."

She gently rejected the book. "Michael, I'm so tired that they are all beginning to look alike."

"I'll make some coffee."

When Michael got up, Jessica let her head fall on the book. It felt good to rest her neck and her eyes.

Michael tapped her on the shoulder. "Come on."

Jessica lifted her head slowly. She studied each face on the page and, when she was finished, she turned to the next. "Why do they all look so mean?"

"They just got busted for doing something illegal. You don't expect them to be smiling, do you?"

"No, I suppose not." She turned the page. "This process is very time-consuming."

"Yes, it is."

She examined several more pages before she looked up. "Can we please continue in the morning?"

Michael pointed to a mug shot at the top of the page. "Does he look familiar?"

"No."

"How about him?"

"No." She turned to him. "What are you going to do? Point each one out for me?"

"Let me get that coffee." He pulled out the carafe of hot coffee and brought it to the table, then returned for two mugs. "This will help," he said as he filled each cup.

Reluctantly, Jessica forced her attention back to the book.

The coffee didn't do any good, because over the next half hour Michael watched Jessica's eyes grow heavy. The only reason her head was in an upright position was because she had it braced with her arm. Her eyes would close briefly and then reopen suddenly. He took the cups and went back to the

128

coffeepot. He heard a thump and turned around to see Jessica's head on the table. Her hair covered her face, the book, and half of the table. "Stanson." She didn't move. He brushed the silky strands aside so he could see the side of her face. "Stanson, wake up."

"No. No more pictures." The objects she had her face buried in muffled her words.

He felt guilty for pushing her. "No more pictures. Go to bed."

"I'm too tired to get up. Let me sleep here."

"You can't sleep at the kitchen table."

"Yes I can." Jessica lifted her head, brushed her hair back, and stood up, then swiped the book off the table and tucked it under her arm. "Good night."

Michael provoked her as he cleared away the coffee. "It's morning."

"Don't remind me," she said.

He gestured to the thick book tucked tightly under her arm. "Where are you going with the book?"

"I'm taking it with me."

"Why?"

"So I can look at it by myself, when I want to, and for as long as I want to. This night is not repeating itself."

"Are you always this cranky when you're tired?"

"I'm beyond tired." She fought the urge to yawn and extend her arms over her head and pass out wherever her body collapsed. "You do realize that I have to be up in a few hours to run your ranch." She jabbed a finger in his direction. "You haven't forgotten that, have you?"

He shook his head. "No, I haven't."

"I'm not nocturnal." She snapped and flung a hand in the air. "I can't stay up half the night like you can. I need a full seven hours' sleep."

"I'm sorry." He tried to move to her, but she took a step back. "I was just hoping that you would recognize one of them."

"If I do, I'll let you know."

Michael hadn't seen Jessica since they had looked at the mug shots, which was two nights ago. He had been too busy checking out some new leads to see how she was doing. He knew that he had kept her up too late because the guys had complained that she had been short-tempered all that day. He had laughed when they told him that she made them clean out the hayloft because they got on her nerves.

He walked into the den to where Jessica was sitting. He noted the black book across her lap.

Jessica glanced up casually. "Hey there, stranger. What have you been up to?"

"Not much."

"I thought the disappearance meant that you were on a hot lead."

"I wish." He threw himself into his recliner and, using the wooden handle on the side, he propped his feet up. "Any luck?"

Jessica finished looking at the last page of pictures. Closing the heavy book, she handed it to him. "Sorry, I didn't recognize one of them."

"Damn." He took the book and drummed his fingers across it. "I'm sorry about the other night. I didn't mean to push you."

Jessica gave him a faint smile.

He set the book on the floor beside the recliner. "How have things been?"

"Very busy."

"I noticed. The parking lot has been full."

"Thank you for talking to Wes. I don't know what you said to him, but it worked."

Michael stretched out his legs. "This is nice. Talking about the ranch."

She took a seat. "Great, if you want to talk about the ranch, I have something we could talk about."

"What's that?"

"Manure."

"Manure?" Michael asked.

"You bet ya. Manure."

Michael wasn't sure that he wanted to know where the conversation was leading. "Do we have a problem with our manure that I should know about?"

"Yes. We're having a parasite problem."

"How big?"

"Nothing to worry about yet, but it could get out of hand. I think we need to rotate the horses more."

"What do you recommend?"

"When it warms up a little more, I would recommend rotating pastures every five days and then don't put the horses back in them for at least three months."

"It's worth a try." He added as a thought occurred to him, "We could also rotate the deworming medications, to prevent chemical resistance."

Jessica nodded in agreement.

"How are the classes going?"

"Good. You'll never guess what we did yesterday. I put on a show. Jake, Richard, and John were the judges. The kids loved it. I explained what was expected of them and the rules. They did fantastic. I wish you could have seen them. They radiated with confidence and poise. You know, the competition did exactly what I wanted it to do. It gave each of them the drive to do better."

His features softened. "How did little Callie do?"

"She won. She's a natural. Everyone received ribbons. I found some in the desk in the office. I hope that's okay."

"Sure." For several moments, Michael watched her. "Where do you want to live? I mean where do you want to build your ranch?"

"I'd like to be close to my family but as long as I'm doing what I love most, I don't think it really matters."

"Tell me about your ranch."

Jessica smiled. "Are you sure you want to hear this?"

"Yes." He reached for a cushion on the sofa and tucked it behind his back.

"Which version do you want, the long, drawn-out one that I've had since I was a kid or the short, realistic one?"

"The dream."

"That's my favorite. It's visually as clear now as it was when I was a kid. Of course, over the years the dream altered according to the latest equipment and styles, but generally not much has changed. I want a big house with a large green lawn. I want weeping willows to stretch down a long driveway with a four-rail white fence behind them. They would disappear behind the house and reappear by the stables."

Michael closed his eyes as he listened to her speak. Her voice was low and soothing, and her words were injected with faint excitement. It was as if she were telling a fairy tale to a group of small children. He scooted down in the recliner. Her voice was lovely. There was no other word for it. He could easily go to sleep and dream of that voice.

"It's funny. The ranch I have always wanted reminds me a lot of your ranch. Michael?" She looked over to his chair. His head was slumped to the side and his chin touched his chest. He was sound asleep. She turned off the lamp next to her. "I don't know how you keep up the hours that you do."

"Good morning." Mrs. Mayfield nodded toward Jessica as she put a stack of folded washcloths in a drawer. She then pulled out a red envelope from the large pocket of her apron and slid it under the empty coffee cup that she took out for Michael each morning.

"Good morning." Jessica pointed to the red envelope that had Michael's name printed on it. "What's that?"

Mrs. Mayfield smiled. "Have you been outside this morning?"

Jessica looked at the envelope and back to Mrs. Mayfield. "No."

"The sunrise looks like it's going to be amazing."

Jessica looked over her shoulder and out the kitchen window. There were a few lingering stars glittering across the dark sky. There wasn't a cloud in sight. The rising sun was turning the black sky a coal gray. Grabbing her cup, she scurried out the back door.

Sitting on the fence rail, she took a sip of the coffee as she waited patiently for the sun to rise and pour its warmth over her. Looking up, there were only a few stars straining to twinkle in the dawn light. An orange hue outlined the mountains in the distance as the sun threatened to peak over the round crest.

She closed her eyes and listened to the wind play a soothing melody as it licked the tall pines. She felt herself begin to sway to the beautiful sound that only nature could make. It was peace in itself. It was a sound that she would never grow tired of.

The massive mountains that bordered the ranch only enhanced its beauty. Lush trees that gave the appearance of fingers reaching into the sky dotted the ridge tops and carpeted

133

the valleys. The foliage filled the background with a spectac-
ular view. Majestic beauty surrounded her on all sides, en-
closing her in a valley of heavenly sights and sounds.

Michael's legs were crossed as he leaned against the
doorframe on the back step. He held the red envelope in
his left hand and coffee in his right as he watched Jessica.
Her back was tall and straight, face turned toward the sun,
drinking in the horizon. She was so unlike any of the other
women he had met throughout his life. She was simple-
hearted and uninhibited. That was what he liked about
her the most. He took a deep breath. He wasn't prepared
for the feelings the unexpected glimpse of her would gen-
erate.

Jessica opened her eyes as the first ray touched her face.
She looked out across the dew-covered pasture, glistening in
the brilliant sunlight. Rainbows of light bounced off the wet
blades of grass. She thought about the red envelope under
Michael's coffee cup. It had to be a birthday card. That was
the only explanation. It was Michael's birthday. She loved
birthdays. She jumped off the fence and ran to the stables.
The crew would be there. They were always there by sunup.
"Hey guys."

John and Richard looked up. "What's up, Jess?"

"Where are Jake and Tom?"

"Jake's still in the house. He should be coming any
minute. I'm not sure where Tom's at. Why?" Richard asked.

"I have some great news." Just as she finished speaking,
Jake appeared through the stable doors.

"It's Michael's birthday today," she said excitedly.

"No shit." Jake looked surprised.

John said, "In all the years we've worked for him, we never
knew when it was."

That was what Jessica had suspected. The thought saddened her. No one should spend his or her birthday alone. "I thought we could have a surprise party."

"Are you sure you want to do this, Jess?" Jake said.

"Why not?"

He lifted his shoulders. "Maybe he doesn't want us to know."

"It's just a little party; it'll be fun. Who doesn't like birthday parties? So, are you in?"

The men nodded.

"Great. I'll call Dan at lunchtime and you tell Tom when he gets here. Jake, you call your wife and tell her to bring the kids." She looked at John and Richard. "You guys bring your girlfriends. I'll ask Mrs. Mayfield to stay late and help me get things ready. Everybody be here at six."

Jessica went back to the house to find Mrs. Mayfield. As she passed through the kitchen, she glanced at the coffeepot. The card was gone. She found Mrs. Mayfield in the den dusting.

"It wouldn't happen to be Michael's birthday today, would it?" She whispered just in case Michael was in the house.

Mrs. Mayfield remained silent. Picking up a book, she dusted under it.

"I plan on giving him a surprise party tonight and if it's not, I'm going to look real stupid." Mrs. Mayfield kept dusting. Jessica proceeded to tell her who she invited and what she wanted to do. "I thought you could stay and help me cook dinner. I also wanted to make a cake."

Mrs. Mayfield nodded and replaced the books. "His favorite is German chocolate."

Jessica smiled and left the room. She had a lot of planning to do. It was going to be hard to get everything done with

Michael in the house. The only time he came out of his office was for lunch, so that was the only time she had to worry about. First on her list to call was Dan. If he could come early, he could keep Michael busy in the office until they were ready. Then she needed to go into town and get a few things.

Chapter Thirteen

Jessica glanced at the clock above the sink as she finished spreading the last bit of frosting on the cake. Dan had arrived fifteen minutes before and was in the study pacifying Michael. In half an hour, the guys would be arriving. That would give her enough time to shower and change.

"Mrs. Mayfield, can you handle everything down here while I get cleaned up?"

"Of course, dear. All that's left to do is set the table."

Jessica surveyed her closet. She hadn't brought any dresses with her. A pair of ivory slacks and sweater would have to do. She swept her hair up, leaving a few curls around her face and neck. Her make-up was minimal, a little blush and lipstick. Twenty minutes later she was back in the kitchen.

"You look beautiful," Mrs. Mayfield said.

"Thank you." She glanced at the set table. "Is everything ready?"

"Yes. Dinner is in the oven and the hors d'oeuvres are out. There are more veggies in the refrigerator and the chips and crackers are in the cabinet."

Jessica hugged Mrs. Mayfield. "Thank you. What would I do without you?" She pulled away. "I want this to be perfect."

"It will be."

Jessica's hand flew to her mouth. "Oh no, I forgot the ice cream."

"There's some in the freezer."

"The bread—"

"Is warming in the oven." Mrs. Mayfield took Jessica's hands in hers. "Everything is taken care of. Relax."

Jessica looked around the room anxiously and began to pace the length of the kitchen. What had she done? What if all this backfired? She turned suddenly to Mrs. Mayfield. "He can't fire me for this, can he?"

Mrs. Mayfield shook her head. "What are you talking about? Fire you."

She went back to pacing. "It's a birthday. Who could possibly get mad for celebrating a birthday?" She hated the feeling of regret. "If I lose this job because of this I'll—"

"Jessica, someone has arrived."

Jessica was pulled from her senseless babble. "What? Who?"

Jake and his two sons were the first to arrive. They snuck in the back door. Jessica managed to push aside her doubts and fears and in hushed whispers she made the acquaintance of his kids. "It's nice to meet you." She squatted down to eye level.

The two kids shyly hid behind their father's legs. They looked just like their dad in jeans and cowboy boots. Their blond hair was combed to perfection and their dress shirts were neatly tucked in. The taller of the two fiddled with his belt buckle. Jake leaned forward to Jessica's ear. "Jennifer couldn't come. She is at home with our youngest. She's sick."

"I'm sorry. Is everything going to be okay?"

"Yeah. Just a cold." He put an arm around each boy. "Go and give Mrs. Mayfield a hug." The boy's raced to the woman. "Quietly." His voice was a loud whisper.

Jessica laughed at the kids' excitement. "They're adorable."

"Spend a day with them." Jake looked to the back door. "Richard's here."

Jessica barely had enough time to meet Richard and his girlfriend before John came in and introduced his girlfriend. The kitchen was crowded as everyone shuffled around, talked, and munched on snacks. The guys stood over a chip bowl and talked horses while Mrs. Mayfield made sure no little fingers found their way into the frosting on the cake.

"The guy at the auction is a local. He has a record." Michael looked at the papers in his hands. "Arrested twice for being drunk in public, once for fighting, and once for D.U.I. I don't think he's our guy."

"What about the guy at the diner?" Dan looked at the clock on the far wall.

"I haven't found him yet. I left my name with the staff at the diner. When he comes in they're going to give me a call. Since I didn't get a license number, it's going to be hard. Are you in a hurry?" Michael said.

"No, I'm just hungry."

Michael wrote some notes down. "We'll grab a bite in just a minute."

"By the way, how are things with Jessica?"

Michael tapped the paper with the pen in an agitated rhythm as he pondered a thought. He wrote down a few sentences before he answered Dan's question. "She's a good trainer."

"That's not what I meant. I was thinking more along the lines of roommate. Is she as good a roommate as she is a trainer?" Dan grinned as he probed Michael and Jessica's relationship.

Michael's head shot up. "What's that supposed to mean?"

He wanted to yell "hello," but feared Michael would leap

across the desk and attack him. "What it means is that she isn't a pain to the eyes. Don't tell me you don't like having her around. Any man would love to live with a woman that looks like Jessica."

"She's annoying." He tossed his pen down. He would never be able to keep a constructive thought in his head now. "But I have to admit when she gets up in the middle of the night to let Quest out I thank the good lord for thin night-gowns."

Dan held up his hands. "Don't tell me any more. I'm already jealous." He looked at his watch. "Can we please go eat now? I'm starved."

Jessica rubbed her hands together with uncertainty. It was almost six and Dan would be bringing Michael out soon. She motioned for everyone to gather around the table. She wanted Michael to see everyone when he entered the room.

She held her breath when she heard the study door open and the low voices of Dan and Michael filter into the kitchen. She didn't know if she wanted to close her eyes or watch his reaction. She decided she didn't care what his reaction would be; she wanted to see the look on his face, good or bad.

"Surprise!" Everyone threw their hands up.

It took Jessica an instant to determine that he looked not only shocked but also pleased.

"I can't believe this." Michael looked over to Jessica before he turned to Dan. "You knew about this, didn't you?"

Dan nodded.

Mrs. Mayfield was the first in line to wish him a happy birthday. "Surprised?"

"That's an understatement," Michael said as Mrs. Mayfield pulled him into her arms and kissed him on the cheek not once but twice.

"Happy birthday." Richard and his girlfriend came up and handed him a bottle of wine. "I hear you can use this."

Michael barely had a moment to thank them before John slapped him on the back and reached for his hand. "Happy birthday, boss. How many is this now we pulled over on you? I think we're pulling ahead."

Michael looked to their girlfriends. "Why are you with these guys?" He smiled. "I think you could do better."

Jessica snapped a few quick pictures of everyone wishing Michael a happy birthday with her Polaroid, before she rushed to the refrigerator to replenish the food. When she turned, Tom was there.

"Here, let me help you."

She handed him a bowl of dip and shut the door with her hip. "Thank you."

"It looked like you could use a hand." He followed her to the table and handed her the dish back when she had freed her hands. "You look mighty pretty tonight."

"Thank you," she gave him a big smile. "Again."

She watched from the sidelines as everybody made small talk. She spotted Michael across the room smiling down at Jake's youngest son who appeared to be telling quite an animated story. She reached for the camera on the counter and captured the touching moment.

"He is good with him, isn't he?" Mrs. Mayfield moved beside her.

"Yes he is," Jessica said as she stood up from her squatting position. She never took her eyes off the pair. She was captivated because this was the only time she had seen Michael let his guard down and let someone in. Everything about him had changed. This was the Michael she had been searching for.

Mrs. Mayfield nudged her. "Come on dear, we need to start serving dinner."

Dinner went as smoothly as she could have hoped. In fact, the entire evening had been better than she had ever dreamed. They only had to get through opening the presents and eating the cake and the celebration would go off without a hitch. And to think Michael was going to let this day pass without saying a word.

After she asked everyone to retire to the living room, she cleared the dinner dishes and set out plastic plates and forks for dessert. She placed the cake on a serving dish Mrs. Mayfield had left out for her. It took several matches, but she managed to light all the candles. She switched off the lights with her elbow and carried the cake into the living room.

A chorus of "Happy Birthday" led her to Michael. As she placed the cake in front of him, their eyes locked. She gave him a touching smile. "Make a wish."

Michael sucked in a deep breath and winced. As all the candles went out, and they were left in the dark, Richard asked, "What did you wish for?"

Michael pulled a candle out and licked the frosting off it. "If I tell you, then it won't come true."

When the lights came back on, Jake's oldest son held out a brightly wrapped box. "Let's open presents."

As Michael looked up to take the present from the boy, he caught a glimpse of Tom standing what he thought was entirely too close to Jessica.

"Open it," the small voice demanded.

"Okay, okay, I will," Michael said as he tore into the paper.

The party died down an hour later. Michael walked outside with Jake, who carried a sleeping boy on each hip, and Richard and John, and their girlfriends. "Thanks for coming.

Drive carefully." He waited until they were out of sight before he went back in.

Dan met him at the front door. "Happy birthday, Mike." He reached for his partner's hand.

"It was at that." Michael took his hand and held it firmly.

"I better get going too." He looked behind Michael. "Jessica, Mrs. Mayfield, thanks for a great evening. Goodnight." He looked back to Michael. "I'll be in touch."

"Happy birthday." Mrs. Mayfield placed a kiss on his cheek when he bent down.

"I'll get you." He spoke the words against her cheek.

She placed her hand over her heart. "I swear I didn't tell."

"Yeah, but you didn't *not* tell."

She gave his cheek a playful pat. "See you in the morning."

When he turned, he saw Tom saying good night to Jessica. He forced a smile when Tom approached him.

"Happy birthday, boss."

"Thanks for coming." Closing the door behind him, Michael stood still. Silence. He hadn't heard that in hours. Though he wasn't complaining. He walked to each room, turning off the lights and picking up cups and plates. Where was Jessica? He climbed the stairs; stopping at the top, he saw the light shining from under her closed door. He made his way back down to the kitchen where he deposited plates and cups in the trash. He immersed his finger in red frosting on the leftover cake and stuck it in his mouth. The night was still young, he could get a few hours of work in. Turning, he went to his study and closed the door.

Jessica tossed the tape and scissors into her top drawer. She fluffed the blue bow on the wrapped gift as she went downstairs. Knocking on the study door, she waited.

"Come in."

She held the gift behind her back. "I thought I'd never get to see you."

Michael looked up from his work, happy to see her. "The way you were running around all night, I assumed you were exhausted and went to bed."

She shook her head.

"Thank you for tonight," he said.

"Then you're not mad?" She didn't look him in the eyes.

He thought for a moment. "No, but don't ever do anything like that again."

"I won't." She exhaled deeply and handed him the present.

"What's this?"

"I didn't get to give you a gift," she said.

He carefully unwrapped the box. He held up the picture frame and looked to Jessica.

"That's why I rushed to my room; I had to put it together."

Michael stared at the frame. There were different snapshots of the party arranged in a single frame. Some were taken at dinner and some were from when he opened his presents. The biggest one in the center was of him blowing out his candles. Everyone was gathered behind him with bright smiles. "Thank you." He placed the frame in the corner of his desk. "That looks like a good place for it."

Jessica didn't want to wear her welcome out. She had already pushed her luck by throwing him the party in the first place. She walked to the door. "Happy birthday, Michael. Good night."

As the door shut, Michael looked at the picture again. It was then he noticed Jessica wasn't in any of the pictures. "Stanson."

Jessica swung the door back open. "Did you call me?"

"Come here." Michael held up the picture. "Why aren't there any pictures of you?"

"Well, I didn't think you would want a picture of me. Besides I was the one taking the pictures."

"Where's your camera?"

"In my room. Why?"

He set the picture back down and rose from his chair. "Go get it. We have a picture to take."

She was reluctant to move. "We really don't need to do this."

"Yes, we do. Now go get it. And meet me in the living room." He gave her a gentle push.

She fled upstairs.

When she returned, he said, "What took you so long? Never mind. Sit on the hearth—no, the sofa." He looked from one to the other. "No, the hearth."

"We don't need to do this. There isn't any more room in the picture frame."

"Then I'll buy another one. Now sit."

She sat and watched Michael turn on every light in the room. The glare bounced off the wall of glass, making the room look double its size. He pushed the coffee table to the side with his leg, giving him more room to work.

"That should do it." He stood before Jessica. Lifting the camera to his eyes he said, "Smile."

"I can't." She turned her head away.

"What do you mean you can't?" Jessica Stanson not know how to smile? That was like the sun not knowing how to shine. It just wasn't possible.

She tried pleading her case. "I don't take good pictures. Just look at every school picture I've ever had taken."

He shrugged. "I figured you would be photogenic."

"Sorry to disappoint you." She stood up.

"Where are you going? You don't get off that easy." He knew it wouldn't take much to get her to smile. "Sit back down. I'll be right back."

She sat down and looked across the room at her reflection in the big window. She did hate having her picture taken. She didn't know if it was the pressure of having the perfect smile or if it was because she felt the picture was fake. Either way, they never came out good. Her eyes turned red or her smile was too big.

"Look who I found." Michael walked in with Quest. When the dog spotted Jessica, he ran to her, smothering her face with wet kisses. She laughed as she fought him off. A flash of light blinded her. "That was rotten," she said.

"I think it will be a great picture."

Relieved that the picture was over, she wrapped her arms around the dog's neck in a big hug. "Can you believe he did that, Quest?" Two more flashes filled the room. She looked up in surprise. "That's it." She jumped up and ran for him. "Give me the camera."

Michael dodged her as he ran around the coffee table. He swung around the backside of the sofa and snapped another picture. Holding up the four pictures he had taken, he said. "I bet you want these." He fanned himself with them as he grinned smugly.

Jessica ran around the table, cornering him against the sofa and end table. "Give me the camera and no one gets hurt." Her smile dissolved the threat. "If you take another picture of me—"

"What? What are you going to do?"

She lunged at him. Trying to grab the camera, she accidentally hit his ribs. The look on his face was what made her stop. "Michael, what's wrong?"

He walked to the hall. Holding up the pictures, he said,

"I'll put these in a safe place." He forced a faint smile for her benefit. "Now, that didn't hurt, did it?"

She followed him. "No, but when I touched your ribs it did."

"I don't know what you're talking about."

"I think you do. Come here." When he stood before her, the look he was giving her was the same one he had given her when she confronted him about the bruise. "Take your shirt off."

His arrogance was quick to return. "Is this part of my birthday present?"

"Do it," she ordered.

"You do it."

She knew he was trying to scare her off. "Okay." She raised her hands to the first button. She could feel his breath on her fingers as she moved to the second button. Undoing the third button, her hand touched the soft growth of hair on his chest, making her fumble on the fourth and fifth buttons. She fought to keep steady.

She looked up and gazed at Michael. He had a look of interest of his face as he watched her unclothe him. She sucked in a deep breath. What sweet torture she was experiencing. Part of her wanted to drag out the task and make it last forever. Another part of her wanted to hurry so she could see him.

"Tell me why your hands are shaking." She was a remarkable blend of strong will and sweet innocence. There were so many amazing aspects of her personality he wanted to discover and experience them all. Desire surged through his body as she slowly looked up at him.

"Are you trying to intimidate me?"

He could tell she was fighting to keep her voice composed. It pleased him to know he could overwhelm her sanity just as easily as she could his. "No. That was not my intention."

"I've never undressed a man before," she murmured.

He was instantly lost in her dark eyes. Jesus, was she even aware of the effect her statement had? He doubted it. To her, she was just being honest. "It's just my shirt."

She looked back down at what she was doing. "I've never removed a man's shirt—" Her words faded as she took each flap of material and moved it aside. "Damn it, Michael." She stared at the yellow-purplish bruise that wrapped around his side. "Are they broken?"

He looked down at the enormous, grisly bruise. "No, only bruised."

She remembered all the times he had looked uncomfortable. "Did you even get a hit in, or did he just beat the crap out of you?" she asked as she examined his side.

"Thanks for the vote of confidence."

She looked his body over. "Are there any other wounds I should know about?"

"That's it."

All at once, she felt responsible for what happened. "I'm so sorry, Michael."

That was exactly why he hadn't told her about getting hit in the ribs. He knew she would blame herself. "It's not your fault."

"Yes, it is. If I had listened to you, none of this would have happened." She looked at the bruise and back to him.

"You didn't make me fight that man," he said.

"No, but I didn't give you much of a choice." Only inches from his frame, she moved to touch him. She glided her fingers over the bruises. With boldness she could only muster when with him, she raised her free hand to his other side. As she moved her hands up and down she could feel each individual rib. Tight, hard muscles stretched across his chest and spread down to his stomach. She did a visual check along with a physical and both gave her great satisfaction. It also delighted her to see the strength contract as she slid her fingers over his flesh.

Her hands felt small and warm as they trembled over his body. He entirely forgot about the pain. He could only feel the incredible sensation her touch created in his body. She revived emotions that he thought had long been buried. He closed his eyes as she ran her fingers through a patch of hair and tried to accept what she was doing, what he was doing. The minute he felt her lips brush over his skin, her tongue reverently taste him, the recklessness of the situation overpowered him.

"What am I doing wrong?" she asked in a pleading, gentle voice.

He eased back as he fought for control. "It's not you."

"Then what? What is it? Tell me what you want."

"You don't want this, Stanson."

Her eyes met his, clinging to the dark depths. "I know what I want, Michael. Tell me what you want."

Without a word, Michael buttoned his shirt and straightened his shoulders. The area where she'd placed her kiss still tingled.

She reached for his hands and stopped him. "Please talk to me." A subtle change came over her face. Her voice quieted as she tried to hide the hurt. "Why are you doing this?"

"This isn't possible." Would it annul what he just said if he reached out and touched her? He wanted to haul her against him and apologize for what he was doing to her, but he couldn't. He didn't have a choice; why couldn't she understand that? He would never be able to give her what she needed. The truth was he didn't have it in him.

"It's possible if you would allow it." Her words were soft with understanding.

It felt like the breath had been knocked out of him. Her heart was at his feet and he couldn't do anything about it. There was sweetness about her that he was slowly crushing. He would rather die himself than watch her wither because of him. "It's not a matter of me allowing it, Stanson." His face went firm and his back rigid as he watched the sparkle in her eyes fizzle out. "I don't want it." With that, he disappeared down the hall. He never turned back to look at her.

Chapter Fourteen

Jessica worked the entire day without any interruptions, and it was a blessing because it had taken a better part of it just to enter all the updated information into the computer. This was the part she liked least about her job, but she knew she had to take the good with the bad. Cleaning up her half-eaten sandwich and empty cup of coffee, she tidied up the desk and put the stack of papers in their proper folders and in the file cabinet. Michael had insisted they handwrite everything for a back-up. She scanned the room to make sure it was all in order before she turned off the light and locked the door.

"Hey, Jess," Tom called out. "I'm calling it quits. The weather is picking up and it's spooking the horses."

She tucked the keys into her pocket. "Okay."

"You want to go grab a burger?" Tom asked as they both walked out of the stables.

Jessica was surprised when she saw the dark clouds that had replaced the clear sky. She looked over her shoulder to the mountains where the setting sun would have been. The clouds hung so low that the lush, green peaks were no longer visible. Although it was dusk, the clouds blocked out any light, making it appear much later than it really was.

The morning breeze had turned to gusts of wind through the course of the day. She hugged herself. "I don't know if that's a good idea."

"It's just a burger."

Disappointment flashed in his eyes. He was right. It was just a burger, Jessica decided. It wasn't like she hadn't ever had a meal with any of the other men. Lifting her arm, she looked at her watch. "I'm not quite finished up. How about I call you when I'm done."

Tom nodded and headed toward his truck. Jessica walked back into the stables, checking all the stalls to make sure the windows were closed and secured. Peeking into the foaling stall, she smiled at the colt. "Look at you, Criss Cross. You're becoming quite a handsome fellow." She reached down and nuzzled his soft head before she turned and went into the tack room. After adjusting the volume to the radio, she left the stables.

Jessica bumped into Mrs. Mayfield in the hall outside her room. The housekeeper's bottom was the only thing sticking out from the hall closet. Jessica tried not to laugh at the sight. The wide rear bounced as Mrs. Mayfield struggled. "Hi," Jessica said.

Mrs. Mayfield's head poked out. "Oh, hi dear." The old woman huffed as she wrestled with the vacuum.

"Would you like some help?" Jessica peeked in the closet and looked at the vacuum. Hoses, cords, and brushes were entangled in huge knots.

Shaking her head, Mrs. Mayfield went back to the undertaking. "No, I've got it under control."

Once in her room, Jessica allowed herself to openly laugh at Mrs. Mayfield's efforts. She changed her clothes, putting on something a little warmer, and ran a brush through her hair. She used a large silver clip her father had given her last Christmas to hold the silken strands from her face.

Mrs. Mayfield was still in the hall when Jessica left her room. "Do you know where Michael is?"

She slammed the door shut with triumph. "In the study."

"The study. Where else could he be?" Knocking softly on the door, she waited for the deep "Yes" that would allow her to enter.

Michael took off his glasses as he looked up. "Hi."

"I closed everything up a little early. I don't think anyone will be coming out. Not in this weather."

He glanced out the window. "Yes, I noticed that it was getting dark out there."

"I'm going to go meet Tom in town for a bite. I just wanted to let you know where I'd be."

Michael's head snapped around as raw possession for the woman leaning in the doorway consumed him. He fought the unfamiliar emotion. "I wouldn't recommend you drive in this. The weather has been unpredictable lately. I'd hate to see you stuck in a storm."

"You think it's going to be that bad?"

"Could be. Wouldn't you rather be safe than sorry?"

"You have a point." She sighed. "I'll go call Tom."

Jessica's back pressed rigidly into the mattress. Her eyes were wide open, ears tuned to every sound. She rolled over for the third time and glanced at the clock. Three twenty-three, only twelve minutes since the last time she looked. It was no use. She would never be able to get back to sleep. She flipped back the covers and got up.

In the kitchen Jessica put the kettle on for a cup of hot chocolate. That would make her feel better. She searched the cabinet for several minutes before finding the little package of instant chocolate. Shaking the contents of the package as she walked back to the counter, she tore the top off and emptied the powder in the cup. Then she paced around the kitchen waiting for the water to boil.

When it was ready, she took the cup to the living room,

switched on the lamp by the recliner, and went to the book-shelf to find something to read. There was everything from *Winter Gardening* to *All You Want to Know About Guns.* She chose an old western. Sitting, she opened the book and tried to focus on what she was reading and not the sounds that were coming from outside.

After reading the first chapter and realizing that she couldn't recall a word of it, she put the book down. She held her cup in both hands and silently wished she were home with her father. Whenever there was a storm at home, her father would fix two cups of coffee with a little Kahlua and they would sit up for hours and talk. They would talk until they were so tired they would drag themselves to bed and fall right to sleep, blocking the storm completely out. "Oh, Daddy I wish you were here." She closed her eyes.

Michael watched Jessica intensely. What was the cause of her insomnia? Did she also have dreams that haunted her at night? Did she lie awake unable to sleep, unable to close her eyes, because she was afraid of what she might see if she did?

"Can't sleep?" Michael voice broke the heavy night air.

Jessica jumped out of the chair. "Michael, good heavens."

He rushed to her side and steadied her. "It's okay."

She pulled away swiftly. "What do you do, go around and scare the hell out of people all the time?"

"I didn't mean to scare you." His voice was much softer now.

"For someone who doesn't mean to scare me, you sure do it often. Will you please stop sneaking up on me?" She turned and tried to identify the abrupt noises coming from outside.

He could see her body shake with fear. He moved closer and watched her pulse pound at the base of her neck. Tracing his thumb over the throbbing vein, his eyes met with hers. He recognized her torment and vulnerability.

154

"I'm sorry." Swinging his arm over her shoulder, he pulled her tightly to him. He laced his fingers through her hair and pressed her head to his chest. She clung to him like he was some kind of lifeline. They stood there for a while, holding each other.

"Where the hell are these storms coming from?" Jessica asked. "I've never seen so many damn storms in my life. And why is it always so windy?"

"My house sits on top of a mountain. It takes the brunt of the wind." He turned her. "Let's sit down." On the sofa he pulled her into his arms.

A huge gust of wind whipped against the house. Michael saw Jessica's eyes dart to the wall of glass. "Can we talk?" she asked.

"Sure, about what?"

"I don't care. Anything. Just as long as we talk." Her eyes darted between Michael and the massive window.

Before Michael had the chance to think of a topic, Jessica spoke. "Do you think that the window could break?"

Michael glided his hand up and down her arm in a soothing manner. "No, it's not going to break."

"What if a tree falls on it?" She curled her feet close against her. Her head rested firmly against Michael's chest. His steady heartbeat was comforting in her ear.

"A tree isn't going to fall on it."

"How can you be so sure?" Jessica said.

"Trust me." He watched as small twigs, branches, and leaves bounced off the glass. The wind was wild, whipping in every direction. Every so often he could hear a huge gust roll through the trees as it built up strength. It would then smash against the house with enormous force. "Why don't you like this kind of weather?"

She turned to him in his arms. "You mean you do?"

"I love it. This is my favorite time of year."

"I like spring. The trees shimmer with new leaves, and wildflowers dot every surface. The earth seems to explode with life and color. The horses get excited too. I love it when you turn them out to pasture and they are full of spirit." A flash of light filled the room. "I could do without all this." Thunder rumbled in the distance.

"How could you not like this?" Michael sounded shocked. "What's wrong with the massive thunderstorms that are the signature of this area? September happens to be their peak."

She smiled. "Great. Why couldn't you have hired me in the dead of winter?"

"Because then you'd be dealing with bone-chilling cold and raw freezing wind."

"You make it sound so appealing."

"It is when you're in a warm, cozy house." He pointed his finger. "Imagine looking out the window and seeing the pasture covered in white. It's so peaceful watching the snow fall gently to the ground."

Jessica snuggled deeper. "It does sound beautiful."

He adjusted his embrace gathering her even closer. "I knew I could persuade you."

"What's spring like here?"

"You know the upper pasture? The one we rode the first day."

"Yeah." She yawned.

"It's covered with purple and yellow wildflowers. The fragrance is the sweetest you've ever smelled. The hills come alive with colors. Town is festive too. Every house and business decorates for Easter."

"It sounds wonderful. Do they have an Easter Egg hunt?"

"Yes, at the park." He watched her eyes grow heavier as her body relaxed and her breath deepened.

"Have you ever gone?" she murmured.

"No."

"Maybe you should." She yawned again. "Can I come back in the spring?"

"You can come back any time you want." Brushing a stray hair off her brow, he watched as her eyes lost focus and faded. With every long, lethargic blink they closed a fraction more. A blast of air pressed against the house and her heavy lids opened slightly. "I'm here, baby."

"I'm sorry," she murmured ever so lightly. Michael had to bend his head down to hear her next words. "My mom died in a storm." That was all she said before she was asleep in his arms.

"Good morning, sleepy head." Jessica's voice was soft as Michael opened his eyes. "How did you sleep?" She had been awake for twenty minutes but refused to move because she didn't want to wake Michael.

Michael rolled his stiff neck. "Fine, considering that I'm sitting up."

"I slept great." She stretched out.

"You're lying down."

"You didn't have to stay with me." She was glad he had. It was wonderful waking up in his arms.

He had tried to leave several times, but she had caught hold of his hand and asked him to stay. "Tell me about the night your mother died."

"I don't recall much." She sat up but didn't move out of his arms. "I remember I was in bed listening to the thunder and counting the flashes of light when I heard a loud knock at the door. I got out of bed and went to my door. From there I had a perfect view of the front door. My dad was leaning against the frame talking to a police officer. I couldn't hear what they were saying over the wind and thunder. All I remember was seeing my dad's face turn white. The officer had to help him sit down on the sofa. That's when I ran out and started crying. I knew something was wrong." She shivered. "After the officer left, Dad and I sat on the sofa holding each other for the longest time. Hearing my dad's cries mix with the loud thunder was heart-wrenching. That's what I hear when I hear thunder. My dad weeping for my mom."

"It must be hard for you."

"I've come to terms with my mom's death. I think what frightens me is remembering the pain I saw in my dad's eyes when he looked at me and told me everything was going to be all right. There was such emptiness and loss in them." Jessica paused. "My dad knew he had to be strong for his four children, and he was."

Michael shifted his weight. "Your father must be a determined man. Some people never recover from a loss like that."

Grudgingly, Jessica stood up. "I think it's sad when people never recover." She smoothed out her shirt and pulled back her hair with a tie that was around her wrist. "When I'm gone, I hope my family and friends don't mourn over me forever. I want them to remember me. I want them to laugh at all the crazy things I did."

"That's a good way to look at it."

"My dad never stopped talking about my mom. He would tell us stories about how they met and how she burned Christmas dinner three years in a row."

Michael laughed. "She didn't."

"She did. When I think of my mom I don't get sad; a smile comes to my face. That's the way it should be."

"I agree."

"Do you want some coffee?"

"Sure. I'll be down to get it after I shower." He got up and stretched his cramped muscles. He hadn't realized how confined he had been. He only noticed the warmth where Jessica's body had rested against his. The light floral scent from her hair filled the air, swirling around him like an intoxicating drug. He could still feel the softness of her skin on his hand that had held her face. The closeness, the contact of her all night was a comfort he thought he had forgotten. It had been a long time since he had the pleasure of having a woman next to him all night.

"Do you need any help?" Jessica teased.

"No, I don't." Michael's voice was taut. Did this woman have no shame?

Jessica walked toward the kitchen and called over her shoulder. "I was only joking. J-O-K-I-N-G, you remember what that is, don't you?"

Chapter Fifteen

Just as Jessica grabbed two coffee mugs out of the cabinet, the phone rang. "I'll get it!" she yelled to no one in particular. She wasn't even sure if Mrs. Mayfield had even arrived yet.

"The Carven residence." She held the cordless phone between her ear and shoulder as she measured out the coffee.

"Hi, Jessica this is Dan. Is Mike there?"

"Yes, but he is busy at the moment. Can I take a message?" She filled the coffeepot with water.

"No, no message. This is very important. Could you get him?"

She heard the urgency in his voice. "I guess I could, but I really don't think he would like to be disturbed right now."

"Trust me, he'll want to take this call."

"Okay, it'll be a minute."

"I'll wait."

Jessica pushed open the bathroom door. Between the steam and the plastic shower curtain, she could scarcely see the huge male body cleaning itself. As she walked closer her vision improved, allowing her to distinguish his large muscular back and his soft white buttocks. He turned sideways to rinse the shampoo out of his hair, enabling her to see his lean torso and large thighs.

Jessica took the towel that was on the sink and stuck it through the curtain when the water shut off. When she felt

160

the towel yanked from her hand, she stepped back to lean in the doorway.

The shower curtain was pulled back abruptly. "What do you think you're doing?"

"You ask that question a lot."

"Answer it."

"I was handing you your towel," she said.

The half-covered body standing before her left her speechless. His unforgettable wide chest was covered with light brown hair that spread down a tight lean stomach and disappeared at the edge of the white towel. It then reappeared on the long legs that stepped out of the tub and stood before her. She retraced her path, this time taking in every minute detail. The bulky swells of his quadriceps were thick with power. They looked as if they were constructed from rock. She skipped the band of white across his waist and rested on his flat stomach. His belly button was sunk in and slightly hidden beneath hair. Her eyes moved to the left and rested on the star-shaped pink scar. The nickel-sized scar looked old but tender.

"Bullet."

"How?" Her brows wrinkled.

He shrugged as if it were no big deal. "I got careless. Do you watch all your bosses take a shower?"

She shook her head. "No, just you."

"Do you like what you see?"

"Does it matter?" She wanted to say, "Would you do anything about it if I did," but thought better of it. She had already seen where that would lead—absolutely nowhere.

"Why did you come?"

She looked him dead in the eyes. "Because of the thought of you up here naked and all alone." The look on his face was what made her stop. Did he really think she

was serious? "Because you have a phone call, that's why."
Turning away she added, "You really need to get a sense of
humor, boss."

Michael watched Jessica fix their coffee as he spoke to
Dan. "Sorry it took me so long. What's up?"

"The waitress at the diner called. She got the license
number of the guy we're looking for. I ran it through the computer and I got an address and a name."

"Good. Do you want to go with me?"

"Sure."

Michael hung up the phone. "I have to go."

"Now? Is everything okay?" Jessica asked.

"Yes." He walked over to the kitchen window and looked
up into the sky. "I don't think there will be a storm today."
He rubbed her shoulders.

She watched him leave. "Michael."

He turned.

"I don't mean anything personal when I tease you." She
wrinkled her nose. "It's just you're so serious all the time. I
don't know . . . If you really don't like it, I could stop."

"I'm getting used to it. See you."

Michael and Dan pulled up to an old double-wide mobile
home. A piece of plywood covered one window and lattice
was placed around the bottom of the trailer for the skirt, but it
never was nailed on. The yard was littered with several old
lawn mowers, a patio set that had seen better days, and a
rusted car on blocks.

Michael looked around. "Nice place. What's this guy's
name?"

Dan looked at the printout. "Abe Sanders."

"Well, let's go see what good 'ol Abe has to say."

Michael hiked through the knee-high grass that led to the decaying deck. Climbing the steps, he tapped loudly on the door. He looked to Dan when he heard movement coming from the back of the trailer.

"What's our little friend up to?" Dan said.

"I don't know, but I'm interested in finding out." Michael unclipped the snap to the gun holster under his coat. He tapped on the door again.

The sound of movement came closer, then they heard a voice, "Wait a goddamn minute."

Michael looked to Dan and said, "I don't think our friend is an early riser."

"It doesn't appear that way, does it?" Dan flashed Michael a big smile. "What's got you in such a good mood? You're acting like your old self." He nodded his head. "I told you, you would come back. I might even resign as chief so we could be partners again. Boy, we sure did have a lot of fun, didn't we?"

The door opened suddenly. They were greeted with a whiff of cigarette smoke and stale beer, and a grumpy voice. "What the hell is it?"

Dan looked at the heavy-set man. He wore a shirt that was two sizes too small. Tiny holes threatened to rip as the white material stretched over his large belly. Black stubble covered his face. "Sorry to bother you this early, Mr. Sanders."

"Who are you?"

"My name is Dan Walker. We would like to ask you some questions."

As if he was slowly waking up, the man looked at Michael. He stared at him for a minute before he took a hasty step into the house and started to slam the door shut.

Michael shoved his foot in the door before Abe had a

chance to close it completely. He leaned his weight against it when he felt Abe start pushing. "What do you think? A little paranoid?"

"That or he's just shy." Dan moved to the door to help Michael keep the vise off his foot.

Michael lifted his head so he was speaking into the small crack that separated him and Abe. "Abe, all we want to do is talk to you." He tried to wedge his foot farther.

"Get the hell off my property, before I call the police."

"We're not leaving until we talk," Michael said. "We are the police."

"We have nothing to talk about. I didn't do anything wrong."

"I didn't say you did," Michael persisted as he pressed harder with his shoulder. His foot was throbbing. He looked to Dan. "Can you push a little harder? I would like to keep my foot."

"Stop your whining." Dan's face was flushed from the strain of pushing. "He has to be over two hundred and fifty pounds."

"Yeah, two hundred and fifty pounds on my goddamn foot." Michael could hear grunting from the man on the other side of the door. "Abe, open the door."

"No way. I didn't mean to cause any trouble. That was the last thing I wanted."

Michael looked to Dan. "Abe, just relax."

"I don't want to fight," Abe pleaded.

"If you stop smashing my goddamn foot, there won't be a fight," Michael snapped.

Michael and Dan stumbled into the room when the door was flung open. Michael looked up to see Abe standing on the other side of the room. "Thank you, that's much better." Michael shook out his leg, rotating his ankle.

Abe backed up a little farther. "All I was doing was having a little fun."

"What the hell are you talking about?" Michael asked. His patience had been exhausted after he lost the feeling in his foot.

"The girl. I was just having fun with her."

"What girl?"

"Your girl. The one at the diner. I didn't know she was yours. If I did, I wouldn't have tried to approach her. I didn't know she was with you until she went to the table. That's why I took off. I didn't want to cause any trouble. I'm not the fighting kind."

Michael looked over his shoulder towards Dan. "Another dead end."

Jessica was stepping out of the tub when she saw it—the biggest rat she had ever seen in her life. It was curled up between the back of the toilet and the wall.

She let out a gasp. Good heavens, it had to be at least five pounds. Okay, maybe not five pounds, but it was huge. How was she going to get past it and out of the door? Had it been there the entire time she was bathing? God, she hoped not. Chills ran down her back, giving her goose bumps at the thought. Reaching for the towel hanging on the shower curtain, she wrapped it around her, feeling a little more protected from the rodent.

Wait. She took the towel off and looked at it. Was this her only weapon? She looked behind her and saw the soap; she clutched it and then put it back down. She wasn't that good of an aim. All she needed to do was piss the thing off. She could throw the towel over the rat and then make a run for it. What other choice did she have?

She looked closer at the filthy rodent. It wasn't moving.

Could it be dead? That would mean she has been sleeping with a dead rat in her bathroom only feet away from her bed. That twisted thought made her toss the towel over the toilet and run out of the bathroom, slamming the door behind her. She fell against the door, heart pounding, gasping for air.

She dressed and went downstairs to get the broom. What she was going to do with it she hadn't figured out. As she marched upstairs, she thought out loud. "Michael, we're having a long talk about exterminators and traps when you get home."

Opening the bathroom door slightly, half expecting the rat to jump out and attack her, she stuck the broom handle through the slit and after several attempts she lifted the towel off the toilet. The rat lay motionless in the same spot. Its size astonished her. What did the thing eat? Cats?

She took a deep breath to build up her confidence and ventured into the bathroom by baby steps. She poked the rat with the end of the broom, then jumped back and ran into her room, stood on the bed, and waited for it. After a few seconds nothing appeared. She slowly stepped off the bed, creeping back to the bathroom.

With the broom in hand, she poked the rat once more. When she poked it again, she realized she had been a fool. She had fallen for it. She picked up the rubber rat and tossed it on the bed.

Michael was sitting at the bar eating when Jessica came in. He looked up. "What's up?"

"Hi, I thought you weren't going to be back until late." She glanced at the clock on the wall.

"I finished up early." He pointed to what she was holding behind her back. "What do you have there?"

Jessica slammed the rubber rat on the counter.

"What the hell is that?" Michael's brows came together at the sight of the rat. He instinctively pulled his plate away.

"A rat."

"Jesus."

"Tell me about it." She slid into the seat next to him. "Imagine sitting in a warm bath, enjoying your day off. Sounds nice, doesn't it?"

Michael nodded, still looking at the rat.

"Now imagine this. You get out of the bath and start drying off; you're thinking everything's grand, you just had a little quiet time to yourself, no interruptions, you're completely relaxed, and then you see it. A big, ugly, fat rat curled up behind the toilet."

Michael tried not to laugh. She was calm and collected now, but what he would give to have seen the look on her face when she had spotted the rat. It was ugly, and its realness was remarkable.

Her smile widened to a full-fledged grin. "Which one of the four respectable boys that I work with could be responsible for this?"

Michael lifted his shoulders. "That's a tough one. All of them are capable of doing it. I warned you. I'm surprised it took this long."

"I have three brothers. This isn't the first joke played on me and it won't be the last. But whoever did this is going to get it good." Her head snapped up. "I have an idea. I want you to find out who did it."

"And how do you suppose I do that?"

"They'll tell you." She leaned forward, looking as devious as ever. "You men share everything."

He smiled.

"Does that smile mean that you are going to help me?"

"Sure, but what's in it for me?" he asked.

167

Nothing came to mind. "It'll be a surprise."

"I don't like surprises, remember?"

"You'll like this one."

Michael held out his hand. "Deal." He slid his plate of munchies toward her. "You want something to eat?"

"Sure." She made a sandwich with two crackers and a piece of cheese. "Mrs. Mayfield's day off?"

"Yep." Michael gestured to the plate. "I had to fend for myself."

"Poor baby."

"I went and visited the guy you saw at the diner."

"What did he have to say?"

"Not much. He was afraid that I was going to kick his ass because he tried to pick you up."

"Was that what he was trying to do?"

"Apparently."

She licked the remains of the barbequed chips off her fingers. "Are you any closer to finding the killer?"

"No. It's so frustrating. Dan and I are doing everything we know to do, and it's still not getting us anywhere." He stood up. "That reminds me, I have to call Dan."

The phone drew Michael out of his deep train of thought.

"Hey boss," Richard yelled.

"What's up?" He held the phone away from his ear.

"We're all at Maggie's having a beer; you up to it?"

"I don't think so."

"Come on, there's going to be women, drinking, and a little bull riding too."

"No, thanks."

"Suit yourself. Is Jess there?"

"Yeah." He had the urge to say no.

"Put her on. You think she knows how to bull ride? I hope

she does. I got fifty bucks on it."

Michael didn't want to hear any more. A surge of jealousy rushed through him as he put the phone down. He found Jessica sitting at the bar doing a crossword puzzle. "Phone's for you."

"Who is it?"

"Richard."

"I wonder what he wants." She took the phone in the kitchen. A few seconds later she heard the extension in the study slam down with a loud thump.

When she got off the phone, she walked down the hall to his study.

"Hi." Jessica stood in the doorway, watching Michael dig through a stack of papers.

"It's okay if you go." He didn't look up from his work. He couldn't keep her locked up in his house indefinitely. And there wasn't any fierce storm that he could use as a reason to keep her here.

"I want you to go too."

"Why?" He had shown no interest in anything she did, but she still wanted to include him in her outing.

"Because you spend too much time in this stuffy room. You need to get out and get some fresh air." She gave him a wicked smile. "Besides, this will give us a chance to figure out who was responsible for the little surprise that was left behind my toilet."

"I have work to do," he said.

"It will be good to forget about it. Just for a few hours." She watched him study the papers on his desk.

"I wish I could forget about it, but it's not that easy."

"What are a few hours?" She gestured to his desk. "It will be here when you get back."

"Sorry, I can't."

She knew him well enough to know that when he didn't want to do something there was no chance at persuading him. "Okay. See you."

Twenty minutes later Jessica pulled off the road into a gravel-filled parking lot. She saw a large neon sign flashing "Maggie's."

A tall, thin man held the door open for her as she went in. "After you."

The bar looked very respectable outside and inside. She thought the boys would prefer something a little trashier. There were a few booths tucked in the corner and about twenty small tables surrounding a hardwood dancing floor. The bar wrapped around two sides of the square room. Neon signs hung throughout the bar advertising various alcoholic beverages. They produced most of the light, along with the light over the dance floor. "Thank you," Jessica said politely as she took another step into the room.

"My pleasure." The man disappeared into the crowd on the dance floor.

Her eyes roamed over the packed bar. She didn't recognize anyone. She walked to the bartender and asked where she might find Richard. He pointed to a dark hall across the dance floor. "In there."

The room was much darker than the one she just came from. In this room the wooden dance floor was replaced with a large mechanical bull surrounded with sawdust and padding. A blond-haired man hung on with one hand, face bright red as the machine twisted and turned in every direction. Men yelled words of encouragement to him while their beers ran down their arms.

It was like she had walked into a completely different bar. The men in here were drunk and loud. There was no dance floor, only a small bar in the corner. Other than the mechanical bull, three pool tables on the left were the only things that filled the room. She decided she liked the other part of the bar better.

"Hey, Jess."

Jessica turned at the call of her name. Squinting through the haze of cigarette smoke she saw Tom making his way to her. "Hi, Tom."

"Come over here with the rest of us." Tom pointed to Richard and John and a few of their buddies as he put his arm around her shoulders and guided her through the thick crowd of people.

"Where's Jake?" she asked as she sat down next to Richard.

"Are you kidding? Jake's old lady doesn't let him within a hundred miles of this place."

Richard filled a mug full of beer and set it in front of Jessica. "Are you ready to have some fun tonight, Jess?"

"I was born ready." Jessica smiled as she took a sip of the cold beer.

John leaned forward so Jessica could hear him. "See that group of guys over there?"

She followed his gaze. "What about 'em?"

"They're from the Rockin' R Ranch. We bet them fifty bucks that you could ride the bull."

Jessica nearly spit out her beer. "Are you crazy?" She looked at the rest of the men. "Is that all my life is worth?"

Richard put his arm around her. "We're talking fifty bucks."

"I don't care if it's five hundred bucks."

"You can do it. All you have to do is trust us," Tom said.

"Trust you?"

"We're not going to let anything happen to you."

Richard looked over to the group of men. "Look at the way they're looking at us. Jess, you got to do this."

Jessica held up her hands, shaking them. "There is no way you are going to talk me into this."

Twenty minutes later, Jessica sipped her beer and listened to John give her a quick crash course on how to ride a bull. "There's more to it than just hanging on for dear life. You have to squeeze with your legs and knees. And whatever you do, don't let your butt come off the bull and don't let your free hand touch it. You got it?"

"I think so."

Richard grabbed Jessica's arm. "It's your turn, Jess. Show 'em what you got."

Jessica got up with them and moved to the bull. Tom slapped her on the back. "Just hang on. That's all you gotta do is hang on for eight short seconds."

Chapter Sixteen

When Jessica got home, the house was quiet. The only light on was the soft glow coming from under the study door. She carefully slid out of her coat. Any sudden movement would result in a burning sensation in her back and shoulders.

She found her way to the stairs without turning on a light. Silently, she climbed the stairs and went to her room. How she managed to get her teeth brushed and change into a nightshirt was beyond her. Her body became stiffer minute by minute. She feared that she was going to have no other choice but to call a chiropractor in the morning, because working was out of the question. She couldn't swing herself into a saddle right now if her life depended on it.

Sleep would make it all better, she told herself. To pull the covers back would take too much effort; flopping on the bed would use fewer muscles. She had already exerted too much energy getting into her nightshirt. She fell face forward across her bed and closed her eyes. Sleep came instantly.

Michael worked for another hour after he heard Jessica come in before he went upstairs. He paused at the door and listened for sound. Not hearing anything, he cracked the door open. He shivered as the light from the hall fell over her sleeping face. She looked childlike, sprawled across the bed. He moved into the room. He stood at the foot of her bed and fixed his eyes on her long slender legs. He fought an impulse to touch her. Instead he found a blanket and covered her. She didn't stir as he tucked the material around her. He checked the alarm clock to make sure it wasn't set. She was going to need all the sleep she could get. He turned off the light in her bathroom and closed her bedroom door behind him.

Michael knew immediately where Jessica was when she didn't show up with the guys to have coffee. He waited for them to clear the kitchen before climbing the stairs to her room. She looked peaceful in the morning light.

During the night she had managed to get under the rest of her covers and roll onto her back. He suddenly felt light-hearted. He moved to her bed and whispered by her ear. "Stanson, you're late for work."

Jessica's eyes flickered open. "What time is it?"

He leaned back slightly, clearing her view of the alarm clock. "It appears you've overslept just a tad."

"Oh, God, is it really that late?" She flung the covers back and regretted it instantly. She moaned as the pain shot through her arms and shoulders. She didn't dare move her legs.

"What's the matter?"

"It's a girl thing," she moaned again as she rolled to her side and concentrated on relaxing. The tight muscles throughout her body were protesting any kind of movement.

"Cramps?"

She didn't doubt he knew the cause of her pain. "Go away." The pillow she pulled over her face muffled her voice. She was too tired and too sore to face the day or Michael. She curled into a ball. The position seemed to be the least painful.

Michael lifted the pillow a little. "They never bothered you before."

"Leave, Michael."

174

He pulled the pillow away from her face. "Are you going to be all right?"

She reached for the other pillow. "Yes, if you go away and let me sleep." Closing her eyes, she relaxed against the softness.

Michael laughed at the agonizing groan. "There's a lot of work that needs to be done today." He knew it was sadistic to tease someone when they were in such pain, but he was having so much fun doing it. Besides, if she had the opportunity to do it to him, she would.

"I'll make up for it." The statement was almost a cry.

"The classes are today."

"Cancel them."

"And disappoint all those kids?"

"Please, go away." She grumbled the low plea as she drifted into a deep sleep. She could faintly hear Michael's voice in the distance, but was too tired to even think about answering him.

Michael stood up and left the room. He came back a few minutes later, calling Jessica's name.

Jessica slowly opened her eyes. As they focused on him, she gasped. "You wouldn't."

He tipped the yellow bucket full of water slightly to allow a trickle to drop onto Jessica's face. "I would."

"This isn't funny, Michael."

"As I recall, you said not too long ago I needed to get a sense of humor. Well, here it is."

"Perfect timing." She laid a lazy hand over her eyes.

"I thought so."

"What do you want?"

"A deal."

"What kind of deal?"

He was going to make her agree to cease all teasing, but he

realized he wasn't sure if he wanted her to stop. He had grown to like her teasing and chatter. He let her off the hook. "The deal is, if I let you sleep, you have to have dinner with me."

"You got it." Jessica rolled over with a loud groan. "Dinner will be ready at six."

"No, you're not making it. We're going to go out."

"That's even better. You're not that good at making deals."

"You haven't heard the rest. It's a benefit for the AHA tomorrow night." He wasn't fond of the big dinner party the America Horse Association put on once a year. But he had to go. It was good for his business, and he was supposed to be one of the bigwigs that were going to make an appearance.

"I'll go." If she didn't feel like she was going to die, she would have been excited about going. She knew the dinner was invitation-only and some of the greatest breeders were going to be present.

"You need to wear a dress."

"Don't push it." Her words were a soft puff as she closed her eyes and went to sleep.

He cracked a smile as he left the room and went across the hall into his bathroom. He returned with a glass of water and some tablets. He set the glass on the nightstand. Touching her shoulder. "Stanson."

She rolled onto her back. "I already agreed I would go with you. I'm begging you, please leave me alone."

"Shh, here take these. They will help the pain." He put the two round tablets in her palm. "You're going to have to sit up to drink this."

Jessica slid up a few inches and reached for the glass. "Maybe I'll choke to death. That'll put me out of my misery."

Michael waited patiently as she tried to force her stiff arm to her mouth. "Here, let me." He set the tablets on her tongue, then held the glass of water to her mouth while she took two large swallows.

"I wish I would just die. Anything would be better than this."

"Roll over." The command was gentle.

Jessica did as she was told, even though her body objected to the movement. Once she was on her stomach she let out a loud sigh. "I had no idea it was going to hurt this badly."

"I know."

"I feel like a gigantic piece of tenderized meat."

"I can't believe you let them talk you into it."

"Not once, but twice. I don't know what I was thinking. I'm going to kill all of them. Actually, this is all my own stupidity."

"You rode it twice?"

"Yes."

"What were you thinking?"

"I obviously wasn't thinking. They went double or nothing. I didn't want to disappoint them."

Michael pulled back the covers just enough to expose her back. He softly scooped up her hair and lifted it out of the way. He rubbed his hands together to warm them before he slid them under her nightshirt. Her flesh was warm and knotted as he began to knead the golden softness. She tensed immediately.

His hands fell against her skin, motionless. "Relax."

"I'm trying. I used muscles that I didn't know I had trying to hang on. At one point I thought my shoulder was going to be pulled out of its socket."

"Close your eyes and try to loosen up. I assure you it will begin to feel better."

She did as she was told. But it didn't block out the fiery pain that consumed her back. She couldn't tell if the burning sensation was coming from her tense muscles or from Michael's touch. She wasn't in any state to try and figure it out. "I'm not cashing in my massage minutes."

Michael laughed. "This isn't a freebie."

"I thought it was worth a try." After several minutes of the constant massaging, she felt her taut muscles ease with relief, allowing her to drift into a sound sleep.

Michael continued to rub Jessica, more for his benefit than hers. He slid his hands down her rib cage to her narrow waist where he kneaded the tender area. She felt small under his large hands. It made him want to protect her even more. Her supple skin melted against his callused palms as he manipulated her muscles.

He rubbed down her entire back, making sure he worked out every last knot before he gently pulled down her shirt and covered her with a blanket.

He found Mrs. Mayfield attacking cobwebs in the den. "Stanson is asleep. She isn't to be disturbed for any reason. I'll be in the stables for the rest of the day if Dan calls."

Michael had wanted to spend some time with the horses, and Jessica taking the day off posed the perfect time. He sucked in a deep breath of hay, grain, and horse as he opened the stable door. He stopped several times when a horse poked its head out to say good morning, affectionately speaking to and rubbing each horse. As he rounded the corner to the office, he looked up to see his crew standing in a small circle, speaking in whispers.

"Hey, boss. What are you doing here?" Tom said, looking a little surprised.

"I live here. Remember?" The men didn't move. "What's up?"

"Nothing. Do you know where Jess is?"

"Wasn't she with you guys last night?" Sure, now they were worried. Oh, how he wanted to yell at them. If he could only scream, "What the hell were you thinking, taking Jessica to Maggie's?" he would feel much better. But then they would ask questions about his anger. Questions that he couldn't answer because he himself didn't know the answers to them.

"Yes," Richard mumbled to John, "I told you to drive her home."

"Don't get mad at me. She said she could drive herself," John said.

"I saw her truck out back," Jake said.

Michael pulled his keys out of his pocket, sorting through them for the office key. "Well, then I assume she made it home." Michael unlocked the door. "Is there a problem?"

Each man looked at each other restlessly. Richard was the first to speak. "No."

John spoke up, "She usually has coffee with us in the morning, and this morning she didn't."

"I'm sure she has her reasons," Michael said.

"If you don't mind, we're just going to wait for her."

"It looks like she's taking the day off. Why don't you just go to work?" They slowly started to scatter in different directions. "By the way, all the stalls need to be cleaned."

"What?" The question was spoken in unison.

Michael looked at each of his men. "I want all the stalls cleaned. Today. Now."

"What happened to the two high school boys you hired?" Richard asked.

"They won't be in this week. I thought I would give them a week's paid vacation." He entered the office and then stepped back out. "Who put the rat in Stanson's bathroom?"

As Jake looked at the ground, the bill of his hat covered his eyes. "Me."

Michael shut the office door behind him.

When Michael opened the back door, he was greeted with a rich, spicy aroma. "Dinner smells good." Jessica was pulling a dish from the oven. She wore one of Mrs. Mayfield's aprons.

"Wait until you taste it. The recipe has been in our family for generations. I hope you like it." She set the dish on the table.

Michael took off his hat and stuck it on the back of his chair. He went to the sink and washed up before going back to the table and sitting.

"I told Mrs. Mayfield to take the day off. I hope that's okay. Since I didn't work today I figured I could make up for it by fixing dinner."

"I didn't expect you to make up for it."

Jessica set a large bowl of salad on the table. "I know."

"How are you feeling?" he asked.

"Sore, but much better. I don't think I would be able to walk if it wasn't for you."

"I was just paying off a debt."

"Thanks anyway. I hope you're hungry."

"Starved." He laid his napkin on his lap as she served him a generous helping. He took a bite.

Before he could even swallow, Jessica blurted out, "Well, how is it?"

He waited until he swallowed and then made a strange, displeasing face. He grabbed quickly for the glass of water in front of him, draining it in seconds. He then reached for Jessica's glass and drained it just as quickly as he had his. Jessica's face went blank.

"Is it that bad?"

Jessica couldn't imagine where she went wrong. She had

made this dish a hundred times. She took a bite of hers. It tasted fine. When she looked up, she saw a faint smile on Michael's face.

She stood up and began hitting him with a dishtowel. "Say you're sorry."

Putting up his hands to defend himself, he yelled, "Okay, okay, I'm sorry. It's good."

She sat back down beside him. "Is this part of your new-found sense of humor?" She commented on his smile. "I like it. It looks good on you."

"It feels good," he said.

"I told you it would."

Michael talked about the class and how much he had noticed the kids' improvement over the few weeks he had been gone. "They like you."

"I enjoy teaching them."

"I didn't realize how much I miss them. It's fun to watch them grow and learn."

She used a piece of bread to soak up some sauce. "I don't usually get to work with kids. This has been a nice treat."

They ate the rest of the meal in silence, enjoying the food and each other's company. Jessica relished the quiet time. It wasn't awkward. It was natural.

"This has to be one of the best dinners I have ever had. You're a great cook." Michael took another bite, chewed, and then swallowed. "Don't tell Mrs. Mayfield I said that."

She crossed her heart as she basked in the compliment. "Promise."

He dished up another helping. "I found out who put the rat in your bathroom."

"Who?"

He couldn't avoid smiling. "You've been waiting for this, haven't you?"

"You bet I have. I can't wait to get him back."

"It was Jake."

"No way. I thought for sure that it was Richard." She lowered her head, cocked it sideways, and looked at him suspiciously. "Are you sure?"

He nodded as he scraped the last bit of food onto a piece of bread. "What are you going to do?"

Jessica took her dishes to the sink and thought for a moment. "I'm not sure. I'll have to think about it. I didn't think it was going to be Jake."

"I was surprised too." He scooted his chair back and picked up his plate and glass. "Go easy on him."

"Not on your life."

Michael chuckled to himself as he prepared the coffee. She was spunky, that was for sure. There was no doubt in his mind she was going to get Jake back, and good.

When the doorbell rang, Jessica looked to him.

"It's Dan." He viewed the table. "Dinner was good."

Jessica was clearing off the table. "I'm glad you enjoyed it."

"Do you need any help with the dishes?"

"I got it. You go ahead."

"You get some rest, you don't want to overdo it." He poured himself some coffee and left to answer the door.

Michael held open his office door for Dan. "You don't look good," he said as he shut the door and sat behind his desk.

"It's nice to see you too." Dan sat in a chair across from Michael.

"What's so pressing that you had to drive all the way out here?"

"You haven't watched TV today, have you?" Dan continued when Michael shook his head. He pulled a newspaper out from under his arm and tossed it on the desk in front of him. "A young girl was raped in Shady Cove."

Michael read the first few sentences of the headlines. "Shit."

"Shit is right." Dan looked at the paper Michael dropped on his desk. "That story is on the cover of virtually every newspaper in the state." He dragged his hand across his face. "You thought the crime scene was a circus, you should see the station. I've never seen so many reporters in my life." Dan stood and continued. "She managed to get away by kneeing the guy in the nuts. Apparently he broke into her house last night."

"Who questioned her?" Michael asked.

"I went to the hospital to question her myself. When I got there she was hysterical, saying that it was our guy."

"It's not him," Michael said immediately. "He wouldn't break into someone's house."

Dan stopped and turned to him. "You know that and I know that, but she doesn't." He waved his hand. "No, let me finish, it gets better. She had already spoken to the press by the time I got there."

Michael hung his head. He knew what was coming. "She didn't tell them it was him, did she?"

Dan's hand went into his pocket where he played with some loose change. "What do you think?"

"What did she say when you showed her the composite?"

"What could she say? She said it wasn't him and left me to straighten everything out with the press."

Michael tapped his fingers against his mouth. "What if the killer responds to the media coverage? What if he wants people to know it wasn't him?"

"We're in trouble." Dan stared out the window into the darkness. "I have a feeling that's what he's going to do."

Chapter Seventeen

After Dan left, Michael gathered every scrap of material collected in the course of the investigation and stacked it on his desk. He spent the next two hours sifting through piles of reports, going over maps, making phone calls, and he still wasn't any closer than when he started. He stared at the mess and rubbed his eyes in frustration. What did he do now?

He would just have to backtrack through the murders and examine each case in detail. He was at a dead end—it was his only chance of finding the killer. Maybe he could uncover some people not previously questioned. He had exhausted every lead imaginable; what he needed was to find a new avenue to investigate. This incompetent feeling was painfully familiar.

He tossed the papers across his desk. It would take weeks to backtrack. And he didn't have weeks. He had already wasted weeks. He had wasted sixteen hours just today. He shoved his chair from his desk. He needed a break to clear his head. And he knew just the thing to do.

Jessica looked up from her book to see Michael standing before her. His complexion was flushed, his image worn. He had an air of weariness about him.

"You want to go for a ride?" His shoulders were hunched forward when he spoke.

Jessica glanced at the clock on the wall. It was a little after nine. After she folded the corner of the page to mark her spot, she placed the book on the table. Then she lifted the green blanket she had tucked around her legs, folded it neatly, and set it aside. When she spoke, she tried to hide her concern. "Sure."

Michael carelessly threw the pads and saddle on his horse. The unkindly way he yanked the cinch demonstrated his annoyance. His thoughts weren't on tacking his horse—they were miles away. He mounted by instinct, his frustration reflected in his posture as he settled into the saddle.

His gaze swept to Jessica. "You ready?"

"Yes."

As they rode out of the barn, Michael kicked his horse into a dead run. It didn't take long for Jessica to catch up with him. The cool night air stung her face as her horse matched his stride for stride. The sky was clear, spilling moonlight across the pastures. The bright light flooded the open field, allowing them to clear it in minutes. Their pace slowed as they entered the edge of the dark woods. Several yards into the dense thicket, Michael stopped his horse. He tied his reins to a branch and motioned for Jessica to do the same.

As they made their way through the low ground cover, Jessica managed to keep up with his punishing pace. They continued to climb; Jessica looked around but was unfamiliar with her surroundings. Where they were or where they were going she wasn't sure. She could barely see Michael in the dark shadows of the trees, but the unhesitating pounding of his steps told her he had a destination.

As they weaved through trees and brush, Michael held an occasional limb, and when the incline became too steep he offered her his hand. "Let me help you." When Jessica reached for his hand, he wove her cold fingers with his, gently squeezing. He pulled her along for several more yards before releasing her hand.

"Look," he said and pointed in front of him.

Jessica climbed a few more feet, slightly out of breath, and stood beside him. She looked across the valley. City lights twinkled from miles around. It was hard to tell where the lights stopped and the stars began. The view was heavenly.

The only sound was the soft hum of wind in her ears and the rustle of the trees behind her. She felt like she was so high she could touch the stars. She looked down at the dancing light of the town and then towns beyond that. They seemed so far away.

Jessica felt Michael move beside her. "It's so serene," she said.

"I like to come here."

"I can see why. It's absolutely beautiful."

She watched Michael move to a boulder and sit. He gazed out at the vista, his jaw set, the corner of his mouth tugged downward. He looked vulnerable.

Michael lifted his eyes to her. They held the stare for several seconds. He unbuttoned his duster without taking his eyes off her and held it open. She moved to him, sliding inside the huge coat. She nestled her back against his chest and stomach and leaned against him as he wrapped his arms around her. His breath brushed against her ear. "I didn't like you going last night."

Jessica didn't move. "Why?"

"I just didn't like it."

"The guys from the Rockin' R were—"

"The Rockin' R?" He didn't know how or when the rivalry started, but the hands at the Rockin' R and his hands were always in some sort of competition. He should have seen this coming. He had no doubt that the rumors soared when they discovered that Jake, John, Tom, and Richard's new boss was a woman.

"Yeah, that's who bet us."

It was a moment before he spoke again. "Promise me you won't do it again."

She turned around in the warm cocoon. Her face was inches from his. "You know what I think, Michael Carven?"

"No, but I'm sure you're going to tell me."

She ran her hand the length of his chin. Her caress was an attempt at eliminating his troubles. "I think you regret not going with me last night."

The cool wind whipped her hair against her face and turned her nose and cheeks a rosy pink. He moved his hand to her cheek. When his thumb touched the silky skin, her big brown eyes locked with his and all the hope and wonder that filled them soaked his heart. "Promise me." He tucked a stray hair behind her ear. "You could get hurt."

"I had fun." She leaned against his hand, her eyes teasing his.

"Promise me."

Her nose brushed his as she lurched forward with excitement. "It was such a rush. Have you ever ridden a mechanical bull?"

"Stanson."

"Have you?" She raised her brows, questioning him.

"Do you ever stop talking?" He lowered his gaze.

She shook her head. "Never."

"I didn't think so," he said.

"Promise." She grinned before turning back around and pulling his arms tight around her. She had gotten him to smile. That was a triumph in itself.

It was moments before Michael spoke. "I come here to think. Up here I have no worries. It's just me. I feel like I'm the only person in the world."

"I see what you mean." It felt like they were in another world. One that didn't have serial killers, painful memories, or heartache. "Have you ever brought anyone here before?"

"No, only you."

Michael resumed resting his chin on her shoulder and closing his eyes. "This is what I needed."

She didn't dare speak. She had prayed for the moment he would let his guard down and open up to her. She wouldn't ruin it with words.

"To hold you and feel you next to me." He paused. "When I'm with you, I feel like everything is going to be all right. You offer me the one thing I truly need: comfort. No pressures, no demands. That's why I brought you here."

She marveled at the view as she listened to his words. "What's wrong, Michael?"

"Stanson, look at me." He waited until she was facing him. "I don't think I'm going to be able to find him."

Worry replaced the joy in her eyes. "What do you mean?"

"I'm not only out of ideas, I'm out of leads to follow. I've got nothing to go on right now."

"So what's this mean? I'm going to have to look over my shoulder for the rest of my life." She withdrew from his coat and took several steps back, studying the ground before looking back to him. "Michael, we both know he saw me."

Michael slid off the rock. "A half a dozen people probably saw him the day he was with Nichole. He's not going to know it was you."

"Damn it, Michael, please be honest with me. Whatever you do, be honest with me."

"Stanson—"

"I was the only one around. He saw me staring at him and Nichole. Or at least in their direction."

Michael was ready to dispute the issue then decided against it. "You're right. He might have seen you."

"If in fact he does know it's me, do you think he'll come after me?"

"I can't answer that question."

"Why?"

"Because I don't—I don't know what the hell he'll do."

"But it's a possibility?"

"Anything is a possibility."

The lull between them felt like it lasted forever. What could one say?

Michael reached out and put his hands on her cheeks. He did worry about her. With the tips of his fingers he pulled her to him. "Don't ever forget what I promised you." His lips brushed her mouth. He had only meant the touch to be soft and quick, but he lingered. Working her lips, he kissed them until they warmed against his. "I'll take care of you." He slid his tongue in and out of her willing mouth, sealing the kiss. He filled the kiss with everything he couldn't tell her. Everything he had wanted to tell and show her over the last few weeks he conveyed in this one moment. He felt Jessica's hand reach for the back of his head, pulling him closer, urging him to continue.

She kissed him back with a yearning that she had never known. She needed him. She wanted him. Her insides smoldered with enchantment as he worked her mouth like a long-lost lover. She had never been kissed with such hunger and longing before.

Michael's hands found their way to her hair. He used every ounce of control he could muster to be gentle. He had waited so long to feel her—to taste her—he feared he might hurt her. A huge weight had been lifted from him. For this brief moment he was free. Free to feel, free to love. Slowly, he brought the kiss to an end. Their foreheads touched as he struggled to put in order the words he wanted to say next. "I don't want you to worry."

The kiss had left her senseless, not to mention speechless. She looked at him with loving eyes and nodded.

"Mike, the Lenwood PD just called. They got a body they want us to come look at. It's a young girl; they think she might be victim number five." Dan's tone was urgent.

Gathering his keys and his coat, Michael said, "If this is the response to the newspaper coverage, he sure does work fast." He stuffed his wallet into his back pocket. "Have they touched anything?"

"No. They said they were going to seal everything off until we get there. The body hasn't been touched."

"You want me to pick you up at the station?"

"I'll be here waiting." Dan paused. "Park around back, I'll meet you out there. You'll never make it through the front entrance."

Michael plucked a sheet of paper from his desk. In the kitchen he left a note for Jessica, explaining where he went. And if she needed to contact him she could call the station and they would know where to find him.

Jessica read the note twice before she turned to the window. The dreaded black clouds were rolling in closer. She hoped it wasn't a thunderstorm. She felt like a tiny speck trapped under something big and powerful.

She carried her soda and a bag of chips into the living room, set the chips on the coffee table, and turned on the television. As she cracked open the Dr Pepper and took a long gulp, she listened to the weather report.

The weatherman stood in front of a large map. "There are

going to be severe thunderstorms. Heavy downpours are likely, so a small stream flood advisory is in effect until tomorrow morning."

"Great." Jessica leaned back and closed her eyes. She listened closely to the wind whipping around outside. It whistled as it blew through the trees, and she could hear an occasional branch snap in the distance. The eerie sound gave her goose bumps. A storm was brewing and there was no telling how big it would get.

A flash of light lit up the room, followed by an ear-splitting boom. Jessica's head shot up. Light flashed again and she tried to remember how to count to see how far away lightning struck. Was she supposed to add five or divide by five? Another rumble shook the house. She didn't have to do any figuring to know that it was close, too close.

Trying to get absorbed in something, she sat on the edge of the sofa and turned the volume up on the television. She rubbed Quest's head as she flicked through the channels. He'd barely moved in the last hour. Why couldn't she be that calm?

She wrapped a blanket around her for security and tried to watch an old black-and-white movie but found herself listening to the unfamiliar noises that were coming from outside. The longer she listened, the more distorted they became. What were they and where were they were coming from?

The wall of glass allowed a perfect view of the storm. She muted the television and watched in amazement as the rain gushed from the sky. She had never seen anything like it. The wind sent the torrent smashing against the window, and the tall pines she dearly loved thrashed around, taking a beating from the fierce weather. While she was thankful for the thin barrier, she would have been even more thankful if the glass was wood or some type of material she couldn't see through. Witnessing the savage storm was frightening.

When the screen door slammed, she clutched the pillow in her lap. Her blood pulsed through her veins with such force she could feel it thump at the base of her neck. She swallowed the knot that had formed in her throat and immediately went in search of candles and a flashlight. It wouldn't be long before a tree took out a power line.

In the kitchen pantry she found several candles. As she set them down on the counter, she heard a noise outside. She stiffened and looked out the window. All she saw was her reflection. The room filled with light again and this time the thunder was so strong she could feel it reverberate through her chest, beating like a drum. She took one candle with her and she went to her bedroom.

Michael sat in the Lenwood police station at a banged-up metal desk. His wet hair lay slick against his head. His clothes clung to his body. The umbrella that had been given to him at the crime scene was useless. The wind had thrown rain in every direction. The search for evidence had been unproductive; the weather conditions put a damper on the investigation, so they had called it quits and came back to the station.

"Where's Dan?" Scott asked.

"He went home from the crime scene. He wanted to beat the storm," Michael said.

Scott nodded. "Do you think this guy is him?"

"I don't think it's him for the simple fact that she had her underwear on. That's his trademark. He's not going to stop doing it. When we find a body, he wants us to know that it's him."

Scott rubbed his chin. "Her age and race is the same as the others. And she was found in a field."

"True, but her body was found closer to town. The rest were found at least five miles from town."

"Do you think we have a copycat on our hands?"

"I hope not."

"I'll be back in a minute." Scott rose and walked across the room.

Michael picked up the white towel that an officer had given him and dried his hair. He wadded it up and tossed it on the desk next to the phone. He stared at the phone. The sound of thunder filtered in through the station. Should he call her?

He tried to tell himself he didn't need to talk to her, that he didn't need to hear her voice, but he had no control over what he felt. He would just call and make sure she was all right, and that would satisfy him.

He dialed his number. A recording came on the line saying that the lines were down. He slammed the phone down and grabbed his coat. "I'm going to the ranch," he told Scott.

"Are you crazy? Mike, you can't drive in this kind of weather." Scott tried to reason with him. "Just ride it out. It'll ease up in a few hours."

Michael started walking to the door. "Tell Dan I'll give him a call tomorrow morning. We probably won't be able to search the scene until it dries out a little." He lifted his shoulders. "But then there won't be much left when it does."

"The weather—" The glint in Michael's eyes stopped Scott. He had seen it before many years ago. There would be no changing his mind. "Drive carefully."

As Michael climbed into the truck, the thought hit him: What if she had tried to call and couldn't get through? What if she needed him?

Jessica turned over onto her back. She wished that the

storm would pass. Or better yet, that Michael would come home. She felt secure in his presence. But neither was going to happen. The storm was growing stronger by the hour and Michael was God only knows where.

She got up and walked into the bathroom to get a drink of water. When she tried the light switch, nothing happened. The flashes of light lit a trail to the sink. She took several big gulps of air as she felt her way back to the bed. She straightened the rumpled covers and lay down.

Michael drove as fast as the weather would allow. He had driven in storms like this before and knew the danger. Debris of all kinds slammed against the truck as he turned down the dirt road leading to the ranch. Huge bolts of lightning spanned the sky, reaching like fingers into the night. He could hear the rumble of the thunder over the roar of the truck's motor. The storm had taken on a life of its own as it roiled above him. A loud crack clashed above him, and he pressed down on the accelerator.

Jessica searched the darkness anxiously, her senses acute. That was not the wind. She pulled the covers closer to her body and waited. There it was again. She reached for the phone. Who was she going to call? The police? What was she going to tell them? She was hearing strange sounds outside in the middle of a violent storm? That would sound insane. She could call the station. Michael had left a note saying he would be there. She pushed the covers back and crawled out of bed. She couldn't call him. He would think she was being foolish.

She lit the candle she had placed on her nightstand earlier and carried it with her as she went into the living room. Her hands shook so badly she had to set the candle down. Calm down, she told herself. She sat on the couch for a long moment trying to focus on pleasant thoughts.

She remembered the poker game she and Michael had shared, the look on Richard's face when she had actually finished the ride, and the rat that had been so cleverly placed in her bathroom. Then a movement caught her eye and she spun around. She looked about the room for something, anything, to confirm she wasn't seeing things. Restless, she stood up. She didn't feel alone, but she didn't see anything either.

Michael struggled to get the key in the door. The harsh wind lashed around in every direction, and rain pounded against his back. When the droplets hit, they felt like sharp pebbles, stinging the side of his face. He tried the light switch as he fell through the door. The power was out. He went to the closet and took out a flashlight.

He called Jessica's name, but it was next to impossible to hear over the wind and rain. Worry set in after he checked the den and living room and didn't find her. He took the stairs two at a time. As he entered Jessica's room, a flash of light lit it up. Michael looked at the empty, unmade bed with apprehension. Without hesitation he sprinted to his room. "Stanson."

Where was she? He ran into his bathroom; it was empty. As he ran back into his room, he caught his knee on the corner of his bed. "Damn." Grabbing his knee, he hopped out the door into the hall. "Stanson."

He ran downstairs again, this time searching the kitchen and the dining room. He sprinted into his office. "Shit. Where are you?"

He rushed back upstairs to search the guest rooms. "Stanson." He flung each door open. "Stanson." As he passed Jessica's room, he thought he heard a low cry. He dashed to the bathroom door. Pushing it open, he shone the light in the room. It was then he saw Jessica huddled in the corner with a blanket around her, shaking like a leaf.

"What in the hell?" He dropped the light and fell to his knees beside her. "It's okay, baby."

Taking her in his arms, he cursed. She clung to him. How long had she been on the bathroom floor like this?

"M-Michael there is someone out there." Her voice was low and shaken.

His arms tightened. "Baby, it was only me."

"There is someone out there. I heard noises." Her voice cracked as tears ran down her cheeks.

"The noises you heard were coming from me. I was looking for you. Didn't you hear me calling you?"

She shook her head.

Michael mumbled inaudible words of relief to himself and words of comfort to Jessica as he picked her up. She was limp in his arms as he carried her to his room. He set her in the middle of his bed and covered her with the thick blue comforter. "Please don't leave me," she said.

He placed a kiss on her brow. "I'm right here."

He hated seeing her frightened. If he had only stayed home, this would have never happened. He slid into the bed beside her, and she instantly rolled over and grabbed him, burying her face into his chest. She had no control over the tears that streaked down her cheeks.

"Shh, it's okay. I'm here." The sound of her crying made him close his eyes and grit his teeth. "Please don't cry, baby."

It was her turn to need him. And just as she had been there for him, he was going to be there for her. He would let her take whatever she needed from him. Emotionally, he would give her everything he had. But her crying was tearing him up inside.

A flash of light filled the room for a second, and then it

shook with the thunder. This was the worst storm he had ever seen. Her arm around his waist tightened.

He rested against the headboard. The mixture of the storm and Jessica's sobs bore into his chest, striking his heart with a sharp pain.

Chapter Eighteen

Michael sat looking at Jessica in the morning light. The blue comforter was tucked tightly around her shoulders and her hair was spread over the pillow with a few strands across her face. She looked peaceful. At last. She had tossed and turned all night, but once he had laid his hand on her shoulder and softly spoken her name, she settled down.

She brushed the hair from her face and rolled to her side, murmuring a few words before stretching.

"You awake?" he asked.

Her stretch stopped. She opened her eyes and looked around the room, then sat up in bed taking the covers with her. "Michael?"

"Good morning."

He looked at ease sitting in the rocking chair. He wore his customary old boots, faded jeans, and a huge gray sweater. His hair had been neatly combed, but he hadn't shaved. Steam poured from the mug of coffee he held in his hand. How long had he been sitting there watching her sleep?

"You had a long night," he said.

She rubbed the sleep from her eyes. "I don't know what came over me. I acted like a child."

Michael pointed to the nightstand beside her where a cup of coffee was sitting.

She reached for the cup. "Thank you."

"How do you feel?"

"Tired."

"You want to tell me what happened?"

"Not really." She took a deep breath. "It was just the storm." She looked out the window. The storm had passed sometime during the night. The dawn was still littered with clouds but the wind had died down and the rain had ceased.

Michael stretched his legs out. "There's more to it than that."

"You'll think I'm foolish." She closed her eyes, trying to stave off the memories of the previous night.

"Try me."

She was a strong person. Why did he have to always see her at her weakest? "I kept hearing noises." She rubbed her head. "I think I'm losing my mind. This whole serial killer thing is freaking me out."

"Are you sure the noises weren't me?"

"Yes. I heard the noises before you came home."

"What kind of noises?" The rocking chair rolled forward as he sat up.

"I don't know. Noises." How did she explain what she had heard? They sounded like noise in a storm.

Michael sensed her frustration and moved on to the next question. "What happened after you heard the noises?"

She rolled her eyes. Why was he doing this? He was making her look crazy. "I ran through the house and locked all the windows and went and hid in the bathroom." She felt foolish. "Go ahead and tell me you think I'm crazy."

"I don't think you're crazy."

"You will after I tell you the rest."

"There's more?" He sounded surprised.

"I thought I saw someone from my bathroom window."

"An actual person?"

"I don't know. It could have been shadows." Her head dropped into her hands. "It was so stormy, I'm not sure what I saw."

"It's okay. You're okay now and that's all that matters." Michael moved to the door. "I'll let you get dressed."

"Thank you for what you did last night."

"Don't mention it."

Jessica flopped back on the bed when the door closed. "That was a good one, Jessica. Could you have acted any more ridiculous if you tried?" She pulled a pillow over her face. "You're going to have to get some help."

Michael was waiting in the kitchen for Jessica. "More coffee?" he asked.

"No. I don't think my stomach can take it."

She looked better, he noted. The only remaining sign that she'd been up half the night were the dark circles under her eyes. "Breakfast? Mrs. Mayfield made some muffins."

Jessica shook her head. "Please, don't think I do this all the time." She rubbed her hands together. "This is so embarrassing."

"Don't be embarrassed."

"That's easy for you to say. I really thought I saw someone."

"I know."

She closed her eyes for a brief minute. "Can we just forget about it? Let's never mention it again."

He couldn't forget about it, but he could lay off the subject for the time being. "The dinner is tonight. Do you feel up to it?"

She appreciated his compassion. "Of course. What time?"

"Eight. If you don't want to go, we don't have to."

"I want to go. I'll be ready." She looked out the window. "The guys just drove up. I'll see you tonight."

Michael was biting into a muffin when he heard the phone in the study ringing. He jogged into the room and plucked the receiver on the fourth ring. "Yes."

"She wasn't alone last night."

Michael's breath stuck in his throat as the low, distorted voice filtered through the phone.

Had he heard this person right?

"I watched her all night."

Michael held the receiver in one hand and the base in the other. Although it felt as if someone had cut off his oxygen supply, he managed to speak. "Who the hell is this?"

"That doesn't matter, Michael. What matters is that I can get to Jessica any time I want."

Michael listened carefully to the steady and terrifyingly calm voice. "I don't believe you." He made sure that his voice held just as much conviction as the caller's.

"Does the fact that I watched her run through the house and lock all the doors convince you?" There was a brief pause. "Perhaps this will satisfy your doubt. She wore a beautiful green nightgown. What is it made of? Silk?"

"That's enough." Michael's knuckles turned white as he gripped the phone tighter.

"She was terrified, Michael. She was terrified of me. You were quite the hero when you came home. Although you did ruin my show." The silence was momentary. "However, it looked like a new and better one had started. Tell me, Michael, what was it like to sleep with her? Did you like it?"

Michael considered the voice that taunted him cruelly. "If you lay one single finger on her—"

201

"Don't make promises you can't keep."

The oath registered in his words. "You can damn well be sure I'll keep it."

"You're forgetting, Michael, which is something you don't do often, I can get to her any time."

The caller's tone held no mercy. "What are you talking about?"

"I saw her at the auction, in the restaurant, at Maggie's. She's a beautiful woman. I would hate to see anything happen to her."

"Is this some kind of sick joke?"

"No, this is no joke."

"How do I know you're him?" A low laugh seeped through the phone. "Damn it. You know what I want to hear, now tell me."

"I'm the one who makes the demands; however, I'll humor you. White lace seems to be Jessica's preference. I'm assuming a size small."

Every muscle in Michael's body seemed to constrict at the same time. "What do you want?"

"You know what I want. Stop the investigation. You do things my way and she won't get hurt. It's as simple as that."

"You won't get away with this."

"I am getting away with it. You leave me alone and I'll leave you alone."

"There's a small problem with that. You're killing people and I'm not."

The icy voice was nonchalant. "It's a simple exchange, Michael. Take it or leave it."

"What—" He heard a click. "Hello? Hello?" Michael slammed the phone down. What in the hell had just happened? The call and the blood pounding in his head played havoc on this thinking process, impairing any ability to reason. "Get it together, Mike."

His eyes shot around the room as he tried to get a grip on the situation. "No." He jumped from the desk in pure panic and ran from the study, in search of Jessica. Chucking open the back door on his way to the stables, he ran into Mrs. Mayfield. He took her by the shoulders to steady the teetering woman, then quickly demanded, "Where is Stanson?"

"Where are you going in such a hurry?"

"Just tell me where she is!"

Mrs. Mayfield pointed behind her. "In the stables, I guess. That's where she's at every morning at this time."

His boots dug into the gravel, grinding and crunching under his feet as he sprinted toward the large building. He slowed his grueling pace as he entered the stables, stopping in front of the tack room not only to take a quick breather but also to calm himself. There were many clients roaming the grounds, and he didn't need to startle any of them.

Regaining his breath and his composure, he found his way to the office. He tried the knob but it was locked. He stifled a curse. He headed straight to the largest arena. Peering through the rails, he didn't see Jessica. A rider who was exercising his horse trotted by Michael.

"Hey Mike. How you been? Haven't seen you around much?"

"Have you seen Stanson?"

The rider looked over his shoulder. "Nope, haven't seen her this morning yet." He loped to the far end of the arena.

Michael pushed off the railing. His nerves quivered and the hair on the back of his neck prickled. He fought the urge to dart through the wings of the stable yelling Jessica's name. She had to be around. He walked aimlessly for a few seconds before it came to him. He knew where she was. When he rounded the corner to the long hall of stalls, he expected to see Jessica staring dreamy-eyed at the foal. When he didn't see her, his pace quickened. He slowed and looked into the stall to see Criss Cross nestled against his mother, but there was no Jessica.

"Damn it, where are you?" He continued down the hall. Cool air greeted him as he pushed open the heavy door. He scanned the area. He saw Jake lifting bales of hay onto a trailer. "Jake, have you seen Stanson?"

"The last I saw her she was saddling Lacy up."

"Did you see where she went?"

Jake shook his head.

I can get to her any time. The words rang in his ears. Calm, Michael. You have to stay calm, he reminded himself. He would find her. Then he turned and caught a glimpse of something out of the corner of his eye. His chest collapsed with relief when he spotted Jessica out in the pasture riding Lacy.

She was all right. His world began to right itself as he watched her gallop in large circles around the green field. As he continued to watch her work the horse, the lingering effects of the brief nightmare diminished completely.

The wind pulled her hair behind her like a chestnut flag. Her body joined with the smooth motion of the lope. Watching her ride was magical. She was mesmerizing.

His back went stiff in realization. What had he been thinking? If the killer were here last night, there would be prints of some kind. He walked down the gravel road several yards. There would be no way to distinguish all the different tire tracks. There were at least a half dozen vehicles in the parking lot, and that didn't include the hands.

He knew his best chance of finding any prints would be around the house, where there was less traffic. He circled the outer boundary of the house, in and out of the bushes, looking carefully for some type of print. He retraced his steps, making sure he didn't miss anything. Could the killer be lying? Finding nothing, he walked back to the house. As he climbed the steps to the front door, he saw them. There were footprints in the mud under the overhang. He followed them for a few steps out into the yard, but they disappeared; the rain had washed them away. He walked around the house, looking under the roof overhang where he knew the area would have been sheltered from the weather. The prints reappeared under Jessica's bathroom window. Looking up at the second-story window, his stomach rolled at the thought of someone staring at her.

He walked back to the porch. "Shit!" He kicked a ceramic planter.

Mrs. Mayfield ran out on the front porch. "What's wrong?"

"Nothing."

She remained on the porch, looking down at the huge flowerpot that looked like it had just exploded.

"Go back in the house." Michael's arm shot out as he pointed to the door.

"He was here, wasn't he?" Her hands came to her mouth. "He was here."

"Damn it. Go back in the house."

"I care about her too. Now tell me."

"Yes, he was here," he said.

She went down the steps and stood by him. They both looked at the prints. "He wants her, doesn't he?"

"Well, he isn't going to get her. He isn't going to hurt her." He sounded as if he were trying to convince himself more than Mrs. Mayfield. "This is between us."

"You have to tell her, Michael, she has the right to know."

He shook his head. "You're going to have to trust me on this."

★ ★ ★ ★ ★

The first thing he did when he got back to the house was call Dan.

Michael tapped his fingers as the phone rang. "Damn it, Dan, pick up." His fingers drummed faster after each unanswered ring. Come on. Come on. "Dan?"

"What's up Mike?"

"He called."

"Who?"

"The killer."

"What? Are you sure?"

"It was him. He was calm, cool, and in complete control. It was him, there was no doubt about it." Michael viewed the folders and maps on his desk and turned away in disgust.

"What did he want?"

"He wants me to stop the investigation."

"And if you don't?"

"Then he'll hurt Stanson." He bit back a curse. "This guy is a crazy mother. He'll follow through. He was here last night."

"Shit, this guy's got some set of balls."

Michael was thinking out loud. "I knew there was a reason for Stanson getting so upset. I just didn't think it would be this. She must have been scared out of her mind."

"Does Jessica know he was there?" Dan asked.

Michael halted and stood firmly in the middle of the room. "Hell no, she doesn't know. I don't plan on telling her either."

"Then what are you going to do?"

"I'm going to take her home first thing tomorrow morning."

"You can't."

Michael gripped the phone tightly. "You wanna bet?"

"Listen to me, Mike." Dan's voice was calm, reasoning. "If this is who we think it is, once Jessica is gone we could risk losing him too. We can't risk that. We need to find him before he kills again. Mike, we're close. That's the only reason he called. He knows that we're going to get him."

"This is a dangerous game, and I don't want her involved. I don't give a shit what the risks are. Do you understand me? You agreed to do things my way; I want her out of here."

"He found you, Mike, and he'll find her if you take her home. Who will protect her then? This guy is for real. He's not playing around."

Michael had to sit. "Don't you think I know that?"

"Then keep her with you where you can keep an eye on her. We'll put a guy on her when you're not there." Dan paused. "Don't change your schedule or he'll know something's up."

Michael hit his desk. "Shit." He knew Dan was right. He didn't have a choice. He had to act like everything was normal. He couldn't let Jessica know what had happened. He covered his eyes with his hand and sighed. "How could I have let this happen? I'm not some young rookie who runs home each night and studies my goddamn note book."

"You're human, Mike," Dan said. "It's not your fault."

"Yes it is. I should have found him by now."

"Don't beat yourself up over this. You have come further than anyone else. You got him scared."

"He didn't sound scared."

"He is or he wouldn't have called. He's going to screw up, and when he does, we'll be there to nail him."

"I hope you're right. Send someone out to make a mold of the footprints. And while you're at it, send a fingerprint technician. I'd like to see if we could find any fingerprints too." He paused and thought for a moment. "Tap my phone while you're at it. And do it quietly. I don't want anyone here to know what's going on."

"You have that dinner tonight, right?" Dan asked.

God, he had completely forgot about that. "Yes."

"Do you want me to send someone with you?"

"No."

The line went quiet and Dan knew that his friend was in deep thought. When Michael broke the dead air, his voice was low. "He just made this personal, Dan."

"I know, buddy. I know. Whatever you want, you got it. Just let me know. Oh, yeah, the girl in Lenwood is still a Jane Doe."

"No one has come forward to identify her?"

"Nope."

"Damn." After Michael hung up he sat, staring into space. Everything started to sink in. He didn't know what he would do if someone hurt Jessica. He tried to imagine how terrified she must have been last night. He pictured her on the bathroom floor trying to convince herself there wasn't anyone outside. The next thing that flashed in his mind was a faceless stranger creeping around the house watching her. The killer's words rang in his ears: *I can get her any time.*

Michael ran his hand through his hair. This couldn't be happening. In one swift movement, the contents of his desk went smashing against the wall.

Chapter Nineteen

Michael slid the gun holster over his crisp white shirt before he put on the black dinner jacket. After adjusting his attire to accommodate the added bulge, he went to the window and gazed into the darkness. Someone had been creeping around his house watching Jessica, intruding on his life, his home. He had been threatened and it infuriated him. He was in a vulnerable position—that in itself would be the driving force that propelled him through this. Faltering wasn't an option. The stakes were too high—Jessica's life.

After talking with Dan, Michael had shifted gears. He wasn't a worried mess anymore, he was madder than hell. He didn't know who was more nuts—the killer or him. He had lapsed temporarily after the call, which was what the killer wanted. The killer wanted him unstable, and he had nearly accomplished that. Well, Michael had his bearings now, and nothing would hinder his promise that he'd made to Jessica. No harm would come to her.

He gathered his thoughts, making sure he hadn't forgotten anything. He turned away from the window and glanced at the clock on the nightstand. If they didn't leave soon, they would be late.

Michael stood at Jessica's door. He rolled his neck and knocked. "Stanson?"

Jessica looked at herself in the mirror attached to the closed door. She could hardly speak. "Yes."

"We've got to go. The dinner starts at eight."

"Um-um—" She ran her hands down the length of the dress as she turned sideways to view a different angle.

"Is there a problem?"

"Yes, actually there is. I think there's been a mistake." She did a complete circle, never taking her eyes off the image in the mirror.

"A mistake? What kind of mistake?"

"In the size of the dress."

He had spent thirty minutes picking out that dress; he knew it wasn't the wrong size. "Let me see." When he opened the door, Jessica was standing in the middle of the room. Stunning. The dress fit her just like he knew it would. The black, slippery material hugged her curves perfectly. It narrowed at her waist and flared just a bit at her hips, then clung around her mid-thigh.

"It's perfect."

"Perfect?" Jessica ran her hands along the soft material, which she feared there wasn't enough of. "It doesn't fit."

"Sure it does." He went to her side. "Turn around and let me help you zip it up." The dress was a few inches shorter than he had thought, but the look only enhanced her long, slender legs. He commended himself on the selection.

She turned around, pulling her hair to the side. "I couldn't reach."

He rested one hand on her waist and took the zipper in the other. A small sliver of black lace visible at her waist marred the gentle curve of her bare back and a matching piece of lace stretched across the middle of her back. This small act most men took for granted he found alluring. The smoothness of her exposed back, the small glimpse of her undergarments, the proximity of his body to hers, formed a sensuous magnetism of desire that started in his loins and spread through him. His hand gripped Jessica's waist. He felt her suck in slightly. As he zipped the dress, the material conformed to her body perfectly. "There."

Jessica let her hair fall. "Thank you."

"Now that you're ready, I'll meet you downstairs." He left without looking back.

Jessica forced herself to take another look in the mirror. She had to admit the dress was beautiful. But it looked strange on her. She just wasn't used to the way it molded to her body.

She walked the length of the room twice to get the feel of the high heels Michael had given her with the dress. She nearly twisted her ankle coming down the stairs. She was going to kill herself if she wasn't careful. It's like walking on your tiptoes, she told herself.

"You can't be serious," Jessica said at the foot of the stairs.

He pulled his coat on. "About what?"

"This dress."

Michael held out her coat. "I don't see anything wrong with the dress."

"You're not joking?" She watched him in amazement as he shook his head. "You really want me to go out wearing this."

"That's what I intended you to do with the dress. Is there a problem with that?"

"Yes. Everyone will think I'm a prostitute."

He started to laugh. "When was the last time you went out?" He had picked the dress because it was a little revealing but very tasteful. There was no way he would have gotten a dress that made her look cheap. Her innocence couldn't be denied anyway. The sway of her hips when she walked was natural, not practiced to perfection. No one could mistake her for anything other than a lady.

"I don't think this is funny, Michael." She had never been to a formal dinner before, and she was a little nervous. "What if people stare?"

He held the coat up again. "If they stare, it's not because they think you're a prostitute. Trust me. Let's get your coat on. We're going to be late if you don't hurry it up." He led her to the garage where a gray Porsche was parked.

"Nice car."

"You sound surprised."

Jessica ran her hand along the shiny hood. "I am. I just don't picture you being extravagant. I thought you were more of a pickup man."

He held the door open. She knew him better than he thought. Cathy was the one who wanted the car. She loved racing around town in it. After she had been killed, he had parked it and hadn't looked at it since.

He watched Jessica slide into the leather seat. He knew that she would look striking in the sports car; that's why he had asked Mrs. Mayfield to clean it the day before.

"My brothers would love this." After they pulled out of the garage, she asked, "What is this dinner for?"

"It's a fund raiser."

"What are they raising funds for?" She adjusted the vents.

"The AHA is putting on the dinner to raise money for ranches that specialize in training horses for the physically challenged." Michael navigated the dirt road with precision. He knew every rut and made sure he missed it.

"Great cause."

He nodded in agreement. "Their motto is: anyone who wants to ride can. The horses are very versatile. From the beginning of training they are exposed to constant stimuli: wheelchairs, crutches, dogs, anything that they might encounter with someone who is handicapped. At the end of the horse's training, he knows three languages: feel, sound, and sight."

"I never realized that there were so many ranches who specialize in this."

"There aren't. It's expensive. The tack alone is very expensive. Custom saddles and balance belts are costly." He turned onto the main road and let the engine of the sports car gather speed. "The horses also need a lot of extra training." He shifted. "They will explain everything in detail at the dinner."

"I can't wait to hear more."

Forty-five minutes later Michael eased into the parking lot. He purposely avoided the valet parking. He wanted to know where his vehicle was if he needed it. Instead of going right to Jessica's door when he got out of the car, he surveyed the huge lot first. scanning it slowly, noticing everything and everyone. The killer said he had seen her at the auction, the restaurant, and the bar. There was no reason why he wouldn't follow them here.

Michael reached for Jessica's door. As he opened it, he held his hand out. When he felt her soft fingers in his, he lifted her out of the low car. Her long legs seemed to unfold as she stood.

"Thank you."

Michael smiled as he pressed the keyless remote. He offered her his arm.

Jessica looped her arm through his. "I could get used to this."

"Watch your step, it's wet." Michael pulled her close while steering them clear of puddles.

Several people at the front door greeted Michael and Jessica. Some smiled politely, acknowledging Michael's presence, then walked off to visit with other people. Others shook his hand and left, but one man stuck out. He was a tall, heavy-set man, who pushed past the others, his hand extended in a greeting.

"Carven, it's nice to see you again."

Michael stuck out his hand. "Nice to see you."

The man's attention jumped from Michael to Jessica when he spotted her. "Well, what do we have here? Are you going to introduce me to this beautiful creature, or am I going to have to do it myself?"

No, he didn't want the slime to even know Jessica's name. Reluctantly he introduced them. "Jack, this is Jessica Stanson, Jessica, this is Jack Stone."

"It's a pleasure," Jack said, as he looked her over.

Michael cursed himself up one side and down the other for picking out the damn dress.

"It's nice to meet you, Mr. Stone." Jessica winced as the clammy hand held hers for longer than necessary.

"I insist you call me Jack. Where did you find such a gem?" His question was directed to Michael, but he never took his eyes off Jessica.

Michael wasn't up to humoring Jack. "She's my trainer." His hands were in his pockets playing with some loose change. He hated coming to these dinners.

"You train horses?" Jack asked.

"Believe it or not," Jessica said. Did he just wink at her? She eyed the man carefully. She didn't like him.

Jack didn't hide his surprise. "So, you know horses."

I know a horse's ass, she thought as she viewed his out-dated suit. She made a sour face; he reeked of cheap cologne. As he raised his hand to stroke his mustache, the light caught two huge diamonds on his ring and pinky fingers.

Michael abruptly took Jessica's arm. "Excuse us."

214

"Jack seems like a nice man," Jessica said sarcastically as he ushered her into the lobby.

"Yeah, great guy."

She made small talk as the mingling people and the huge, elegant room swallowed them. She had never seen anything like it. Brilliant chandeliers that must have each weighed a ton hung overhead. The light reflected off thousands of tiny crystals. The carpet was plush red with a gold accent.

Jessica looked to Michael after the last introductions were made and the couple had left. "You obviously spend a lot of time with these people."

He looked around the room, indifferent. "No, I just do business with them." He spotted an attendant and told him his name.

"Yes, this way, Mr. Carven." The boy led them through a series of halls into another room, where he weaved them through a maze of tables. He stopped at a table located in the front near a stage. Three other couples were already seated. The boy pulled out a chair for Jessica. "Dinner will be served shortly."

Michael again made note of his surroundings, carefully looking for all the exits. Just in case, he told himself. He touched the gun under his coat, just in case.

Introductions were made and polite conversation flowed as appetizers were served. The conversation leaned toward the theme of the evening during the main course and dessert. Jessica was intrigued.

Everyone's attention was brought to the podium as a spokesman from the AHA elaborated on the topic. The speech was both interesting and educational. A roar of applause broke out as the spokesman ended his speech and introduced one of the biggest contributors. Jessica was surprised when Michael slid his chair out and moved to the podium. She hadn't realized that his name had been called.

Michael's lecture was brief but efficient. His demeanor was confident as he thanked everyone for attending. He left the audience with a brilliant smile and final words of enjoyment.

The lights were dimmed and coffee was served. One by one the other couples at the table excused themselves to the dance floor.

"Wow, if I knew you were so important I wouldn't have yelled at you the first day I met you," Jessica said.

"Somehow I doubt that."

She smiled. "No, really. If I'd known that you were *The* Michael Carven, my behavior would have been a little more respectable. I might have even bowed."

Michael took a sip of his coffee. "I think you were right."

"About what?"

"The dress."

She had looked at the other women's dresses, and was surprised to find the one she wore was much more conservative. Realizing that she was not overdressed had given her a little satisfaction and confidence. "I think it's a great dress." She gave him a wicked smile.

"And so do half of the men in the room." He put down his coffee. "Would you like to dance?"

"I'd love to."

Michael took her hand and led her out to the dance floor. It wasn't long before they were lost in the music, gliding across the floor. Their motions were refined, as if they had been choreographed and practiced for many hours.

By the time the song ended, Jessica was winded. "That was fun."

Michael pulled Jessica into his arms when the slow song started. He held her so close he could feel her heartbeat against his chest and her breath on his neck. The light fragrance she had applied behind her ears hovered around his nose. Christ, she smelled good. He took a deep breath and relished the moment. It felt wonderful just to hold her. To feel her body sway next to his was consuming.

Jessica thought if there was a heaven on earth, this was it. She slid her hand under his coat and ran her fingers over his ribs. "Do they hurt?"

Shaking his head, he kissed the top of her head and pulled her close. "No, they don't hurt."

As Jessica moved her hand to his waist, she touched the tip of his gun. She pulled away quickly and looked at Michael. Her words were spoken in a whisper as her eyes darted around the room. "Why do you have a gun?"

Michael pulled her back to him. "Don't worry about it."

"Is there something I should know?" she insisted.

He turned her and smiled. "No."

Her feet shuffled to keep up with him. Her mind wasn't on dancing. "Don't ignore me. Tell me what's going on."

"Nothing's going on." He leaned into her ear. "People are starting to stare."

She didn't care who was staring at them. "Everything's okay?"

"Everything's fine." He whispered into the top of her head. "You know you ask too many questions."

She looked up at him. "You never answer them."

He winked. "Let's just enjoy the dance."

Michael didn't want the song to end, but when it did and another slow song immediately followed, he said a silent prayer. A tap on his shoulder interrupted his unspoken words.

"You plan on keeping her all to yourself, Carven?" Jack asked.

"That was the plan," Michael said in a low mumble.

Jack looked at Jessica. "You don't mind if I cut in, do you?"

Jessica wanted to scream, "Yes, I mind." She looked to Michael. He released her hand. "No, I suppose not."

Michael walked back to the table and sat. He watched Jack hold Jessica for a few seconds before he picked up his wine glass and drained it. He raised his hand. "Excuse me."

A waiter came to his side. "Yes."

Michael handed him his wine glass. "Give me something stronger."

"What would you like?"

"Brandy."

"Yes, sir."

Michael looked back to the dance floor. Physically, she was beautiful—tall, slender, and elegant. Her hair tumbled down her back in soft waves and she was just as beautiful inside. Her inner charisma shined continuously. If someone was to ask him what quality he liked about her most, he wouldn't be able to pinpoint just one. She was a mixture of so many things. She was candid and innocent, fun and uninhibited. He looked around for the waiter and his drink.

Jessica tried to relax in Jack's embrace, but she couldn't. She made eye contact and smiled politely as he continued to list all the wonderful things he owned. His breath smelled of the cinnamon breath saver he rolled around in his mouth. Every now and again it would click against his teeth with an annoying sound. He had applied so much gel to his hair that it looked bulletproof. After several minutes of his non-stop boasting, she looked in Michael's direction helplessly.

Michael watched Jessica over the rim of his glass. He was surprised when she pushed her bottom lip out in a childish pout. He put his glass down and continued to watch. When she came around again, she stuck her tongue out. When he smiled at her antics, her eyes seemed to dance.

Her whimsical behavior didn't end with the single episode. The next rotation she crossed her eyes, reminding him of a circus clown. He watched as Jack tossed his head back and laughed at something he just said. He was so wrapped up in himself that he didn't notice what Jessica was doing.

Jessica pretended to yawn. Michael leaned back in his chair and winked at her. "I know he's boring, baby."

Jack moved his hand lower around Jessica's waist. "A pretty thing like you shouldn't be out in a barn."

Jessica brought her attention back to Jack. "Where should I be?"

"In the arms of a man who knows how to treat you right." He gave her a squeeze.

Jessica forced herself to smile. "I like to be out in the barn."

Michael leaned forward in his chair when he saw Jack pull Jessica closer. Jessica rolled her eyes as she looked across the dance floor to Michael.

Jack cleared his throat.

Jessica looked up, blushing.

"Like I was saying, you should come out to my place—" Jack turned around. "Carven?"

Chapter Twenty

Jessica couldn't stop laughing.

"What's so funny?" Michael turned on the headlights and sped out of the parking lot.

She used the back of her finger to wipe the tears under her eyes. "The look on Jack's face when you asked if you could cut in." She paused to take a breath. "I thought he was going to cry." She turned to him. "You should have never cut in. It wasn't polite."

"He cut in first."

"Yes, but you're not supposed to cut back in." Another bout of laughter caused her to tear up again. Her stomach muscles protested her enjoyment by cramping.

Michael downshifted as he rounded a corner. "How could I not when you practically begged me to?"

"I did no such thing." She reached for the dash and leaned with the car.

He took his eyes off the road to look at her. "Then what were the sad puppy eyes for?"

The creases around her eyes intensified. "I didn't have sad puppy eyes."

"You did too." He would have cut in even if she hadn't wanted him to. He wasn't going to sit back and watch Jack maul her the entire dance. He looked at her as she repaired her make-up in the lighted visor. He had no doubt that she could have handled Jack. That wasn't the issue; he simply didn't want the man touching her.

"Can we slow down?"

Michael glanced at the speedometer. "Sorry." On the other hand, he had wallowed in Jessica's frequent glances. The few annoyed expressions she had thrown his way he had thoroughly enjoyed. He liked knowing she preferred dancing with him.

"There's a little coffee shop about a mile up the road I saw on the way here. Let's stop." She snapped the visor shut. "Let me take you out. I owe you something for finding out who put the rat in my bathroom. Besides, I don't want this night to end, I'm having so much fun."

He didn't want the night to end either. "Where is it at?"

Jessica smiled as a waitress in a white apron approached the table with two cups of coffee: straight black and a tall mocha. She sat a cup in front of each of them and left quietly. Jessica picked up the cup and asked, "What made you get into the horse business?"

"My grandpa." He cast a quick glance around the room before he continued. "As you know, after my parents died I went to live with them." His eyes settled back on her.

"Did they have a ranch?"

"No, couldn't afford one. My grandpa owned a small construction business. He team roped on the weekends with his partner." He smiled. "My grandpa always told me that I was a natural. He was a good liar."

Jessica lifted her cup so she could smell the delicious mixture of coffee and chocolate. "You weren't?"

He shook his head and chuckled. "I don't know if you would call it natural. After the hundredth fall I was beginning to think I would never get the hang of it."

"Yeah, but the great thing about it is, it's kind of like

riding a bike. Once you learn, you never forget."

A bell rang as someone walked through the front door. Michael moved his hand to his side and watched the man. He didn't take his eyes off him until he saw the waitress lean over the counter and kiss him. "Once I got the hang of it, I was hooked."

"It's easy to get hooked." She paused, glancing at the man who had just come in. "Can I ask you a personal question?"

Michael wasn't one for personal questions. "Sure."

She recognized the fight or flight mode he so easily slipped into, but continued anyway. "Will you give me an honest answer?"

Michael nodded.

"Do you miss being a detective?"

Michael dropped his eyes to his coffee. He would be honest with her. It was the least he could do. "I miss it every day."

"Then why don't you go back?"

"I can't."

"Who said?" There was no sympathy in her voice.

"I say." The statement held a trace of challenge. "You'll never understand, Stanson, so don't even try."

She hesitated and then decided to lean forward. "Help me understand."

"I don't know how to." He shrugged. "I don't even understand myself." His eyes reflected deep confusion.

Jessica gave him a slight smile; she knew there was truth to his words, but she understood more than he thought.

The waitress came back and refilled Michael's cup. "Is there anything else I can get you?" she asked.

"Do you have any apple pie?" Michael asked.

"I sure do."

Michael looked to Jessica. "Would you like a piece?"

"Sounds wonderful."

Michael held his fingers in a V. "Two slices please."

Jessica decided against continuing with the topic. The night was too perfect to try and work through painful issues. "Thanks for inviting me to the dinner. I had a wonderful time."

"Thank you for coming. You made it bearable." Michael tore open a small packet of sugar and emptied it into his coffee.

"Bearable? How could you not have fun? I had a great time. I ate a wonderful dinner, danced with a handsome man, and I got to talk about horses all night. I don't think it gets any better than that."

"When you put it that way, it doesn't sound that bad. The food was good and you do look—" he searched for the right word.

"You better finish that sentence good."

His eyes sparkled and his smile lingered, "Amazing."

She touched his hand and grinned. "Good answer." She raised her eyes to view the coffee shop. It was quaint. The room was long and narrow. Small round tables covered with white cloth cluttered every inch of the floor. A huge, shiny roasting machine sat across from them. A number of water-color paintings from a local artist hung from the walls.

He studied her as she looked around the room. "What were you thinking about?"

She turned her attention back to him. "I was thinking how nice this is. How nice the entire evening has been."

He reached for her hand. "You were getting bored, weren't you?"

She nodded. "Don't get me wrong. I love my job—"

"But?"

"But, I usually go out on the weekends." That was her reward to herself. She would work her butt off all week and live it up on the weekends.

Michael squeezed her hand. "Like on a date."

She laughed. "No. I usually go out with my girlfriends. We go dancing or to the movies."

He fiddled with a small container that held several packets of sugar. "Do you date much?"

"No. I have three brothers. Have you forgotten? It doesn't matter if I'm two hundred miles or two miles from home, everyone knows that I have three big brothers who watch out for me whether I like it or not."

"You don't like it?" He sounded surprised.

Without thinking, she turned his hand over and stroked the calluses on his palm. "Let's just say having three protective brothers inhibited any chance of having boyfriends."

"It couldn't have been that bad."

"You want to bet?" she countered. "They had to pick who I went to the prom with."

The waitress returned with the slices of pie. Michael waited for her to leave before he spoke. "That's bad. Are they still that way?"

"Yep," Jessica said.

"Don't they realize that their little sister isn't so little any more? That she's all grown up and has a life of her own?" He took his fork, broke off a piece of flaky crust, and put it in his mouth.

She toyed with the whipping cream on her pie before taking a bite. "I don't think they'll ever see me as grown-up."

"Should I be worried about these three big brothers?"

"I think they would like you." Her voice was warm as she pictured the four of them together. Yes, her brothers would approve of Michael.

"I hope so." He laughed. "So there's never been anyone serious?"

"It's hard to get serious when you move around so much." She gave him a hopeful glance. "Maybe someday."

The waitress came by and filled Michael's cup and set the tab on the table. As Michael reached for it, Jessica put her hand on his. "It's my treat, remember."

"This evening is on me. You can treat some other time." He took the bill. "Have you figured out what you are going to do to Jake?"

"No, not yet, but I'm working on it." She puckered her lips before she took a bite. "It's going to be good."

Michael smiled. He knew that she had been mulling over what she could do to get him back. "I'll pay the bill, then we'll go."

"Okay."

Michael nodded to the waitress, who was clinging to the man who had come in earlier. When she saw Michael, she smiled and moved toward the cash register. "Was everything okay?"

"Yes, everything was fine."

She picked up the receipt and began punching in numbers. "Will this be all?"

Michael looked to Jessica, whose back was to him. "Yes. Wait, I'd like the flowers."

The waitress looked a little confused. "What flowers?"

"Those." Michael pointed to the bouquet behind the girl.

"Those aren't for sale. It's a display."

Michael glanced around the room, at Jessica, and then back to the flowers. He reached into his back pocket and pulled out his wallet. Taking out a fifty, he set it on the counter.

The waitress took the money. "Would you like the vase too?"

"No, just the flowers." Michael walked back to the table. "These are for you."

Jessica stood up and took the bouquet. "Michael, they're beautiful." She inhaled the soft fragrance.

Michael placed his arm around her waist and guided her back to the car. He pulled away from the curb and steered into traffic.

Jessica watched the full moon dip behind the clouds and out again. "You know, when I was a little girl I thought the moon followed me. I know all little girls think that, but I really believed it." Her voice was thick as she spoke. "My dad used to tell me my mom was up there somewhere watching over us; that's why it shined so bright."

Michael turned off the already low radio and glanced over at her. He loved to hear her talk. Her voice was like a beloved melody. What would it be like when it no longer filled his home? He couldn't imagine going a day without hearing her infectious laugh.

Jessica pressed her hand against the window. "I believed him too. I loved it during the summer; after dinner we would go out on the porch swing and sit and look at it for hours. I even talked to it just like I was talking to my mom. My brothers used to tease me about it." She laughed. "My dad would scold them, but you know it never really bothered me." She looked over at him suddenly. "Sorry for babbling."

He shrugged. "I don't mind. I like to hear about your family. You miss your dad, don't you?"

She nodded.

"Give him a call when we get home. It won't be too late," he suggested.

Jessica smiled and rested her head against the seat. "Thank you, Michael."

"You know you can call him any time."

"No, I meant thank you for letting me work for you. The two months are just about over and I'm going to be going home. I know I've been a pain to live with."

"You haven't been the pain; I have." She was rare and special and he wouldn't let her leave thinking she had caused him any grief.

Her smile was slow at first but then grew wide. "How about we split it fifty-fifty?"

His smile matched hers. "Sounds fair to me."

"I'm going to hate leaving," she admitted. "It's never been hard for me to go. It's going to be different this time. Don't ever repeat this, but I'm going to miss Jake, Richard, Tom, and John. I'm going to miss Mrs. Mayfield and Criss Cross too." She sighed. "And the kids. It's going to be so hard to say good bye." She looked down at the beautiful flowers in her lap and tilted her head toward Michael. "I'm going to miss you the most."

Chapter Twenty-One

Michael sat in his study and poured himself another drink. How many was this? Not enough, he decided, as he drained the glass and refilled it. He looked at the door when he heard the knock. He made no motion to answer it; he didn't want to see anyone. All he wanted was to be left alone to wallow in his self-pity.

"Mike?" Dan tapped on the door again.

"He won't answer," Mrs. Mayfield said. "I've been knocking all day."

Dan's concern was clearly written on his face when he tried the doorknob and found it locked. He had seen Michael snap before, and this was how it started. He turned and spoke in a low voice. "How long has he been in there?"

"Since last night, I think." She looked over her shoulder and up the stairs. "His bed is made, so I don't think he even went to his room."

A frown formed on his face as he searched Mrs. Mayfield's eyes. "Did he and Jessica go to the benefit last night?"

She took a deep breath and nodded.

"Well, did something happen? Is Jessica all right?"

"Jessica is fine. I saw her this morning as she was leaving for the stables. She said they had a nice evening together."

He ruffled his hair with his hand. "He hasn't come out at all today?"

Mrs. Mayfield shook her head. "Not once."

"Have you heard any sounds?"

"Lots of them when I first came in this morning." She shook her head sadly. "I'm worried, Dan. I haven't seen him like this in years. I don't know what to do."

Dan put a comforting hand on her shoulder. "I'll see if I can talk to him."

Mrs. Mayfield covered his hand with hers. She had known Dan as long as she had known Michael. He was a good man and she knew he would take care of Michael. "I don't know what's wrong with him."

"I think I do," Dan said.

Feeling helpless, she said, "I'll be in the kitchen if you need anything."

Dan turned back to the door. "Mike?" He knocked once more and, when he didn't receive a response, he pulled out his pocketknife and worked the lock until the door opened.

Michael looked at him with a scowl. "Go away."

"What are you doing?" Dan closed the door behind him.

"Go."

"Mrs. Mayfield called me because she's worried about you."

"There isn't anything to worry about." Michael tried to scoot up in the large leather chair, but found the slouching position felt more comfortable and fit his mood.

Dan went to Michael's desk, picking up an empty bottle in one hand and a half-empty bottle in the other. He looked at his friend. "You think you can drink her off your mind?" Dan's voice was husky as he spoke.

"I'm gonna try." He swiped the half-empty bottle from Dan's hand and filled his glass again. If his friend wouldn't leave, then he'd try and drink him away too.

Dan's voice softened. "It won't work." He turned and looked around the room. It was in shambles. The waste can was lying on its side in the corner, books teetered from the shelves, and it smelled like the drunk tank down at the station. "God, Mike what are you doing to yourself?"

"I don't need a lecture right now. If you want to stay, then stay, but don't say one goddamn word." Michael's words were slurred, but he meant every one of them. He didn't want to talk. He couldn't talk. Not right now.

Dan watched as Michael's eyes fell onto the picture of Jessica and Quest sitting on the corner of his desk. Twisted anguish flashed across Michael's face. "Mike—"

"Save it. I don't want to hear anything you have to say." He held up a weaving hand. "I said no lectures and I meant it."

"All right, no lectures."

Michael motioned to the chair. "Sit." He filled an extra glass and slid it to him.

Dan angled a chair toward the desk and sat. He took the shot Michael handed him, regarded it for a moment, and then swallowed its contents in one smooth gulp. He slid the glass back to Michael when he finished.

Michael filled the glass again and slid it back to him. "That's better. In no time you'll be feeling no pain."

"How long have you been in here?" He drank the drink like the first and set the small glass down. Michael looked like shit. His dinner jacket was slung over the chair he was sitting in. One sleeve to his shirt remained snuggly buttoned against his wrist while the other was rolled halfway up his arm. The black tie was still threaded through his collar, but it was undone, and several buttons down his chest were missing. His eyes were red with dark circles underneath.

Michael stared aimlessly at a speck on the wall. "I don't know and I don't care."

"Mike, I got the results back from the shoe print." He

leaned forward. "It was a perfect match. You were right; he was here. It's him."

Michael wiped his mouth with the back of his hand. "I know. I knew it would be."

"Have you told her?"

"No."

"Do you plan to?" Dan asked.

Shutting his eyes tightly, he pinched the bridge of his nose. "Yes." He exhaled a long breath and then opened his eyes. "When the time is right."

Dan's gaze leveled with his friend's. "And when is that going to be?"

Michael slammed his hand on his desk. "God damn it, I don't know." He swore under his breath again. "I don't know anything anymore." He refilled his glass and then Dan's.

"I can tell her if you want me to," Dan offered.

"No," Michael snapped. "I don't want you to say anything to her. When she finds out, she's going to find out from me."

Dan slouched down in the chair and propped his feet on the desk. "What are we going to do?"

"About what?"

"Finding the killer."

Michael raised his fingers until they were about a half an inch apart. "We're this close to finding this guy. We have shoe prints, we have his height and weight, we have a witness, I've even spoken to him. You'd think we could get him."

"You'd think."

Michael gritted his teeth. "It's like he's invisible."

"This is no different from any other case. Sometimes you get 'em and sometimes you don't."

"Bullshit. If you believe that, you're only fooling yourself. This is completely different. How many times have we had a killer call?" Michael had been taunted by letters in the past, but he had never had a killer call him.

"Never."

"That's right. And can you think of anyone we've tracked that was as shrewd as this guy is?"

"No." Dan took another drink. "He's good. There's no denying that."

Hefting himself forward, Michael managed to sit straight up. "Good is an understatement. This guy is like nothing I've ever seen."

"The Jane Doe in Lenwood has been identified. It appears her boyfriend killed her because he thought she was cheating on him. Lenwood PD has him in custody."

"We don't have to wonder who his next victim will be."

"You're not suggesting it's Jessica, are you?"

Michael took a drink and held it in his mouth as he thought about his chestnut-haired beauty. "I'm not suggesting anything."

"I don't see what the big deal is," Dan said three hours later.

Michael couldn't fathom how for the last hour he talked to Dan about his feelings for Jessica. He hadn't wanted to examine why he cared about her, but somehow he had opened up and found himself stuck in a heated debate with Dan. There was no doubt that the alcohol played a major role in giving himself the liberty to speak. He leaned back in his chair. The slight movements made his head spin. "The big deal?"

"So you care about her. I think it's about goddamn time." Dan wobbled on the end of his chair as he leaned forward to stress his point.

"What if he takes her away from me?" He knew that it was the alcohol talking, because he would never have spoken the words sober.

Dan looked into his friend's glossy eyes. "He won't. Because we're going to get the bastard."

Michael shook his head furiously. "I wish I could believe that." His eyes lowered as he looked at the picture in his hands. "She makes me want to be with her."

"What's wrong with that?"

"For starters, when I'm with her the pain goes away." His voice fell. "I forget about Cathy."

"That's okay."

Michael balled his fists. "It's not right."

"Goddamn it, Mike. Do you think that you're supposed to suffer for the rest of your life? What's wrong with not feeling the pain? What's wrong with falling for a beautiful, young, intelligent woman?" He swung his arms around the room. "Show me where it's written that you can love one woman and one woman only."

If he heard any of Dan's words, he didn't acknowledge them. "She was so young. She didn't even have a chance to live."

"And you feel that since she didn't get to live and experience life that you shouldn't either? That's fucked." He poked his finger in the air between them. "It was her time to go, not yours."

"I see her sometimes," Michael said solemnly. "When I close my eyes, she's there."

"It's guilt! If you would quit feeling so fuckin' guilty, you wouldn't be going through any of this." Dan started to rise, then decided against it. He nodded as he put everything together. "I see what's going on. You want Jessica and you think because of that you're betraying Cathy. You feel like a big piece of shit for caring. Am I right? And don't lie to me, Mike, we have been through too much together."

Michael nodded.

"And because you never found her killer, you feel even worse."

Michael nodded again.

His thunderous voice switched to a subdued tone. "You did everything you could do, buddy."

"And it wasn't enough," Michael said.

"You're not Superman."

He fooled around with the empty bottle, spinning it. "I was taught and trained to think like the bad guy, to investigate him, track him—"

"And you did. You were good at it."

The bottle dropped and Michael looked up. "Yeah, until it came to the most important one. I can't go through it again."

"You're not going to have to, because we're going to get him."

"I hope you're right."

"I know one thing I'm right about." His smile grew. "You're in love with Jessica. It's plain and simple. You better get used to it, my friend." He took a big drink.

Mrs. Mayfield opened the door and made a disagreeable face. She looked sternly at the two men, who could scarcely keep their heads up and their butts in their chairs. "I knocked several times, but you didn't hear." She glared at Dan. "It's so nice to see you're taking care of things."

Michael looked to Dan with an expression that said: we have been busted, but what the hell.

Dan whispered to his friend in a slurring tone. "I've got it taken care of."

Michael nodded and gestured with his hand. "Go right ahead." He leaned back in his chair.

Dan looked back toward the door at Mrs. Mayfield. "Everything's okay."

She frowned. "Smells like it. Would either of you care for dinner?" She tapped her foot smartly as she waited for an answer.

"Sure." Dan pushed the items on the desk aside. A stack of papers, the stapler, and a cup holding pens and pencils fell to the floor. He pointed to the cleared spot. "Bring it right here."

Michael leaned toward his ear and whispered. "Glad to see you've got it under control. She looks madder than a wet hen."

Mrs. Mayfield slammed the door and went to the kitchen. She took out a tray and began loading food on it. She made a pot of strong coffee and put the carafe on the tray next to some stew she had made just a few hours ago.

Jessica came into the kitchen and noticed the tray. "They're not eating out here?"

"No, it appears that they are working late." She carelessly piled items on the tray. "I don't expect them to come out all night."

Jessica started to fix her own meal. "They must be on to something with the case."

"Yeah, they're on to something all right," she mumbled as she spread butter on several slices of bread.

Jessica looked over to her. "What's that?"

"Nothing, dear." She lifted the heavy tray and walked out of the room.

Chapter Twenty-Two

Jessica straightened the short black leather skirt she had found at the thrift store in town and applied another coat of the chokingly bright red lipstick. She plumped up her hair, trying to squeeze a little more fullness and height out of it before she knocked on the door.

"Hi Jess," Jake said as he swung the door open. "Where the hell are you going looking like that?"

Jessica ignored his distorted expression, stood on her tiptoes, and placed a kiss on his cheek. "Hi, sweetheart."

Jake looked at her curiously. "What?"

"I said, 'hi, sweetie.' " She used her thumb to wipe the lipstick off his cheek. "Aren't you happy to see me?"

"Why are you dressed like that?" He viewed her attire.

"Who's there, Jake?" Jennifer, Jake's wife, came up behind him, placing an arm around his midsection.

Jessica looked at the woman and then back to Jake. "Tell her who I am, honey."

Jennifer pulled away from her husband and stared at him. "Yeah, how about you tell me who she is, h-o-n-e-y?"

Jake shrugged. "I don't know what she's talking about. This is—"

"May I come in?" Jessica shoved past the couple and into the house.

"I don't believe you were invited in," Jennifer said in a severe tone.

236

Jessica moved about the room, surveying the family pictures on the walls. She took her time admiring each one. They were a good-looking family. A happy family.

The pieces of furniture were mix-matched, some old, some new, giving the home a cozy feeling. Children's toys were tucked neatly away. She turned to Jennifer. "You must be Jennifer."

"Yes, I am." She looked to Jake and then back at Jessica. "Would you mind telling me who you are? My husband can't seem to pick his jaw up off the floor."

"Have you ever heard of a place called Maggie's?" Jessica twirled a piece of hair at the base of her neck around her finger. "I'm sure you've heard of it. That's where all the guys go, to hang out, drink beer, have a little fun." She gave Jennifer a wink. "You know what I mean."

Jennifer glared at Jake, who had managed to close his gaping mouth. "I've heard of it. Please continue."

"I met your hubby there a few months ago." Jessica paused and strutted to Jake's side. She rubbed up against him. "Go on, tell her about it, honey. Tell her how we met."

Jake shook his head like someone had hit him. "What's wrong with you, Jess?"

"He's a little shy." She ran a finger down his chest and slithered closer. "You sure weren't shy the other night, were you?" Jessica turned to Jake's wife. "I'll tell you all about it."

"Please do."

"It was a few months ago when we first met and it was the most romantic night of my life. I was sitting at the bar with some of my girlfriends when Jake asked me to dance." Jessica's eyes glazed over like a lovesick puppy. "Come on, honey, you tell the rest."

Jakes eyes were wide as he stared at Jessica. He found it hard to swallow and even harder to speak. "Why are you doing this, Jess?"

"She's going to have to find out sometime." She looked to Jennifer. "Where was I? Oh, yeah, we slow danced five songs in a row. It was love at first sight."

Jennifer balled her fist up. "Just what in the hell is she talking about, Jake? I want some answers and I want them now."

Jake looked at his wife with hesitation. "You don't actually believe her?"

Jennifer moved over by Jessica. "You haven't denied anything she has said."

"Because it's so outrageous. She's crazy, Jen. I haven't been to Maggie's in I don't know how long." His state was borderline hysterical. He looked directly at Jessica. "This is absurd Jess, stop."

Jessica looked to Jennifer, somewhat taken aback. "He said that he was going to tell you everything."

He stomped his foot. "I did no such thing. There's nothing to tell." He was almost yelling.

Jessica knew Jake was close to snapping because he had swiped the green hat off his head and wadded it in his hands. Her agony had been long and drawn out and so would his be. She continued. "And when he did, he was going to leave you and come to me."

"You did what?" Jennifer threw her hands up.

"I never said that. Look, I don't know what she is talking about. When would I ever have the time to see her? Think about it, Jen."

"When was the last time I saw you, Jake?" Jessica said suddenly.

"Yesterday."

"You saw her yesterday?" Jennifer started crying. "How could you do this?"

"I saw her at work. Work." His voice was drenched with desperation. "I work with her. This is Jess. I've told you all about her."

Jennifer covered her face and started sobbing. "I thought you loved me."

"I do. Jen, don't listen to her. She doesn't know what she is saying." He looked at Jessica. "Tell her you're lying." Beads of sweat broke out across his forehead. His hands started to shake. "Listen—"

Jessica and Jennifer put their arms around each other like they were long-lost buddies. They smiled as they spoke in unison. "Sucker."

Jake's head shot up. "What?"

Jessica gave Jennifer a high five. "That was perfect. Thanks for playing along."

"No problem. I had fun."

Both women bent over with laughter. Jessica pulled out a Kleenex from her purse and began wiping off her make-up.

Jake looked from one woman to the other. "What? This was all a joke?"

Jessica smiled and nodded. "Pretty good, huh? I called Jennifer last night and we set it up."

Jennifer and Jessica started laughing again.

"This isn't funny," Jake said.

Jennifer kissed her husband. "Yes, it is."

"How could you do this to me?"

Jennifer pulled Jake into a tight embrace. "It was easy." She kissed him soundly again. "I can't believe you put a rat in Jessica's bathroom."

"Neither can I." Jessica gave him a dirty smile. "But I think all's fair now." She looked back to Jennifer. "Can I use your bathroom to change?" Her attempts to remove the rest of her make-up with the small tissue were futile. "I have to get this stuff off."

"Right through there." Jennifer pointed.

When Jessica returned, face clean and in jeans and a sweater, Jennifer asked Jessica if she wanted some coffee.

She looked at her watch. "Okay, but only one cup. I need to be getting back to the ranch. I still have a truckload of feed to unload."

Jake came up behind Jessica. "You can't tell the guys about this. I'll never hear the end of it."

Jessica motioned to the chair next to her. "Sit and have a cup of coffee with me. I'm sure we can work something out."

Jake pulled out the chair. "You're ruthless."

She shot him a quick smirk. "You know what they say about paybacks."

Where the hell was she? Michael sat in his chair, his elbows on his knees, his fists balled under his chin. He stared out the window at the driveway. It was getting dark. If she wasn't home in ten minutes, he was going to get in his truck and tear the town apart if that's what it would take to find her. He looked at his watch and back to the window.

Not knowing what to do with himself, he walked from one end of the house to the other trying to control his anxiety. "Damn it, Stanson where are you?" He rubbed his eyes and went into the kitchen to make some coffee. As he waited for it to brew, he looked at the phone. Why wasn't she calling? She would call if she were going to be late. It wasn't like her to stay out and not call him. Unless she couldn't.

He braced his arms on the counter and hung his head. "Shit." She should have been back hours ago.

He pushed away from the counter and poured a cup of

coffee. What he wanted was a drink, but he had drunk himself insensible the previous day and there was no need to repeat it. He wouldn't be able to handle it anyway. His hand went to his head; he could still feel the lingering effects of the alcohol.

He took a seat at the bar and looked at his watch. Five more minutes. If she wasn't here in five minutes, he was going to look for her.

After he finished the coffee, he got up and started pacing again. Maybe he should call Dan. Would he be overreacting if he called and organized a search party? He would be if she were out shopping. But if something did happen to her, he didn't have time to waste. When he went for the phone, he heard someone pull into the driveway.

When he spotted the truck, his relief was shadowed by intense anger. He flew to the door and flung it open when she got to the steps. "Where the hell have you been?"

Jessica had never seen Michael this mad before. His features were a mask of dark anger. His eyes consumed her; his stance intimidated her. Stunned and worried, she didn't move. "I went to get feed."

He met her in the middle of the porch. "It took you all day to get feed?"

"No, not the entire day."

"If you don't tell me where in the hell—"

"Jake and Jennifer's." She slid past him. "I also went to Jake and Jennifer's." Jessica turned around and watched him sweep the door shut with a powerful hand. She jumped when it slammed.

His fingers went to his temples. The ache in his head gained strength. "Jesus Christ. You've been at Jake and Jennifer's all this time." His eyes turned dark, brimming with anger. "Why didn't you call? You could have called and let me know where you were."

241

Jessica removed her coat and moved into the living room. "I'm sorry. I didn't realize how late it was." She paused. Feeling the need to justify herself, she said, "Time just got away from me."

Michael stuffed his hands in his pockets because he was afraid that if he didn't he would put them around her neck. "All this time I've been worried about where you've been and you were at Jake's."

She crossed her arms over her chest and watched him closely. "What's the matter?"

He moved around the sofa to put some distance between them. "I thought something happened to you."

"Nothing has happened to me." The creases across his brow told her that he was not only aggravated but also genuinely concerned about her safety. "Why are you so upset?"

In two steps Michael cleared the space between them. He took Jessica in his arms and crushed her against his chest. "You scared me half to death." He sucked in a deep breath. His nostrils filled with her scent and went straight to his head. The pounding of her heart echoed against his. "Stanson, you can't just come and go as you please. You have to let me know where you are at all times so I can protect you."

Jessica struggled out of his embrace and stumbled backward. All her features transformed into concern. "Protect me?"

"Shit." Michael closed his eyes and brought his hand to his head. "That's not what I meant."

Jessica stepped back as Michael came toward her. She raised her hand in an attempt to stop him. "Who do I need protection from?"

"Come here, baby." Michael tried to reach for her but she drew back.

"Who do I need protection from? Answer me, Michael."

242

She stumbled over the coffee table and aimed a loathing look that penetrated right through him. "Answer the God damn question."

He raised his hands. "Calm down." He needed to touch her.

Her head snapped to attention. "I will not calm down. Don't tell me to calm down." Her muttering tone halted. Her gaze wandered around the room and slowly came to rest on Michael. "He knows who I am." Her words were low and grave. "Oh, God."

Michael didn't look at her. He didn't need to see her face to know her pain or her fear. They were laced in her words as she spoke.

Jessica staggered back in a daze, trying to get as much distance between them as possible. She didn't want to be near him. "When? How long have you known?" She swiped at the hair in her face. "Damn it, Michael, if you're not going to answer me, you could at least have the balls to look me in the face."

Michael slowly lifted his head and looked at her across the room. His stomach quivered at all the emotion playing on her face. "Two days."

Jessica leaned against the wall for support. "Why didn't you tell me?" Betrayal replaced most of her anger.

Michael moved to her and planted his arms on each side of her head to prevent her from moving away from him. His face was inches from hers when he whispered, "I didn't want to scare you."

"Do I have reason to be scared?"

Michael only nodded.

"He was here, wasn't he?" She closed her eyes and took a deep breath, afraid of his answer.

"Yes."

Her anger was swiftly restored. "I thought I was going nuts, imagining things. I can't believe you knew and you didn't tell me." The words came out as a cruel strike against him.

"What did you want me to do?"

"Tell me the truth. The truth." She shook her head, fighting off her tears. "That's all I ever wanted from you." She tried pushing him away, but didn't have the strength. "This is my life we're dealing with; doesn't that mean anything to you?"

Michael closed his eyes. *It means everything to me.* "It's your life that I'm trying to protect."

Jessica's voice went four octaves higher. "By not telling me? That's sick, Michael." Her tone was biting as her body started to tremble. She swallowed, trying to suppress the wave of realization that swept through her. "He was at the dinner, wasn't he?"

"I don't know," he said mildly.

She searched his eyes as her insides shook. "But you thought he might be, and that's why you had a gun?"

"Yes." He would tell her everything. He had no right to keep it from her. "He's been following you, Stanson."

"Where?" she said impatiently.

His blue eyes were fixed on hers. "Everywhere."

"What do I do now?" Any attempt at trying to contain her composure was lost. Her words were borderline hysterical.

"Wait."

"Wait and see if he gets me? Wait and see if I end up like Nichole Blake?" She couldn't breathe. She needed some air. She needed to move. She tried to duck under his arms but was held firmly in place.

"I don't want to hear you talk like that," Michael said.

"It's true," she said in an uneven voice.

"No, it's not. I'm not going to let anything happen to you."

She let her hands fall on his large biceps. His muscles yielded under her touch. She wanted to be angry with him but she couldn't. She gave up. Her head fell forward and rested against his. Her body went limp. "I can't handle this."

He tucked her hair behind her ear. "I know."

She didn't care if he didn't want to hear it. She needed to say it. "I need you, Michael."

He traced a finger over the arch of her brow, down her nose, and across her lips. He tucked the same piece of hair behind her ear again. "I need you too," he murmured.

She pulled herself forward, placing her lips on his, in a slow, questioning kiss. Michael laid his splayed hand on the center of her chest, giving her a slight push against the wall. His lips followed in hot pursuit, crushing her mouth in a painful frenzy. She felt his tongue plunge into her mouth, tasting her, discovering her, demanding everything from her.

Raw hunger for her drove him to unearth every secret and every mystery her body held. He had gone over it in his mind a dozen times what it would be like to touch and love this woman's body, but nothing had come close to this.

The firm hands that entrapped her slid down her torso, roaming and touching. In his exploration, he gathered her shirt and began pulling the tucked material out of her jeans. He eased the material over her head and tossed it on the floor. His fingertips caressed her flushed skin, wild to learn its feel. Gliding over perfect mounds covered with silk, he sucked in a deep breath. "God, how I've wanted to touch you." His hand moved to her back, where his fingers fiddled with the small metal clasp.

Jessica was lost in his caresses. The anticipation of his touch set her body on fire. His mouth found her nipple, sucking until a little bud formed. He rolled it across his tongue, bit, and held it between his teeth. When Jessica gasped with pleasure, he moved to the other breast.

With his mouth, he kissed, tasted, and aroused a fiery trail down to her abdomen. His tongue flirted with her belly button. His hands slid down the contours of her rib cage to her hips, committing to memory her every curve. For as long as he lived, he would never forget the way she felt under his hands. Unbuttoning her jeans, he slid the zipper down. He placed a tender kiss just above the white lace as she stepped out of the unwanted article of clothing.

Never breaking contact, he found his way back to Jessica's face. He took it in his hands. She could read his unspoken words. The yearning he felt equaled hers. She could feel not only the urgency tugging at his heart but could also hear the inner voice that told him this was okay. There were no more barriers between them. Michael was giving himself to her.

His eyes searched hers for an instant, before pulling off his shirt. He took her hands in his and rested them against his chest. He guided her fingers over the soft growth of hair, across his nipples, down to his midriff. "Touch me."

It was only moments before he felt her hands begin to move on their own, no longer needing guidance. Her shaky fingers played with the hair that trailed down his abdomen and disappeared behind faded denim. Jessica's eyes went dark as she leaned forward and placed her lips on his skin. His toned stomach tightened under the caress.

Michael collected her hair in his hands, enjoying the softness of it. He wound it around his fingers, lifting its weight. His hands grasped her shoulders, as her kisses moved lower. Her name came out in a long moan. "Jessica."

"I like the sound of my name on your lips." She spoke the

words against his navel as she tugged the denim from his body.

He felt like a bomb that was going to explode any minute. Passion seeped from every pore in his body as he drew her up and kissed her fiercely. "I like your lips, they taste good."

Jessica didn't know if her legs would support her much longer. Heat rippled through her body in small waves, causing her to slowly slide down the wall. In one swift movement she was no longer standing. Michael lifted her to him, pinning her against the wall. Fire spread between her thighs as he pulled her knees up, wrapping them around his waist. A small cry escaped her lips as she felt him fill her. She buried her head in his neck and clung to him as her body bucked out of control.

Michael clutched her buttocks with both hands as he pulled her away from the wall. He balanced her on him as he climbed the stairs to his room. Each step buried him farther inside her. The feel of her around him, inside and out, was powerful. To hear her moan his name over and over as he loved her was overwhelming. He couldn't wait any longer. He came as he fell against the wall and drove into her.

Exhausted, he kissed her tenderly as he carried her into his bedroom and laid her on his bed. "Did I hurt you?"

She shook her head as her mouth sought his.

Chapter Twenty-Three

Michael's face lit up when Jessica walked into the study. A rush of desire spread through him at the sight of her. His robe consumed her small frame and her hair tumbled around her face in soft disorder. "Good morning."

"You weren't there when I woke up, so I came looking for you." She shut the door behind her and twisted the lock.

"I was going to stay with you, but I thought you were going to sleep all day." He had lain next to her, watching her, adoring her all morning until it hurt. Reluctantly, he had gotten up to work.

She rubbed her sleepy eyes as she perched herself on the edge of his desk. "If I did, I would have had a good reason."

Oh, baby, stop looking at me like that, he thought. "Why is that?"

The question almost made her purr. "I had a long night."

A brow shot up as he dropped the pen in his hand, the notes he had been taking forgotten. "Is that so?"

She nodded, her lips twisting into a shy smile. She disregarded the flutter in her belly and scooted closer to him. Her eyes smoldered with affection.

A thrill rippled through him. How he managed to keep his hands to himself, he would never know. "Care to tell me about it?"

She wedged herself between Michael and the desk. Her

heart began to beat wildly. "I would prefer to show you," she said.

He peered over the tops of his glasses, completely mystified. "Show me?"

She nodded slowly. "I have a few war wounds."

"Wounds?"

She loosened the belt around her waist and let the oversized robe fall. As Michael took off his glasses and leaned back in his chair, she slid off the desk and stood. "See these?" She turned slightly and pointed to four small slices on each hip. She got pleasure from his grin as he remembered. "And this." She moved her hand up to her breast and pointed to a tiny red mark. Michael started to speak, but she cut him off. "I'm not through." She turned around and pointed to a small indentation in the middle of her back. Michael looked at her, questioning. "You don't recall that one, do you? Look a little closer. Doesn't it resemble the hall light switch?"

Michael stood up. "I had a rough night too."

"What a coincidence."

He took off his shirt and, turning his bare back to her, he exposed long red marks that ran the length of his back. Jessica looked up. Had she really made those? "Sorry."

"I'm not." He had to touch her. He traced a line from her throat down to the soft patch of hair. "Don't ever be sorry." What did he ever do to deserve her? She was beautiful, compassionate, and all his. She was also standing before him naked, eyes heavy with want.

She kissed the center of his chest and then nibbled a trail to the base of his neck. "Will you do it again?"

"Do what?" His eyes were closed as he took pleasure in the feel of her lips against his skin.

"Make me feel the way you made me feel last night?" Her

pulse began to throb. "I have never felt anything so wonderful in my life."

Her words were soft on his neck as she spoke. He lifted her on to the desk and kissed her tenderly. Using his tongue, he probed until her mouth opened for him. The kiss was thorough and intimate and she responded to him by giving all she had.

"You felt so good last night." She managed to say in between kisses. "You made me feel so good—"

The phone rang.

She held him tightly in place, refusing to let him go. "Don't answer it." Her lips were no longer tender when she reached up to him. She worked his mouth mercilessly. "I'll make it worth your while."

Michael groaned. There wasn't anything more he would love to do than lay her across his desk and make love to her. "I have to get that."

Jessica's fingers found their way to his jeans; ignoring the phone and Michael, she stroked the tight bulge. Her lips glided over his chest; she didn't care if he had a shirt on, as her body fit itself to his. His body turned taut in response to her caresses, shuddering twice as her fingers stroked repeatedly.

Michael took her hand by the wrist and brought it to his lips and kissed it before he snatched the phone up with the other hand. "Yes."

Jessica smiled as she got off the desk. She watched Michael talk while she put the robe back on and cinched it around her waist. There was something different about him and she liked it. He had surrendered, she decided. The haunting memories that inhibited every aspect of his life were set free. He had managed to accept them and then let them go.

When Michael hung up the phone, he looked to Jessica. "Why are you looking at me like that?"

"Because I can't seem to help myself."

He touched her chin with a finger. "I have to meet Dan in town."

"Is everything okay?"

Michael pulled her close and rested his chin on the top of her head. "Yes."

"You would tell me, wouldn't you?" She lifted her head and looked at him.

"Yes. I'll never keep anything from you. That's a promise."

"When are you going to be back?" She wrapped her arms around his waist.

"Tonight."

"I'll fix dinner."

"Sounds good." He kissed the top of her head and moved away. "I don't want you to leave the house today." He scribbled numbers on a piece of paper. "This is my cell phone. This is Dan's cell phone. You already have the station's number."

She nodded.

"Call me if you need anything." He gathered items on his desk. "I have someone watching the house, so don't be afraid."

"I'm not." And it was the truth. Nothing could touch them. Not now.

He kissed her soundly one last time before he left.

Michael sat across from Dan in his office and listened to him closely.

"I got a call this morning from a guy saying that he knew where the killer's hide-out was."

Michael stifled a laugh. "Hide-out?"

Dan shook his head. "I know it sounds ridiculous, but that's what he said." He looked at the paperwork before him. "This guy was nervous. Scared shitless, I think."

"What did he do when you asked him to come down?"

"He freaked. He said that there was no way in hell he was coming down to the station. I asked him if I could meet him somewhere." He shrugged. "That didn't work. He just kept muttering that he liked his life and there was no way he or anyone in his family was going to end up like the girls." Dan paused. "I tried to calm him down, but no matter what I said he wouldn't listen. He refused to answer any personal questions, so I asked him if he could give a description."

"What did he say?" Michael moved to the water cooler and filled a cup.

"He said that he shouldn't even be making the call and hung up."

"Did you get a recording of the conversation?"

Dan let out a breath. "No."

"Do you think he knew anything?" Michael sat sipping his water as he watched the muted activity of the squad room.

"I think he knew a lot. He was just afraid to say anything."

"You can't blame him." Michael couldn't count how many times there was someone out there who knew something about a case but wouldn't speak up because they were afraid for their life or their family's. Which was understandable—there were times when a witness was found dead. "Do you think he'll call back?"

"When he gets his nerve up again, I think he will." Dan stood, went to the door, and held it open. "It's one goddamn brick wall after another."

Michael nodded and walked out of Dan's office.

"We're having a meeting at the grange this afternoon.

There are going to be representatives from several different PDs. You want to come?"

"Sure."

Jessica peeked out the kitchen window and ran to the table when she saw the lights from the truck pull into the driveway. She lit the candles at each end of the table, dimmed the lights, and sat down. Smoothing her hair, she waited with anticipation.

Michael hung his coat and began looking through the mail as he headed for the kitchen. "Did you miss me?" he called out as he reached the entryway. When he didn't get an answer, he slowly looked up. The mail drifted to the floor unnoticed as he sucked in a deep breath. "I guess so." He focused on the slender leg that was artfully draped across the table. He followed silken curves to her round thighs, his gaze moved momentarily to the dark shadowed mass of soft hair before returning to her abdomen. Her tender round breasts were responsive to his gaze, straining for his touch. He feasted his eyes on her delicate flesh that was carpeted in dancing candlelight.

His eyes captured hers, holding them until he could speak. "I was just thinking on the way home how great it felt knowing that someone was here waiting for me. I never dreamed of this."

A smile crept to Jessica's lips. "Come here."

He went to her and fell to his knees. She swiveled around in the chair and held him to her chest. Tears streamed down her cheeks. She tilted his head up and kissed him with all the love that billowed inside her. She undressed him, savoring every touch.

Michael took Jessica's hands in his. "Slow down, baby."

"I can't."

He kissed her tears dry and lifted her onto the table. As he laid her down, he straddled her. He nibbled on her swollen lips, deepening the kiss so he could taste her sweetness. Jessica stroked his back, and, gripping his buttocks, she wrapped her legs around his waist, lifting herself to him. She needed to feel him deep inside her.

The joining was powerful and passionate. In the aftermath, they lay exhausted on the table. Jessica ran her fingers across Michael's stomach; it rumbled in protest. She looked up.

"I thought you said that you were going to fix dinner."

"That was dinner."

He tilted Jessica's chin up. "Then it was delicious." He sat up on an elbow and watched her.

She smiled. "Why are you looking at me like that?"

"I love you."

"What?" She pulled away with surprise, wishing the candlelight wasn't so dim. Her heart fluttered in her chest.

He only had to look into her eyes for all his fears to disappear. "It's been a long time since I've said that, but it's true. I love you, Jessica Stanson, more than you will ever know. I want you to be here every day for the rest of my life." He drew her back to him. "I love knowing that whatever kind of day I'm having, good or bad, at the end of it I can come home to your smiling face." He kissed her fingertips. "I want your laugh to fill my house and my heart. Promise me you'll never stop taunting me, teasing me, mocking me."

She blinked twice as she listened to him.

Michael touched her tears. "No, don't cry." His thumb touched the corner of her eye. "No tears, baby."

She sucked in a deep, shaky breath. "I love you too. I have loved you from the first time I saw you." She felt liberated. "I never thought I would be able to tell you." She wiped at her fresh set of tears. "I never dreamed you would allow me to."

He linked her hand with hers. "I know I was hard on you—"

"Shh, it doesn't matter."

He kissed her long and hard, as if sealing his words. "How does a hot shower sound?"

"Wonderful." She looked at the goose bumps that had formed on her skin. "And warm."

Standing under the hot water, Jessica watched Michael as he lathered the soap up.

"Come here." He held open white foamy hands.

She stepped out of the water into Michael's waiting hands. It felt wonderful having them roam all over her. He didn't miss an inch. When she was completely covered in soft white lather, she scooped a handful off and began to cover Michael.

"Rinse." His command was a husky whisper.

Once the soap was rinsed off, he guided Jessica to the back of the shower. Pressing her against the cold tile, he kissed her long and hard. The kisses blended into one as he slid down her neckline to her breasts.

She buried her hands in his hair and cupped the back of his head. She couldn't believe the pleasure she could derive from such a small act. She looked down and watched the man she loved ravish her body. She enjoyed watching him please her.

Michael licked the water off her flat stomach on the way down the soft patch of wet hair. His body grew with excitement as he looked up at Jessica. Her head was leaning against the tile, eyes closed, waiting. He savored the taste of her and the moans of pleasure that escaped her lips.

"Please, Michael." She felt like she was going to die if he didn't give her some type of release. Was it possible to want something so much? "I want you in me."

Michael smiled up at her as he rose and fulfilled her request.

In bed, Michael cradled Jessica in his arms and stroked her wet hair. "How did everything go with Jake?"

Jessica had forgotten that she hadn't found the time to tell him how well the prank went. Their last twenty-four hours together had been a whirlwind of anger and passion. She snuggled next to him as she told him all about it.

Michael's laugh was deep and hearty. He kissed her soundly on the head. "That's my girl." He would have loved to have seen the look on Jake's face.

"I couldn't have done it without Jennifer."

"She's a nice woman. I think you'll become good friends."

"I hope so." Jessica raked her fingers through his chest hair. "I love you."

He looked down at her. "Where did that come from?"

"I don't know. I've just wanted to say it for so long, and now that I can, I can't say it enough."

"You can say it as much as you want. I'll never get tired of hearing it."

Her lips curved as she closed her eyes; she was content. "Tell me this isn't a dream."

"It's better than a dream."

It wasn't long before she drifted into a deep sleep. Michael slipped out of her embrace and went downstairs to his study.

He picked up the telephone and dialed Dan's number. "Hey, buddy, I know it's late, but we need to talk."

"What's up?"

"I want her out of here now." His mouth was set in a hard line as he spoke.

Dan cleared his throat. "I don't think that is wise."

"I don't give a damn what you think. I don't want her

here." Michael let his head fall into his hand. "Shit. I'm sorry. I can't shake the feeling that something is going to happen."

Dan tried to reason with him. "You can't just send her away and expect her to not see her family or work. We don't know how long it's going to take us to find this guy."

"We can relocate her somewhere far away for a few weeks. That's all I need." His eyes lifted, thinking about Jessica in his bed. "If I know that she's safe, I can find him."

"Okay, where do we put her?" Dan asked.

"I don't know." He shrugged. "I don't care just as long as it is away from this house and this town."

"Let's wait until morning. We can't leave in the middle of the night."

"Okay, but first thing in the morning we're leaving." His fingers automatically reached for the picture on his desk. "I'll think of a way to tell Jessica."

"Jessica?" Dan sound surprised. "I've never heard you call her Jessica." He paused, then said, "Don't worry, Mike, we're not going to let anything happen to her. I'll see you in the morning."

Michael racked his brain trying to think of a place he could take Jessica that was safe. Maybe she could go to Mrs. Mayfield's daughter's or to Dan's parents' house in California. He could send her on a cruise. What about a trip overseas?

The ring of the phone broke his thoughts.

"Yes."

"You can't hide her, Michael. I'll find her. That I promise you."

Michael gripped the phone with both hands. "I'll find you before you have the chance to kill again."

"How do you know I haven't? I'm always one step ahead

of you, Michael." The faceless, distorted voice let out a daunting laugh. "You'll never get me. You're good, but not that good."

"I'll get you and when I do, I'm going to rip your fucking head off and shove it down your goddamn throat." Michael stared out the window into the darkness; he didn't recognize his own reflection.

"I told you to stop the investigation." The next words were slow and precise. "Now, you pay the price for not complying."

The cool voice didn't quiver once. His calmness made Michael shake. It was like he knew his every thought. He held his breath trying to block out what the man was saying. Think Michael, goddamn it, think. He had to keep him on a little longer to trace the call.

"I guess all I really need to do is kill Jessica to stop the investigation. Right, Michael? See you around."

The phone clicked dead.

"Fuck."

Michael raked his hand through his hair. "This guy is crazy. He is fucking nuts." Impatiently his eyes darted around the room. He looked at the walls, the shelves, the window, trying to gather his thoughts. He focused on the phone before it registered that it was ringing. He plucked it up quickly, expecting the emotionless voice of the killer.

"Carven, this is Hanson at the station. I thought you should know that the tipster called back. He was a little anxious, but one of my men managed to get some information out of him. He works for the local taxi service. He said that he has taken a man that fits Ms. Stanson's description to a building in the old part of town. He said that he'd come to the station and speak with us. I thought you would want to be here when we question him. Carven, you there?"

"I'll be there A.S.A.P. Send a man out to watch Jessica. I'll leave when he arrives."

Michael hung up the phone and dialed Dan's number. It was busy. He was most likely talking to the station, getting all the details. He went to his room and quietly opened the top drawer of his dresser and pulled out his gun. He stuffed an extra clip into his coat and went to the bed and looked down at Jessica. She looked lost in peaceful dreams. He sat on the edge of the bed and watched her, memorizing every feature.

"Baby, wake up." He kissed her cheek. "I have to go."

Jessica's long lashes fluttered open and her eyes found his. "Now? You have to go now?"

"Yes. I think we found him."

She sat up. "Where?"

"I'm not sure. I'll know all the details when I get to the station." He watched her get dressed. "It's going to be over soon." He looked toward the window when he heard a sound. "That's the officer I had sent out."

Michael met the young officer at the door and invited him in. Taking Jessica's hand, he made introductions. "This is officer Scalf."

"Please, call me Jason."

Jessica shook his hand. "It's nice to meet you, Jason."

Michael turned Jessica to him. "I'll be back in a few hours." Dark panic shot through her eyes as she clutched his hands tightly. "Everything is going to be fine."

She nodded but the torment in her gaze never vanished.

"Jason will take care of you."

She nodded again.

He pressed his thumb against her lips and then replaced it

259

with a gentle kiss. "I love you."

"I love you too."

Michael motioned Jason to follow him to the door. "If anything happens to her, it's your ass, is that clear?"

"Yes, sir."

Chapter Twenty-Four

Jessica kept herself busy by fixing a pot of coffee and arranging some cookies that Mrs. Mayfield had made the day before on a plate. "Are you married?" she asked Jason as she set the plate on the counter.

"Yes. Going on four years now." Jason helped himself to a cookie. "We just had a baby girl six months ago."

"Congratulations. What did you name her?"

"Saddie. She has red hair just like my Grandmother."

"She sounds beautiful." She took two cups from the cupboard. "How do you like your coffee?"

"Black is fine. She has the sweetest smile you've ever seen. Her eyes light up when I walk through the door. It is the best feeling in the world."

Jessica handed him a cup. "It must be hard to be away from her."

"It is. But you know how much babies cost these days." He laughed. "Diapers alone can put you in debt. That's why I'm working all the overtime I can." He lifted his shoulders. "Besides, I want Kate, my wife, to be able to stay home with her." He took a sip. "You know, women don't do that much these days. Kids are raised in daycares and it's just not right."

"I agree. Children need their parents."

They both heard the noise at the same time. Jason put his coffee down and stood. He moved to the window. "I'm going to have a look." He turned to give Jessica a reassuring smile.

"Just a quick look. Lock the door behind me."

Michael shoved open the door to the police station. The room buzzed with commotion and the mood was tense as people hurried about. He searched the squad room before he spoke. "Is Dan here?"

"Not yet." A young officer in the back of the room stood up as he replaced the receiver on the phone. "He just called and said he's on his way."

Damn it. He looked at the group of detectives and recognized one of them. "Scott, you're coming with me if he doesn't get here in time."

Scott stepped forward. "No problem."

Michael moved to the nearest desk. "Someone fill me in. Where is this place?"

A piece of paper changed hands until it was handed to Scott. "It's an old abandoned hotel on Sixth Street."

Michael looked at the address as Scott passed the paper. "Is it the one behind the dry cleaners?" He looked up.

Scott nodded. "That's it."

Michael chewed on his bottom lip. "That's a big building."

Scott leaned against the desk. "It was condemned a few years back. I have someone trying to track down blueprints right now."

Michael looked around the room and then back to Scott. "How many men do we have?"

"About a dozen."

"I have a feeling we're going to need them," Michael said.

Michael and Scott looked up as a man walked into the room holding a long tube. "I got the blueprints."

Scott spoke to the group of men across the room as he spread the map across the table. "Gather around, men, and get familiar with the building."

Michael studied the map until he had every floor, room, exit, elevator shaft, and fire escape committed to memory. He looked at the small group of men circling the desk. "Scott and I will go in the front." He looked up. "You two take the fire escape." He pointed to the map. "Here. You two go check the basement out, and you guys go around the back." He leaned back and glanced from face to face. "If anyone has any questions, now is the time to ask them."

No one did.

"Remember who we're dealing with. This guy is capable of anything." Michael paused. "Is Dan here yet?"

An officer moved to the window. "I don't see him."

Michael stood. "We don't have time to wait for him." He looked at each officer again. "I want him. If you find him, I want him."

Jessica paced back and forth in the kitchen. What was taking Jason so long? She glanced down at her watch but realized that she hadn't looked at it when he left so she wasn't sure how long he had been gone. Realistically, it hasn't been that long. Oh, but it felt like an eternity.

Walking aimlessly, she found herself in the living room. Eyeing Michael's recliner, she sat. "Be patient," she told herself. "He could be awhile if he decides to search the stables and the barn." She ran her hands up and down her thighs.

A light tapping on the front window broke her thoughts and the heavy silence. The tap shuddered through her ears, making her heart sink into her stomach and come back up with a horrible ache. She turned around to face the window and gasped. A man's face was pressed against the glass. Her breath caught in her throat, stifling her scream. She froze.

★ ★ ★ ★ ★

Michael killed the lights as they pulled up to the building. Everything on the street was closed except for a twenty-four-hour restaurant and a bar several blocks down the road. He moved around the back of his truck and pulled out a large black duffel bag he had tossed in before leaving the station. He looked over to Scott and handed him a flashlight. "Everyone here?"

Scott looked at the row of cruisers and the men as they prepared and organized. "Looks like it."

"Let's do it," Michael said as he zipped the bag and tossed it back into the truck.

Like shadows in the night, everyone scattered in different directions. Moving without a sound. Scott used a crowbar one of the other officers had given him to open the front door. He whispered, "Go ahead."

Michael drew his gun and slowly entered the building. The first room was the lobby. The streetlights weren't bright enough to light his way, so he flicked on the flashlight. The room smelled damp and dusty. The sagging, exposed beams and the disintegrating floor displayed the building's frailty.

"Be careful where you walk; this place is a death trap," Michael said as he pointed up.

"You're not shittin'." Scott glanced down. "I think I can see the basement through the floor."

What was left of the main counter was directly in front of them. The elevator was to his left and the stairs were to the left of that.

"Stairs," Michael pointed.

Scott nodded.

Michael put a single foot on the first step, testing its strength. "I think it will hold."

The warped steps creaked under Michael's full weight.

They climbed the flight of stairs carefully. When they reached the landing, the hallway split. Michael motioned for Scott to take the left, while he took the right.

The first room Michael came to was littered with trash. Wallpaper peeled away from the walls in long sheets. Any type of light fixtures had been removed, leaving wires dangling from the ceiling and the walls. The next four rooms were the same. He looked up. He could hear the other officers on the top floors. He searched a half dozen more rooms before he came to a room at the end of the hall. He shined the beam of light around and stopped when it caught a rumpled green blanket in the corner. He moved into the room and began to search it. A small gas burner and a portable radio sat on a makeshift table constructed from crates. It was shoved against the wall to his right.

Michael's head rotated instantly when he heard a noise in the adjoining room. He shone the light on the closed door in front of him. He assumed it was the bathroom. He raised his gun and moved to the door, then reached for the knob and turned it slowly. He heard the noise again.

He flung the door open and looked down the sight of his gun. "Damn." It was empty. Moving inside, he looked around the small room. It stunk of urine and feces. Michael wrinkled his nose at the potency of the odor. He shone the beam of light at the stained tub were he saw a nest of rats. They scattered when the light fell on them.

Michael moved the beam to the sink. A toothbrush and a comb lay on the chipped porcelain. He caught a glimpse of himself in the rusted, shattered mirror of the medicine cabinet and stopped abruptly. Something wasn't right. He didn't feel right. He went back into the room and scrutinized its contents. His thoughts were a scrambled mess. Complete confusion engulfed him briefly before realization struck. "Fuck."

"Mike?" Scott hollered. "Mike, are you okay?"

"In here. I'm in here."

Scott came running in. "What? What's the matter?"

Michael kicked the portable radio. "It's him." He shoved his gun back in the holster. "Damn it, why didn't I think of it before?" He pounded his palm against his forehead.

"What are you talking about?" Scott asked as he looked around the room.

"The caller. He's the tipster." He sucked in a long breath. "He knew we would come." Suddenly Michael's head shot up. "Shit. He's going to get her."

Scott raised his hand. "Calm down, Mike."

"He's going after her." Michael took off in a dead run.

"Wait." Scott took off after him.

Jessica cringed at the sight of the man's flattened face. The churning in her stomach and the dull hammering at the base of her head had fermented into a sick, queasy feeling that left her lightheaded. The room was beginning to spin. The furniture and pictures on the walls were getting hazier and hazier until they blended into one massive colorful print. She couldn't distinguish if the nauseous sensation was due to the cramping in her stomach or dread.

"Jessica."

Forcing herself to focus, she blinked. Was it the man's voice she had heard?

"Open the door, Jessica."

Jessica heard the voice, but it sounded strained, distant. She felt as if she were thawing out. The numbing sensation was slowing wearing off, breaking her paralysis, sending warm blood through her body, enabling her to move.

"Let me in, Jessica." The voice was calm.

She glanced at the window. The man standing outside was

the man who was with Nichole Blake.

Michael jumped in his truck. Scott barely got into the passenger's seat before Michael sped down the road. "Buckle up."

Scott grabbed his seat belt and yanked it across him. "Let me get this straight. You think the tipster is the killer?"

"I don't think, I know."

"Why would he give away his hiding place? Oh shit." Scott reached to the ceiling, trying to grab the handle as they slid around another corner. Securing himself in his seat, he continued, "What does he have to gain by it?"

"What do we have to gain by it?" Michael paused while he slid around a corner. He waited until he felt his back tires gain traction before he spoke. "Besides, the killer has never stayed there."

Scott flinched as Michael passed a car on a one-way street. "Then who has?"

Michael braked slightly and then ran the red light. "I don't know. Maybe a homeless person lives there. Perhaps it was all just a set-up."

Scott shook his head in disbelief. "What you're telling me is that he has had this planned from the beginning?"

"Ever since I started on the case."

Scott relayed the story as he saw it. "His plan was to call you tonight and get you livid, then call the station pretending to be the frightened tipster who finally got up the nerve to call again. I assume that he was the first guy who called."

"Yep."

"This guy is a nut." Scott leaned as they skidded around a corner. "He gave us the location because he knew you would go there. That would give him time to go to the ranch and get Jessica." He paused to take a breath. "And if he gets Jessica, he figures you'll stop the investigation like you did with Cathy."

"You got it."

"How did he know about Cathy?"

Michael shifted. "He did his homework."

"Boy, this guy is fucking cunning."

As he headed out of town, Michael looked down at the car phone. Why hadn't he thought of it sooner? He picked it up, guiding the truck with one hand as he dialed his number.

Jessica jumped when she heard the phone ring. She dragged her eyes away from the wall of glass and forced herself to search for the phone. She silently cursed the cordless phone. After several rings, she was able to locate it. She clutched it with both hands.

"Jessica."

"Michael, it's him. The guy that was with Nichole Blake." Her voice came in short gasps, both relieved and frightened.

"I know, baby. You're going to be fine. We're on our way, ten minutes. I'll be there in ten minutes."

Jessica didn't look back to the stranger. "I don't think he's going to wait."

Michael talked slowly and clearly. He remained completely calm for her sake. "Jessica, I want you to take the phone and go up to my room. Lock the door and stay there. And whatever you do, don't hang up. Jason will protect you until I get there."

"Jason went outside and hasn't come back."

Michael put his hand over the phone and looked at Scott. "Christ, he got Jason." He removed his hand. "Jessica, listen to me. Everything's going to be fine." He knew that was the furthest thing from the truth. "I won't let anything happen to you. I want you to go to my room as fast as you can." Michael jammed his foot on the accelerator. "Five more minutes."

She was already walking toward the stairs. She could still hear the stranger who was now yelling outside. "Michael." She whispered his name not because he was at the end of the line but because the feeling of comfort and safety came with it.

"I'm coming, baby."

Jessica heard a loud bang on the door and began to run. She took the hall behind the stairs to avoid walking by the front door. She looked over her shoulder as she heard the door being bashed in. Catching her foot on a piece of furniture, she tripped and flew through the air, landing with a thud. The phone landed a few feet away.

"Jessica! Jessica!" Michael yelled.

Jessica sat up and wiped the blood from her nose and mouth and looked around for the phone.

"Jessica, are you all right? What happened?" His voice was frantic.

"I tripped," she said. Rapid footsteps pounded toward her.

Michael had a hard time hearing her over the engine. "What?"

She slowly lifted her head up. When she saw the shadow at the end of the hall, she began to scoot away. "No, no. God, no."

"Tell me what's going on," Michael said.

"No!"

There was a loud crash in Michael's ear and before the phone went dead he heard her scream.

The stranger was on top of her in one swift movement, pinning her to the floor with his hands. "It's so nice to see you again, Jessica."

Digging her heels into the floor, Jessica reared up as far as she could. The action was enough to throw the man off balance. When he fell to the side, she drew her knee up and drove it into his groin. Free from his grip, she scrambled to her feet, grabbed hold of the banister, and swung herself around up the stairs.

A hand shot up through the railing, grabbing her ankle. She fell, smacking her head on a step. Dizziness consumed her but just as quickly self-preservation kicked in and propelled her to fight. Twisting, turning, and pulling her ankle did no good. There was no way of breaking free from his death grip. She didn't like the thought of touching him, but she couldn't think of anything else to do. She reached down and groped for anything she could get her hand on. Winding her fingers through his hair, she pulled as hard as she could. She was surprised when the tension broke and she stared at the hairpiece in her hand. Dropping it, she reached down again. Her finger fumbled over his face and as she tried to gouge his eyes, he let go.

She managed to make it to the top of the stairs by crawling and climbing but was so lightheaded she couldn't walk. With the back of her sleeve she wiped at her eyes, trying to clear her blurred vision. The attempt only smeared the blood dripping profusely from her nose. She reached out and felt for the wall, using it as her guide as she stumbled down the hall.

"Jessica."

Jessica turned at the sound of her name. She could barely make out the dark shadow at the end of the hall. Adrenalin exploded through her veins, forcing her forward. Suddenly her entire body was consumed with pain. She stumbled, trying to maintain her balance. The throbbing at the back of her head was too much. She fell. Grunting, she rolled onto her back. The dark figure was coming toward her. From the corner of her eye she saw the dark, blunt object that had been tossed at her head. Warm blood ran down her back.

Raw survival instinct took over as she reached out and took hold of the doorframe. Pulling herself with all the strength she could muster, she fell into the room. Kicking the door shut, she twisted the lock. Dizzy and unable to walk, she crawled to the other side of the bed. She shut her eyes tight against the pain, wrapped her arms around her knees, and began rocking.

The truck slid sideways as Michael turned the corner onto the dirt road. He was less than a mile from the ranch. Gripping the steering wheel, he fought to keep the heavy vehicle under control as it bounced over pothole after pothole. His body was dulled with a deadly mix of fear and hate.

Scott held on tightly to the dashboard. "What's the plan, Mike?"

Michael never took his eyes off the road. "Find the son of a bitch and kill him."

"Open the door, Jessica," the cold voice said. "Make this easy on yourself."

Hearing the man's voice made her sick. He sounded so calm and so familiar. Jessica watched the door as the man on the other side rammed it repeatedly. The sound of cracking wood made her heart pound frantically. She shut her eyes as tightly as she could and put her hands over her ears. To her amazement, the noise stopped. She lifted her head over the bed and looked at the door. Had he gone away?

The slight movement made her woozy. She moved a shaky hand to the back of her head but couldn't feel anything but a wad of blood-soaked hair. Her eyes filled with tears. She looked down at the floor. It was peppered with her blood.

A smashing noise forced her to look up again. She watched in horror as a large chunk of wood split away from the door and an ax blade struck into it. A sliver of light glistened through the now-large crack; a few more whacks and he would be through.

The voice was now irritated. "You're making this," he paused and the ax slammed into the door, "harder than I planned."

Michael cursed as they rounded the last turn before they came to the ranch. As the truck slid to a stop, both men jumped out, guns drawn. They raced toward the front door, stopping briefly when they saw Jason's body in the middle of the walkway. Stepping over him, Michael released the safety on his 9mm.

In the house, Michael motioned for Scott to search the downstairs while he went to the second floor. As he took the stairs two at a time, he could hear only the strong hollowness of his heartbeat quicken. It vibrated loudly in his ears—an inanimate sound that he could not shake.

A small, dark object rested halfway up the staircase. Picking up the wig, he fingered the coarse hair before dropping it and continuing on. It was easy enough to know where they went. All he had to do was follow the trail of blood.

He made his way down the hall, his steps quick but cautious. His breath caught in his throat when he reached his bedroom door and saw that it was torn to shreds. He swallowed hard as he slowly raised the gun.

Jessica crawled into the bathtub and closed the shower curtain with unsteady hands. She was going to lose it any minute. She lifted her blood-covered hands in front of her and felt strangely disconnected from them. As the nauseous feeling devoured her, she closed her eyes.

The noises in the other room mixed with the warm sensation that filled her body. She relaxed and welcomed the much-needed comfort. She knew that she should fight the feeling, but it was too inviting.

Michael stepped into his bedroom and watched as a man lifted an ax over his head and let it fall into his bathroom door.

"Hey!"

The killer turned around, the ax still in hand.

Michael went numb. "Dan?"

Dan didn't look surprised. "Hey, Mike. What took you so long?"

"Dan," Michael said again. He raised his gun and looked at his old partner through its sights.

"Are you that surprised?" Dan let the blade of the axe fall to the ground and leaned against the handle as he caught his breath. "Didn't think I had it in me?"

Michael's eyes narrowed. "Why?"

"Because I can." He smiled. "Or because I'm—how did you so nicely put it—a crazy son of a bitch who's whacked out and fucking nuts."

"I can think of a few more to add to the list." He walked across the room, allowing Scott to have the other side. "How long?"

"A few years after we became partners." He shrugged and looked at Scott. "Enjoying the fun, Scott?"

Scott held his gun level and didn't speak a word.

Dan looked back to Michael. "I got tired of you always solving the crimes." He made a bitter face. "Sure, you'd share the credit, but you and everyone else knew you were the best."

He laughed. "So I thought I would give you a challenge."

Michael's head swirled with confusion. "A challenge?"

"Yeah, a challenge. Thought I'd toss a little something at you that would really make you think." His brow arched. "I was doing you a favor. I was pushing you to see how good you really were. I demanded from you what no one else could." He shifted his weight, which caused both Michael and Scott to flinch. "Besides, I was bored. It's not really fun when your partner can solve anything that comes across his desk."

"Cathy?"

Dan smiled. "She was a nice woman."

"What about Cathy?" The acidity of bile backed up in his throat.

Dan shrugged. "That was one of the ones you didn't."

"You goddamn bastard." Michael's nostrils flared as the words oozed from clenched teeth.

"You threw me with that one." He shook his head. "I thought you were stronger. I would have never guessed you'd freak out and leave the force."

"Why the other girls?"

"I had to bring you back. I was getting bored. I knew you would follow the story. Solving crimes and finding the bad guy is in your blood."

Michael lowered his gun. "Give me one good reason."

"Because we're old friends." Dan laughed.

"You really are sick."

Dan swung the ax up and flung himself forward, swinging the ax wildly. Michael stumbled back a few steps, aimed his gun at the madman, and pulled the trigger. He kept firing even when the body fell to the ground. He watched as each bullet sunk into Dan's flesh. He fired until there were no more bullets.

Scott stood behind Michael. He made no move to stop him.

Michael's gun fell from his hands, landing with a thump. Sirens and the crunching of gravel in the distance grew louder. Moving to the bathroom door, he punched through the splintering wood and unlocked it. He could see the blurred shaped of Jessica in the tub. "Jess—" His voice trailed off when he pulled back the shower curtain and saw her. As his eyes assessed Jessica, he felt like he was watching a motion picture where the projection was slowed to an almost nonexistent speed. His body went numb.

Her head rested on the side of the tub. Her skin was pale against the white porcelain. Her clothes were coated with blood. In a deranged voice he yelled, "Jessica!"

He stepped into the bathtub and took her in his arms. He pressed his fingers to the base of her neck and felt a light pulse. "Wake up, Jessica. Don't you dare go to sleep on me." His voice rose. "Do you hear me? Jessica." He propped her up in his lap and he shook her limp body, and then raised his gaze slowly to Scott. "Go call a goddamn ambulance." He rocked Jessica in his arms; tears streamed from his eyes.

Scott came back several seconds later. "They're on the way." He wet a towel in the sink and handed it to Michael. "How's she doing?"

"She's hanging in there."

"She's going to be okay, Mike."

Michael took the cloth and wiped some of the blood from Jessica's face and head. He could hear the skidding of tires, the slamming of car doors, and footsteps in his house. "I don't want them in here. I don't want them to see her like this."

"I'll take care of it."

275

Michael lifted Jessica in his arms. He tore the blankets off his bed. He threw one over Dan's body and wrapped Jessica up in the other. He sat on the edge of the bed, cradling Jessica. "Hang on, baby. Hang on." He pinched his eyes closed and silently begged, God don't take her, not now. Don't do this to me.

Epilogue

The sky was big and blue. Birds chirped overhead and a gentle breeze carried the sweet aroma of grass, pine trees, and flowers to their picnic. The sunshine warmed the blanket they had spread in the middle of the meadow.

Jessica lay stretched on her back next to Michael. "You were right."

"About what?"

"Autumn."

"You say that every year," Michael said as he popped a handful of grapes into his mouth.

She sighed as she turned her head and looked around. Horses in the distance dotted the hillside. "I don't know if it's possible, but it gets prettier and prettier each year. The leaves seem to be brighter, the flowers more fragrant, the breeze a little softer. I love it."

"It is nice." He examined the peanut butter sandwich, tossed it aside, and stuffed his hand into an open bag of chips.

Jessica rolled onto her side and propped her head up with her hands. "Thank you for the picnic." She smiled at him. "How did you know I needed this?"

Michael dusted his hand off and slid one across her stomach. He played with the material until it came untucked. He glided his hand over her flat stomach and cupped her breast. "Because I know my wife." He bent his head down and kissed her. "And I know what she needs."

"I love you," Jessica whispered against his lips.

"I love you too." He took her face between his hands and kissed her tenderly. He slowly pushed his fingers through her hair as he tilted her head back, exposing her neck. He nibbled on the tender area before moving to her ear. He whispered words of love to his wife as he teased her with his tongue.

Michael pulled away. "I can't believe I'm saying this, but I need to get back to the house. Scott is picking me up so we can go catch some bad guys."

Jessica noticed the sparkle in her husband's eyes when he spoke those last words. Her hands found their way to the front of his jeans. "Can we pick up where we left off tonight?"

"Do you need to ask?"

Jessica gave him a wide grin. "You're right, that was a dumb question." She sat up and began loading the uneaten food into a basket.

Michael shook the blanket out and folded it. He looked across the field of wildflowers and stared for a moment.

"What?" Jessica asked.

Michael pointed. "Look."

Jessica smiled when she realized what he was looking at, then went back to cleaning up.

"Anneliese, it's time to go," Michael yelled.

Anneliese looked up. Peering through long golden locks, her bright blue eyes met Michael's. "Look, Daddy." She smiled as she held up one fist full of yellow flowers and the other full of purple flowers. Navigating the high grass was hard for her short legs, but she managed to reach Michael without falling. "I picked the yellow flowers for you Daddy and the purple flowers for Mommy."

Michael took the bouquet of flowers and kissed his daughter. He watched Anneliese walk over to her mommy and present her with the bouquet. Jessica squatted down and took her daughter in her arms. She then pulled away and began tickling her. They rolled around in the grass laughing and tickling each other. Michael smiled; they were his two girls. They were his life.

About the Author

Aris Whittier is a freelance writer who lives in northern California with her husband and two children. She is the author of the hilariously funny book: *The Truth About Being A Bass Fisherman's Wife*. She is also a member of the Romance Writers of America. Aris enjoys reading romance just as much as she does writing it. To learn more, please visit www.ariswhittier.com.